SUN ON FIRE

SUN ON FIRE

VIKTOR ARNAR INGOLFSSON
Translated by Björg Árnadóttir and Andrew Cauthery

Text copyright © 2009 Viktor Arnar Ingolfsson

English translation copyright © 2014 Björg Árnadóttir and Andrew Cauthery

Sun On Fire was first published in 2009 by Mál og Menning as Sólstjakar. Translated from Icelandic by Björg Árnadóttir and Andrew Cauthery. Published in English by AmazonCrossing in 2014.

Published by AmazonCrossing, Seattle

www.apub.com

Amazon, the Amazon logo, and AmazonCrossing are trademarks of Amazon.com, Inc., or its affiliates.

ISBN-13: 9781477823125

ISBN-10: 1477823123

Cover design by Paul Barrett

Library of Congress Control Number: 2013923614

Vala, Emilía, and Margrét Arna:
Thank you for all your patience.

MONDAY, OCTOBER 12

01:45

D o you remember me?"

The voice came from the restroom doorway. Inside, the fat guy rinsed his hands at a shiny steel sink.

"Yeah, we talked earlier this evening," he replied without looking up.

"Yes, but I mean . . . do you recognize me from the past?"

"Should I?"

"Maybe you can't, Anton. It was a long time ago—I was only nine years old."

Anton picked up a clean towel and carefully dried his hands. Then, lifting the towel to his puffy face, he wiped the sweat from his brow.

"Nine, huh," he said, pausing to check his reflection in the mirror. "That's a good age."

03:05

The cell phone on the bedside table played the ever-popular "Air on the G String" by Johann Sebastian Bach, quietly at first, but growing louder and more distinct despite the phone's poor sound quality.

It took Arngrímur Ingason, counselor at the Icelandic embassy in Berlin, a few moments to figure out what he was hearing as he became fully conscious. The bedroom was pitch black, so he knew it was the middle of the night. His body wasn't ready for this interruption of his deep sleep, and his nerves bombarded his brain with a firm message: "Go back to sleep," they kept repeating, to the accompaniment of the phone's soothing ringtone. Arngrímur shut his eyes briefly before finally reaching for the phone.

He looked at the illuminated screen. It was past three o'clock. The music grew louder still but abruptly stopped as he pressed the "Answer" button.

"*Ja?*" he said in German.

The voice at the other end also spoke German. "Sorry for disturbing you, Herr Ingason. This is the Nordic Embassies' night watch. Main reception. Chief Security Guard Achim Wolf speaking."

The counselor sat up in bed.

"Hello, Herr Wolf. What can I do for you?"

"I'm sorry, Herr Ingason, we have a little problem at the Icelandic embassy."

"Problem?"

"Yes, Herr Ingason, but it's nothing serious. Ambassador Björnsson had visitors earlier this evening."

"At the embassy?"

"Yes. It seems there was a meeting at around six o'clock, but it went late. The ambassador ordered in some food and the visitors stayed longer than expected."

The counselor sighed and swung his legs out from under the sheets.

"Are they still there?" he asked, fumbling around for his glasses.

"No, sir. The ambassador left twenty minutes ago. His wife was with him."

"OK. I hope there wasn't too much of a disturbance."

"Oh, no. No disturbance at all."

"So what exactly is the problem, Herr Wolf?"

The guard hesitated, looking for the right words. "I'm afraid that one of the visitors who checked in to the embassy has not checked out."

"You mean he's still there?"

"Yes, sir. His name is Eiríksson. We have his passport here at reception."

"Eiríksson? An Icelander?"

"Yes, sir. His first name is Anton."

"Anton Eiríksson. I'm not familiar with that name."

"I didn't really think you would be," the night guard said. "Please excuse the presumption. He could have fallen asleep inside the embassy without the ambassador noticing. My colleague says that the ambassador and his wife were pretty tired when they left. He called cabs for them and the other guests."

"I see. So this Eiríksson gentleman is still inside the embassy?"

"Yes. Unfortunately, we didn't notice that a guest pass was missing until after the ambassador had left. So far we've confirmed that he isn't in the common area. He must be in the Icelandic building."

"I see."

"Herr Ingason—we're not allowed to enter the embassy unless it's an emergency. So if it's just that the man fell asleep, sir . . ."

"All right—I understand. I'll come look for him." He found his watch on the bedside table. "I'll be there in twenty minutes."

With the call completed, the counselor clutched the phone while considering the situation. Then he called for a cab.

"It'll be right there," a voice at the other end said.

"Thank you very much," Arngrímur said before hanging up.

"I've got ten minutes," he thought aloud. Carefully, he stood up, supporting himself on the tall headboard as he took his first step. He was feeling his age: sixty-five this past June. His joints weren't yet awake enough for energetic movement, and the room was cold. He'd left the window open, so it had cooled off overnight.

Fall was making its presence felt.

He walked stiffly into the bathroom and flipped the switch. As his eyes adjusted to the light, he used the time to brush his teeth. Then he combed back his silver hair and decided he didn't need to shave for this particular errand. He could do it before the embassy opened for the day—and if he couldn't make it back home first, he'd shower at the embassy before the other staffers showed up for work. He kept a toiletry bag and clean underwear in his office locker.

Eight minutes later, he'd pulled on neatly pressed pants and a shirt, and he was putting on a tie. By the time he left the house, his posture was upright, his mind alert, and his movements polished. His workday at Berlin's Icelandic embassy had begun.

03:20

The cab was parked outside with headlights on, its engine gently purring; the driver had climbed out for a cigarette. He opened the back door for Arngrímur and said good morning. Then he extinguished his half-smoked stub and placed it in his jacket's breast pocket before sliding back behind the wheel.

"The Nordic Embassies," Arngrímur said, "Number One, Rauchstrasse."

"The Nordic Embassies," the driver repeated quietly while driving off.

There was hardly any traffic at this time of night, and within five minutes they were driving north along Klingelhöferstrasse, with the east wall of the Nordic Embassies complex illuminated before them on the left. An instantly recognizable and distinctive feature of the complex is its fifteen-meter outer wall clad with green copper plates. Mostly, the plates are vertical and close the wall off, but in places they slope outward at an angle of either forty-five or ninety degrees, allowing light from within the compound to filter through. The wall forms a snaking, horseshoe-shaped enclosure for the five separate embassy buildings.

The driver made a left onto Stülerstrasse and again onto Rauchstrasse, driving almost a full circle round the complex before arriving at the south side, which was constructed very differently: A glass wall with an illuminated canopy provided a view into the open central plaza, while the main entrance was on the right in a building clad with pale wooden horizontal slats—the Felleshus, or Pan Nordic Building.

Arngrímur paid the driver and waited for the receipt before getting out of the cab. He spotted the night guard watching him through a window as he approached the illuminated doorway, which swung open as he came near.

He entered the lobby and was greeted by the guard's tinny voice coming through a loudspeaker from the reception desk, which was screened off with thick glass. "Thank you for coming, Herr Ingason. Would you like someone to accompany you into the embassy?"

"No, Herr Wolf. I'll call if I need assistance."

"Very well, Herr Ingason. We'll be ready for you."

Arngrímur took the security pass card hanging from his neck and inserted it into a reader next to the first of double doors into the embassy compound. The door opened and, as he stepped through it, immediately shut behind him. He repeated the process for the inner door, reemerged into the open, and inhaled the fresh night air as he walked across the plaza between the embassy buildings.

They were all the same height. On the right, nearest the entrance, was the Finnish embassy, and across from it the Danish embassy. At the far end on the left was the Icelandic embassy, the smallest building by area, but with walls of pale-brown rhyolite that made it stand out from the glass, steel, wood, and dark stone of the other buildings.

The plaza was at least thirty meters across, and Arngrímur soon felt cold in the chilly night air. Despite that, he stopped to think for a moment when he reached the Icelandic embassy's entrance. He needed to plan his next step. Maybe he should have accepted an escort. That would also have complicated matters, though, as the night guards had to log their movements in a diary. This was the main reason Wolf had asked him to come over. If the German security guards entered an empty embassy building on their own after hours, that would require complicated reports involving multiple people. Hopefully, this friend of the ambassador's just needed a bit of prodding and escorting out to a cab. That wouldn't be a problem, and the security staff could quietly forget the night's events without filing a report.

A dark-colored shield bearing the Icelandic coat of arms hung on the rhyolite wall to the left of the entrance. To the right a corrugated concrete wall stretched along the entire ground floor of the building.

Arngrímur slipped his pass card into another reader and tapped a number onto a keypad. With a soft beep, the glass door's lock opened, and he entered the building.

The corrugated pattern of the outer wall continued through the entranceway and formed the body of the reception area desk, behind which were a chair and a side table with a computer on it. Apart from that, nothing. Nobody was usually here during the day except for the embassy driver, when he wasn't dispatched outside the embassy. Visitors would ring a bell and introduce themselves on the intercom.

Bright illumination from outside shone in through the windows of the stairwell, so Arngrímur didn't need to switch on any lights. He glanced at the security system's control panel and saw that it had not been activated. *The ambassador must have been very tired when he left,* Arngrímur thought. Next, he contemplated the two half-empty wineglasses on the desk. He was about to deal with the glasses, but then he changed his mind. Probably best to first find the guy and get him out. He could straighten up after.

It wouldn't take long to search the building—though there were four stories and a basement, the floor area was quite small. Each story only comprised a hallway and three or four rooms.

File cabinets were always locked, and the folks who worked there locked their own offices when they left for the day. That meant he'd only have to check the conference room, the kitchenette, the washrooms, and possibly the ambassador's office. Maybe the basement as well, but he would leave that for last.

On the ground floor were just the reception area, a single washroom, and some locked storage rooms. *There can't be anybody here*, the counselor thought, and he took the stairs up to the second-floor hallway and switched on the light. To the right were four doors—three of them locked. The fourth was half open and led to a conference room with a large table and ten chairs. The ambassador had obviously held an impromptu dinner party here the evening before. Dirty plates and leftover food in paper wrappers littered the table, as did a number of wineglasses. Two brandy bottles stood in the middle of the table. The lid of a cardboard box that had contained twelve bottles of red wine had been roughly torn off. In the box were eight bottles—six empty and two unopened. Two bottles stood on the table, so that meant two were missing. A powerful odor of spilled wine mixed with the smell of tobacco pervaded the room's atmosphere. A dirty plate had been used as an ashtray.

"Lovely," Arngrímur muttered as he surveyed the room. He looked under the table and observed a box that had contained a brandy bottle lying under one of the chairs.

"It doesn't get much better than this," he added, returning to the hall.

He peeked into the washroom on the other side of the hall. Someone had thrown up in the toilet and not bothered to flush. The smell was rank.

"Wrong, still more treats to come," Arngrímur corrected himself. He took a deep breath, leaned over the toilet, and pushed the lever with one finger. The stench grew stronger still as the jet of water stirred things vigorously around before the bowl emptied.

Up on the third floor, all rooms were locked except for the staff kitchenette. In there the lights had been left on, the cupboards were open, and plates and glasses had been removed. A silverware drawer was also open. Arngrímur closed the cupboards and drawer, and crossed to the window to look out over the plaza. The night was still dark, and nobody was out in the common area. He could see a light in the security guards' window in the Felleshus. It was the only sign of life. This should have been a quiet night.

He left the kitchenette and crossed the hall to investigate the washroom. Everything was as it should be, or nearly so. The toilet lid was up and a cigarette butt floated in the bowl. Arngrímur flushed and watched as the water vortex sucked the butt away. Then he carefully closed the lid and returned to the hall. He stood still awhile and listened. He had worked in this place for many years and knew all the sounds. Every building has its night sounds, and the silence is never complete. If anybody was around, he would hear it immediately. But he couldn't detect any unusual noise at all.

He headed upstairs and peered along the top floor's unlit hallway. He fumbled for the first two doors on the right and found them locked. The washroom on the left was open and deserted.

The only remaining room was the ambassador's office; its door was half open, and Arngrímur moved closer and looked in. The room was dark except for the flickering light from a large candle in a candlestick standing on a table at the near end of the room. The drapes were closed and all the lights were switched off. Arngrímur stepped inside and examined the candlestick. It was tall, made of fired clay, and more or less cylindrical with a solid base. Beside it was another very similar candlestick, its candle not lit. The candlesticks were strangely craggy and clearly intended as objets d'art.

Sensing that something was off, Arngrímur felt a chill creep up from his spine to the top of his head. Warily, he turned round and looked into the shadows at the ambassador's desk. A large man, with head bowed, sat in the chair behind it.

The blood drained from Arngrímur's face, and he froze for a few moments.

"Hello," he said as his blood flow recovered, not really expecting a reply.

"Hello," he repeated, and when the visitor still didn't move, he fumbled to flick on the light switch by the door.

It took him a while to work out the situation. The man leaned forward in the chair, his hands hanging by his sides. It looked as though he was contemplating his enormous stomach, which had been slit open from the chest down to the groin. The shaft of a large knife protruded from the wound like some lewd symbol. Looking closer, Arngrímur realized that the pool that had formed on the pale wooden floor beneath the man was not merely blood, but also included a substantial part of his intestines and the contents of his stomach. The disgusting stain was incredibly big, but for some reason Arngrímur turned his gaze and fixated on the fat cigar the man held between his fingers, its two centimeters of ash indicating that it had burned in this position until its glow died.

This visitor had the nerve to smoke in here? was the only thought Arngrímur could manage. He felt that his increasing nausea must be the result of unwelcome tobacco smoke instead of the stench emanating from the filthy pile on the floor and the gaping cleft in the man's belly.

10:30

"How many times do I have to tell you—I'm not answering any questions from some fucking half-caste," the prisoner said for the fourth time, grinning across the table at Birkir Li Hinriksson. They were in an interview room at the Reykjavík detective division's headquarters.

"What were you doing the night before last?" Birkir asked a fifth time, his dark-brown almond eyes unblinking. His work as a detective often exposed him to insults like this, and, though he would have preferred not to have to put up with such remarks, he had long since learned to ignore them. He was unfazed by mere words, especially when there was a lack of intelligence behind them. To him, this was no more than a bark from an untrained dog.

Birkir Li was born in Vietnam toward the end of 1970—his first name at that time was simply Li. In Iceland's National Register, however, his birth year was recorded as 1972 because people didn't know any better, and his birth date was recorded as January 10, which was the date in 1979 when he'd arrived in Iceland with a refugee group from Malaysia. By that time, he had lost his whole birth family, and later he was left behind on his own by his Vietnamese adopted family when they disappeared to the United States. After that he was brought up by an old Icelandic couple, and he had taken his patronymic from his foster father, Hinrik.

"What were you doing the night before last?" Birkir asked yet again.

"OK, I'll tell ya. I was watching your whore of a mom down at the harbor getting fucked by a bunch of Russian trawlermen with the clap." The prisoner roared with laughter and smirked at Detective Gunnar Maríuson, who sat at the end of the table, cheek in hand, bored out of his mind; his bald patch shone pinkly under the ceiling light, and his thick double chin sagged onto his chest as he tipped his head to one side.

"Is it lunchtime yet?" Gunnar asked when Birkir seemed like he wouldn't continue talking.

"It's only ten thirty," Birkir said.

Gunnar looked at the prisoner. "Shall we get this over with?" he asked, and straightened himself up in his chair, towering his large frame threateningly over the table.

In downtown Reykjavík, an international culture center had been broken into and set on fire, and a cashbox (which was, in fact, empty) removed. A security camera at an embassy right across the street had captured a good shot of a blond guy in a sleeveless leather jacket dropping the box twice before managing to stuff it into the back of an old station wagon of obscure make. In the background, flames could be seen through the building's windows.

It had taken a day to investigate the scene and negotiate permission to access the security-camera footage, after which the case was cracked—they recognized the blond guy as a well-known psycho, and Gunnar had found him at home at six thirty that morning.

Looking at Birkir, the prisoner made monkey noises and scratched at his sides. Then he hooted with laughter.

Birkir examined the man's face. Its proportions were odd, with eyes set far apart and the head cone shaped; the nose was thick, upturned, and protuberant with flared nostrils.

"Degeneration," Birkir said.

The prisoner stopped laughing. "You what?" he screeched. "Does the half-caste know fancy words?"

"Inbreeding," Birkir explained.

"Whaddya mean?"

"Are your parents brother and sister?" Gunnar asked.

The prisoner's face contorted with fury, and he threw a punch at Gunnar's head. But Gunnar had evidently been waiting for this. He dodged the blow, grabbed the arm and twisted it, and slammed the prisoner face down onto the table.

"Aargh!" the prisoner screamed as Gunnar pinned him down with his weight.

"This freak's hair still smells like smoke," Gunnar said. "It doesn't even wash."

"Let me go, or I'll smash your face in," the criminal whimpered.

"You already tried."

"I'll sure as hell get you later."

The door opened and Detective Superintendent Magnús Magnússon, head of the violent crime unit, entered the room.

"Jesus, men," he said, sizing up the situation. "What's going on in here?"

Gunnar stood up carefully, maintaining his grip on the prisoner with one hand while taking handcuffs from his pocket with the other. "Assaulting an officer on duty," he said formally, and cuffed him.

"Ouch!" the prisoner said. "That hurts!"

"We have the arrest warrant for this suspect," said Magnús, "but it can wait for the time being. When you get back from taking him to lockup, come and see me. Something else has cropped up."

11:45

"We have a problem," Magnús said, his customarily sunny demeanor clouded with concern. Though close to sixty years old, he was—aside from a little thickening around the waist—in pretty good shape. The suntan he still had after his August vacation in Italy looked nice against his clean-cut gray hair and thick mustache, but today he was missing his usual crispness and seemed pale and unwell under his tan.

He closed the door to his office and looked gravely at Gunnar and Birkir for a moment before saying, "I need to send you on a quick trip to Berlin. There's a direct flight early tomorrow morning."

"To Germany?" Gunnar shook his head. "No way. I never go abroad."

Magnús was dumbfounded. "What do you mean?"

"I'm not going abroad," Gunnar repeated.

"You speak German—and you've been abroad, surely? You have a passport?"

"Yes and yes and no."

"What do you mean?" Magnús asked again.

Birkir replied for Gunnar. "You know his mother is German. Of course he speaks German."

"And he has been abroad?" Magnús looked questioningly at Birkir.

"He went to Majorca once—ate and drank too much and got indigestion. Since then he hasn't wanted to go abroad. He doesn't have a passport."

Gunnar looked angrily at his partner. "I didn't eat too much. I got salmonella poisoning. I had the runs for six weeks."

"And you're always looking at German websites," Magnús continued.

"He only looks at football news and naked women," Birkir said.

"And the news," Gunnar said, bridling. "I got sunstroke, too."

"Where?" Magnús asked.

"In Majorca."

Magnús sighed wearily and said, "Berlin is hardly Majorca. You're in no danger of getting sunstroke at this time of year, and if you eat in moderation you shouldn't get diarrhea."

Gunnar replied peevishly, "I also get claustrophobic on airplanes. The seats are so cramped."

"Right," said Magnús, "but I'm not *asking* you to go. This is an order."

Gunnar's face turned bright red. "I haven't seen anything in my job description that says I have to do police work in other countries," he said. "Why the hell do you need to send people to Berlin to do stuff for you?"

Magnús hesitated before replying, "A murder was committed in the Icelandic embassy last night. I got called in to a meeting at the Foreign Ministry this morning."

Gunnar shook his head and said, "That's not our problem. Just let the Berlin *Kripo* deal with it."

Magnús said quietly, "We can't do that. This is a sensitive matter for the ambassador and for the ministry. We can't just leave it to the *Kriminalpolizei*."

Birkir asked, "How the hell are we supposed to solve a murder in Berlin?"

15

Magnús replied, "Assess the situation, question witnesses, and write a report. After that, we'll see. Anna will go with you to take charge of CSI—I've already spoken to her. I need my most trustworthy people on this job—people who can do the work and keep their mouths shut. Nothing can get out to the media except through the ministry."

"I'm not going," Gunnar said.

"That's what you think." Magnús was angry. He threw open a desk drawer and grabbed the sheet of paper that lay on top. He thumped it onto the table and said, "If you want to discuss job descriptions and such formalities, let's not leave anything out. I received this complaint from a law office in Kópavogur last Friday. They say you made a nuisance of yourself, poking your nose into a deceased person's estate they'd been hired to settle."

"Is this about that lawyer that was shot out west? The goose hunter?" Gunnar asked.

"Yes. Anything else I should know about?"

"It was about the farm. I promised the folks there that I'd arrange for them to buy back the buildings and the farmland. They've been treated really badly in this situation."

Magnús banged the table with his hand. "The attorneys tell me you made a threatening phone call to people who were about to make an offer for the farm."

Gunnar screwed up his nose and said quietly, "I just told those vultures that the place was haunted by evil spirits."

"The attorneys say they had to sell the farm at half price."

"That sounds good enough, given the economic situation in Iceland. The farmer and his daughter had to take out a large loan to pay for it. That's not so easy these days."

"OK, but does your job description say that you should discourage people from going about their everyday business by scaring them off with some mumbo jumbo about ghosts?"

"My job description says to do what's right and proper wherever it applies."

Magnús shook his head. "The normal response to a complaint like this is to send you on unpaid leave while the matter is under investigation. If it turns out to be true, you will probably be dismissed from the squad. If the law office doesn't press charges, you might be allowed to return to uniformed police work."

Gunnar was about to reply, but Birkir gestured him to silence and asked, "Is there another way?"

Magnús said, "I have certain connections with these attorneys. I'm very reluctant to pull those strings—but if you agree to go to Berlin immediately, I can try to straighten things out."

Birkir said to Gunnar, "Sounds like a good deal for you."

Gunnar thought for a good while. "OK, then," he eventually replied, "I'll go, but only this one time."

"Beat it, then, and go get yourself a passport," Magnús said, picking up his phone. "I'll tell the head of the agency you need it expedited for travel on official business."

TUESDAY, OCTOBER 13

05:30

It was pitch black and pouring with rain. A cold wind blew from the east. Old snow, thawing in the wet, spattered from beneath the wheels of the few cars driving around Reykjavík so early in the morning—or late at night, depending on how you looked at it. Winter had arrived on October 1, with a sharp frost followed by a strong northerly wind bringing snow to the whole country. Now a new low-pressure area hung to the west of Iceland, dragging in warmer air from the south and raising the temperature above freezing, though the forecast predicted that it would soon track eastward across the country, deepen, and bring more icy weather from the north.

As scheduled the previous evening, Birkir and Gunnar met at the bus terminal and were joined by Anna Thórdardóttir, a forensic officer at the detective division. In the present economic situation, the police force had to cut their expenditures, so there was no available money for a taxi to the airport. The bus would have to do.

After the usual good mornings they had no further need to converse. They were all shivering and were missing their sleep. Birkir went and bought the tickets for them all, asking for a receipt.

In the meantime, Gunnar got himself a couple of buns and a coffee from the cafeteria.

Anna went outside to smoke. This was going to be a long day for her. On a normal day she went through three packs of cigarettes, but now she had to endure a smokeless bus ride to the international airport at Keflavík followed by a flight to Berlin. Her habit had left its mark: Her face was thin and drawn, and though her ID revealed that she wasn't even fifty-five, she looked at least seventy.

"What did Magnús have on you?" Gunnar asked when Anna came back inside. He couldn't imagine that anybody would agree to go on this trip unless forced to.

"Three reprimands for smoking indoors in official buildings," she replied and coughed. Her voice was deep and hoarse. "He promised to withdraw them if I agreed to go with you. What did he have on you?"

"Some rude phone calls to lawyers."

"Rude calls?"

"Yeah, well, maybe not exactly. More like advice on how to deal with a certain case."

"Is that against the rules?"

Gunnar shrugged. "I didn't think so, but it seems nowadays everything is banned unless it's authorized by some regulation and a certificate."

Anna nodded and popped a nicotine gum into her mouth.

"How are you going to survive the flight?" Gunnar asked. He had once been a longtime smoker and was familiar with the craving.

"Sleeping pill and gum," Anna replied.

Birkir motioned for them to follow him out.

"I think I may have forgotten to bring an extra pair of pants," Gunnar said, patting the old sports bag that was all the luggage he had.

"You'll just have to buy yourself another pair in Berlin—if you decide you need them," Birkir said. "I'll help you choose."

Birkir was immaculately dressed in neatly pressed gray trousers and a jacket. He wheeled a new-looking black suitcase; a shoulder bag housed his laptop. Anna had two pieces—a small suitcase and a sturdy tool case made of rigid plastic.

"I don't have any money," Gunnar said after a short deliberation.

"I'll lend you some if you need new pants," Birkir said. He knew that Gunnar had cut up his credit card and only carried cash. When he had any, that is.

They watched their bags get loaded into the luggage hold, and Anna lit a cigarette. Gunnar and Birkir climbed aboard while Anna smoked outside.

"I wonder if you can smoke in the embassy?" Gunnar asked with sympathy.

"I don't know," Birkir replied. "They're sending a driver to meet us. We can ask him."

"*Jawohl*," said Gunnar, leaning back in the seat. He promptly nodded off and slept all the way to Keflavík.

On arrival at the airport, they were retrieving their bags from the bus when a taxicab stopped behind it and a young man in a black suit got out. He came straight over to them and asked, "Are you the police team going to Berlin?"

"Yes," Birkir replied.

"Great," the other one said. "I was told I could recognize you by your . . . well . . . that someone in the group looked . . . uh—"

"That one of us looked Chinese?" Gunnar finished the sentence for him.

"Uh, yeah. I'm from the Foreign Ministry. We'll be going together. I'll handle the legal aspects and relations with the German Foreign Ministry. Good morning to you all—I'm Sigmundur." He shook hands with the three of them.

"This is a very difficult case," he went on. "The minister and the chief secretary are eager for it to be dealt with in a professional manner. That's why they chose me to manage it."

"So maybe we don't need to go?" Gunnar asked, his voice full of hope.

"Well, yes, you do. The chief secretary wants the Icelandic police to investigate the case. You're the one that speaks German, right? Hopefully we'll solve the matter quickly."

"Do you have any experience with investigations like this?" Gunnar asked.

"No, not with murders, but we have had to deal with a number of very difficult cases at the ministry. I've had many dealings with police authorities in Europe."

"I feel better already," Gunnar said, stomping off into the check-in area.

They walked down the Jetway to board the plane and a stewardess greeted them.

The ministry official turned to the police team and smiled apologetically. "I'm afraid this is where we part ways. I've got enough air miles that I was able to upgrade my ticket to Saga Class." He nodded toward the front of the plane. "I'll see you in Berlin."

He turned left and disappeared into the forward seating area. The other three continued to the right, along the aisle to row 23. Anna, leading, immediately slipped into the window seat, fastened her seat belt, and popped a nicotine gum.

Birkir asked Gunnar if he wanted the aisle seat.

Gunnar looked with horror at the seat that was meant to accommodate his huge frame, and then at Anna, who, despite being small and slim, seemed to fully occupy the space allocated to her.

"Am I supposed to sit here?" he asked Birkir, pointing at seat 23C with a stubby finger.

"That's the only option," Birkir replied and shrugged. He sat down in the middle seat. He was also slim and smaller than average, but even so there wasn't much space left.

"Excuse me for a minute," Gunnar said, and turned around. He inched back toward the front of the plane, pushing his way past all the people going the opposite direction. He barked "*Afsakid,* excuse me, *entschuldigen bitte,* sorry" as he went.

When he reached the stewardess standing at the entrance to Saga Class, he flashed a broad grin and pushed past, ignoring her confusion and saying, "Sorry, I just need to have a word with my colleague."

Sigmundur's seat was much more spacious than the one assigned to Gunnar. He was talking to the passenger next to him, a young woman Gunnar recognized from pictures in glossy magazines. He couldn't remember what she was famous for.

Gunnar tapped Sigmundur's shoulder, saying, "Hey, buddy." The ministry official looked up in surprise.

"We need to fix a problem."

"Indeed?"

"I get claustrophobic in those tight coach seats." Gunnar pointed toward the back of the plane.

"Claustrophobic?"

"Yeah. It makes me lose control, and I make these peculiar animal noises. Can't help myself." He demonstrated with a quiet "*Moooohhh.*"

Sigmundur looked around quickly.

Gunnar continued, "I'm afraid that the captain will kick me off the plane before we can take off."

"What?"

"That wouldn't be good. You know the chief secretary was adamant I should be on this case. I speak German, you know."

"Yeah?"

"We'll have to do something about it, won't we?"

"You want me to speak to the captain?"

"No."

"What, then?"

"Change seats with me."

"What?"

Gunnar made another quiet mooing noise and flashed a smile that made the gap between his front teeth particularly prominent. The young woman sitting in the inner seat stared at him in terror.

The man from the ministry looked around again and saw that the passengers in nearby seats were watching them. He stood up, opened the overhead bin, and got out his briefcase.

Gunnar said, "23C. See you in Berlin."

Birkir saw the man from the ministry approach along the aisle, scanning around for seat numbers. He stopped by row 23, opened the overhead bin, and stuffed his briefcase in—with some difficulty, as the compartment was almost full. Then he sat down in the empty seat without uttering a word, and fastened his seat belt.

"It was kind of you to change seats with my colleague," Birkir said.

The man from the ministry was quiet for a while before turning to Birkir. "This associate of yours—is he OK in the head?"

"He's a good detective, he is scrupulous and honest," Birkir replied. "He sometimes uses unusual methods to get what he wants. I hope he wasn't impolite."

Sigmundur looked at Birkir and said, "He behaved like a maniac."

Birkir smiled apologetically. "He is as mentally healthy as you or I. But he can be a bit impulsive sometimes."

Sigmundur unclasped his seat belt. "Right, I can't let him get away with this," he said, standing up.

"Wait, wait," Birkir said, grabbing his arm. "It would be great if you could fill me in during the flight. It would save us time in Berlin."

The ministry man sat down again and sighed. "Well, I just hope he's not going to be a problem when we get to Germany. This is all highly sensitive. The minister is very worried." He refastened his seat belt.

"No there won't be any problems, I can promise you that. Gunnar knows when to behave properly. Tell me what you know about this case."

Sigmundur pulled out a small laptop computer and fired it up.

"Look," he said. "Here's an e-mail I got this morning. It's a statement that's going to be read at a press conference they're giving at the ministry this morning—nine o'clock."

Birkir read from the screen:

Early yesterday morning an official at the Icelandic embassy in Berlin came across a deceased gentleman in the embassy quarters. It was evident that the death had not occurred naturally. The deceased is of Icelandic nationality but not an embassy employee. His name cannot be released at the present time. Icelandic detective officers are now on their way to Berlin, where they will investigate the case in collaboration with the Nordic Embassies' security force, the Berlin police, and the foreign ministries of the two states.

"It would have been better to delay this statement," said Sigmundur, "but the story began to leak out yesterday and we started getting media calls."

He switched off the laptop as the plane backed away from the terminal.

"What else do you know?" Birkir asked.

"Embassy Counselor Arngrímur Ingason called the chief secretary the night before last to report the incident. The chief secretary called a crisis meeting at the ministry very early yesterday morning, and we decided to carry out an initial investigation ourselves."

"What happened exactly?"

"An embassy visitor was knifed to death in the ambassador's office."

"Who was the victim?"

"Anton Eiríksson, an old friend of the ambassador's. A very wealthy man who mainly worked in Asia. An agent of some kind."

"Why didn't you ask the German police to investigate?" Birkir asked.

"This business doesn't look very good for the ambassador. He hosted a party in the embassy building that evening, which is not supposed to happen. He'll have to answer for that."

"What kind of a party?" Birkir asked.

"He'd organized a reading and reception Sunday afternoon in the Felleshus auditorium—the Felleshus is a public building that belongs to all five Nordic embassies. After that he seems to have invited a small group of people for dinner and drinks in the Icelandic embassy building. He apparently started off holding some kind of meeting, and then ordered in food from a restaurant. That in itself is inappropriate, because the premises are not suitable for parties like that. The ambassador's residence is, on the other hand, specially designed to accommodate receptions, and of course he should have taken the visitors there—or to a restaurant—if the occasion demanded it."

"Any idea why he decided to stay at the embassy?"

"No. That's one of our many questions. After dinner, the group apparently continued drinking until sometime after two a.m. When the party finally broke up, the ambassador seems to have forgotten to count the visitors out. The German security guards eventually realized one of them had been left behind inside the embassy, and they contacted Arngrímur."

"How large was this group?"

"At first there were eight—and then nine when Hulda, the ambassador's wife, joined them just after eleven o'clock. Arngrímur sent the list of names yesterday. The security team monitors all visitors that pass through into the embassies' compound, holding their passports while they're in there and logging their details. These particular visitors were all Icelandic nationals, which is one reason we're keeping this case to ourselves."

"Tell me who is on the list."

"First and foremost, the ambassador and his wife," Sigmundur replied. He paused as the plane thundered along the runway and took off. When it was in the air, he continued, "Are you familiar with them?"

Birkir replied, "I've heard of him. Wasn't he a politician?"

"Yeah, that's right. Konrad has been the ambassador in Berlin for just over a year, but before that he was a member of parliament for twenty years or so. At the last party conference, he challenged the sitting chairman and almost defeated him in the party leadership election. He lost by one vote."

"I remember that," Birkir said.

"Yeah, it was a memorable weekend in the political landscape. Two months later, the party unexpectedly found itself in power, even though it had suffered heavy losses in the elections. But there was no way that Konrad would get a ministerial post. Then they came up with the solution to make him ambassador to Berlin. Apparently, he studied at an East German agricultural school when he was young, so his German is pretty good."

"Did everything work out?"

"No major mishaps until now. The foreign service's most experienced and reliable counselor, Arngrímur Ingason, has been at the Berlin embassy for years. He oversees the embassy's work

28

and has mostly managed to prevent any embarrassments. Until yesterday."

"What do you mean by no major mishaps?"

"Konrad functioned well as a typical constituency go-getter when his party was in the opposition. He was actually never in a position to commit any major blunders, but his career was pretty flat. Younger folks had begun to run against him in the primaries, and he needed to do something to draw attention to himself and establish a position within the party. His big break was totally by chance—the party chairman encountered an unexpected crisis involving careless handling of party funds, and Konrad was the only one who'd been preparing to run against him. So he rode the crest of the wave that arose at the party conference and nearly won the leadership election. At the embassy, he's at his best when he isn't doing anything. Fortunately, that's the normal state of things."

"Doesn't that get tiresome?" Birkir asked.

"Konrad is sober for two hours a day. He shows up at the embassy around ten o'clock and has a drink around noon. After that nobody has to worry about him. Somebody told me he spends most of his time writing his autobiography. Hulda, his wife, on the other hand, likes to set up events for Icelandic artists she invites over to Berlin, leaving it to the embassy staff to organize the details, often on short notice. And then nobody knows who's going to pay, and that can cause problems. Especially after the banking crisis. It's difficult to find sponsors these days."

"You said his wife was at the party, too."

"Yes. Hulda turned up at the embassy later that evening, as I said, and left with Konrad when the gathering broke up. She's something else, that woman. The story goes that Konrad finagled her into that pivotal party conference—with full voting rights, even. She represented some women's group. But she went off to get her hair done for the last-night ball, and forgot to vote in the leadership election. Her missing vote would have resulted in a tie, in which case they would have had to draw lots between Konrad and the sitting chairman. The ambassador and his wife sometimes discuss this fact at awkward moments."

Birkir asked, "How will this murder affect the ambassador's position?"

"He'll be recalled home, for the time being at least. I will act on his behalf until he returns or a new ambassador is appointed."

"Who else is on your list?"

The plane had now reached cruising altitude, so Sigmundur woke up his laptop.

"Let's see. Here's Arngrímur's list. First is the guest of honor, Jón Sváfnisson, 'the Sun Poet,'" he read from the computer screen. "Do you know him?"

Birkir said, "I know his poem 'As daylight grows longer and dreams multiply,' et cetera."

"Ah, you know that one," Sigmundur said. "A book of translations of his work was just published in Germany. The ambassador's wife had him come to Berlin and do a reading at the Felleshus auditorium. He came with his old friend, the artist and book designer Fabían Sigrídarson."

"Did the Sun Poet plan to do any other readings in Germany?"

Sigmundur checked his computer screen. "Yes, according to Arngrímur's summary, he's finishing up at the Frankfurt Book Fair next weekend."

"Any more names?"

Sigmundur read, "David Mathieu, the Reykjavík fashion designer—and his husband, Starkadur Gíslason."

"Numbers five and six," Birkir counted.

"Then Helgi Kárason, a ceramic artist, and Lúdvík Bjarnason. They are preparing for an exhibition in the Felleshus to be held in the new year. Lúdvík sometimes works as an overseas exhibition manager for Icelandic artists. He deals with transportation of the works and their installation in the space."

"That makes seven and eight."

"And then there was the deceased, Anton Eiríksson."

"Nine. So, no women?"

"No, apart from the ambassador's wife, of course, and it depends on how you classify the two gays."

"What do you mean by that?" Birkir asked sharply. "Their gender is male, so they are men. Isn't that how it works where you're from?"

"Yeah, I suppose."

"OK, then. Could there possibly have been other guests in the building?"

"It's very unlikely. The security people are checking their logs and security-camera footage. There's an entrance from the underground parking lot, and the cameras pick it up if anybody goes through there—of course, you need a key and a security-access number."

"So the perpetrator's definitely one of these eight?"

"Yes. Has to be."

"Do we know where all these individuals are now?"

Sigmundur looked at the screen and said, "The ambassador and his wife are in Berlin, and the poet and his friend have gone to Frankfurt. The other four are probably on their way back to Iceland or already there, according to what the ambassador told Arngrímur."

"Didn't anyone try to contact them yesterday?"

"Not to my knowledge. The ministry's immediate response was not particularly well coordinated. When they got things sorted out, they realized that the men had left Berlin, and we're hoping they'll show up back in Iceland soon."

Birkir said, "It would have been better to talk to them right away yesterday morning. Individually. The German police could have taken care of that. We could have followed up with interviews today."

"It might have been a bit extreme to ground all those people in Berlin," Sigmundur replied hesitantly.

"Oh well," Birkir said after a pause, "hopefully we'll get hold of them all before long."

Sigmundur became engrossed in his laptop while Birkir thought about the case. Anna quietly snored in the window seat.

13:50

The plane landed, and over the PA a flight attendant announced, "Welcome to Berlin Schönefeld Airport. The local temperature is twelve degrees Celsius."

Birkir, Anna, and Sigmundur had reached the walkway in the terminal building before they caught up to Gunnar, who was trying to tuck his shirt back into his pants.

"Honestly!" he said apologetically. "I must have slept the whole way."

Birkir guessed Gunnar had probably gotten himself two in-flight meals from the attendants and drunk three or four beers before spending most of the journey fast asleep. "You should be well rested, then," he said.

Sigmundur watched Gunnar's behavior with disdain, but said nothing. He pressed his cell phone to his ear.

Anna made a beeline for the corner where smoking was permitted and lit a cigarette. She waved the others on as they passed, saying, "I'll be with you in a minute."

"The embassy chauffeur is here at the airport," Sigmundur said, pocketing his phone. "He'll meet us by the exit."

Birkir eyed Gunnar as they walked toward the baggage claim.

"How do you feel about being in Germany?" he asked.

"It's kinda strange," Gunnar admitted, looking around. "I mean, I'm used to hearing people speak German in Iceland. Tourists, and all. But here it's everywhere. I'm fond of this language—I picked it up from my mom before I learned Icelandic."

Gunnar's voice trembled slightly as he spoke.

"I know you don't like traveling," Birkir said, "but why the hell haven't you ever made the effort to come here before?"

"My dear old mom has had a phobia about the country ever since she fled to Iceland," Gunnar replied. "She went through something really bad at the end of the war, and I understand that the situation here was terrible. She came to Iceland from Lübeck, but her roots were in the eastern half—that was her Germany. She was sure she wouldn't be allowed to leave the country if she came back to visit here."

"But after the fall of Communism in East Germany? Wasn't she happier after the reunification?"

"No, not at all. She thought it would all go down the drain. She's totally convinced there's going to be another war in Europe. It's kind of an obsession. She was always very unhappy when I brought up the idea of going to Germany, and I just got used to the idea that it wasn't going to happen."

"So how did she react to this trip now?" Birkir asked.

"I told her I was going to the east of Iceland, to Egilsstadir," Gunnar said. "You'll back me up on that, won't you?"

"I'll try," Birkir replied.

14:30

The embassy driver stood outside the customs area holding a card with "Icelandic Embassy" printed on it. He was a neatly dressed, shortish, middle-aged man with thick dark hair carefully combed back. Sigmundur greeted him in English and introduced his companions as "the Icelandic police."

Gunnar nodded familiarly at the man, who bowed in greeting.

"Please follow me," the man said in English, leading the way out of the terminal building. Birkir nudged Gunnar and they fell behind the others. "Try to get to know this guy. He could be useful to us."

Gunnar nodded. "Let's hear what he's got to say."

The embassy car, a spacious BMW, was waiting for them in the short-term parking lot. The driver skillfully shoehorned all five bags into the trunk and then opened the driver's side rear door for Anna, who stubbed out her cigarette before getting in. Sigmundur was about to climb into the front passenger seat, but Gunnar tapped him on the shoulder.

"Hey, buddy, I have longer legs than you, and my butt is wider." He smiled, revealing the gap between his front teeth.

Sigmundur hesitated, but then climbed into the backseat next to Birkir and Anna.

"Thanks for meeting us," Gunnar said to the driver in German as they drove off. "I hope it hasn't been too much of an inconvenience for you."

"Oh, you're German?" the driver said. "How long have you lived in Iceland?"

"All my life," Gunnar said. "My mother is German. She moved to Iceland after the war."

"I see. She has taught you good German."

"We always speak German together. I understand that we sound somewhat old-fashioned."

"You speak excellent High German," the driver replied.

"Thank you very much for the compliment," Gunnar said as he studied the distant outline of the city out the window. Then he added, "You have a bit of a problem at the embassy, huh? Do you know anything about it?"

"No, hardly anything. We've only been told that a deceased man was discovered in the ambassador's office yesterday morning. All the staffers are devastated. The Icelandic embassy building is locked, and they have to work in a couple of borrowed rooms in the Felleshus."

"So you don't know who the deceased is?"

"No, I haven't heard anything else about it. Embassy Counselor Herr Ingason had a brief meeting with all the staff yesterday morning and told us that the deceased was not linked to the embassy, but that he was some kind of acquaintance of the ambassador's."

Gunnar was silent for a while, enjoying the sights of the big city. He hadn't experienced an urban environment like this, and found it a little overwhelming. He also wondered where to take the conversation next, as he sensed that the driver was not a very willing participant in a discussion about his workplace, but too polite to make this obvious. Probably best to go down a completely different road. He said, "What's the latest soccer news? I saw on the Internet that Hertha tied scoreless against Bochum Saturday."

"Ah, you're a soccer fan?" The driver's face lit up.

"Yes, Hertha is my team."

"Is that so?"

"Yeah, ever since 1995, when Sverrisson joined the club."

The driver grinned broadly. "Ah, Jolly Sverrisson," he said. "Everyone remembers him. Sverrisson was a great player. Maybe not the most skillful, but he was hard-hitting and reliable. He did a lot for the team."

"Yeah, it was a great team when it finally got into the Bundesliga."

"I agree. The team is very strong again now in my opinion."

"Yeah, but it's lame that they didn't beat a low-ranked team like Bochum," Gunnar said, grabbing the handle above the door as the driver took a sharp curve.

"Yeah, that was bad. If you're still here on Saturday, you can go to the Olympic Stadium. Hertha's playing at home against Stuttgart. The ambassador sometimes goes to soccer games, and he invites me if there aren't any visitors. I'll tell him you're a fan."

"I'll definitely be back in Iceland by then, but thanks anyway," Gunnar said. After a short silence, he asked, "What's he like, the ambassador?"

The driver hesitated, then said, "He has many good qualities."

"Such as?"

"He's always very friendly and grateful for everything you do for him. He speaks very good German, and he's kind."

"Any flaws?"

"It's hardly worth mentioning. He's a bit . . ." The driver let go of the steering wheel with his right hand and pretended to drink from a glass. "You understand," he said.

"Ah. But he's always compos mentis, isn't he?"

"Um, yes, but he does sometimes fall asleep in the car when I'm driving him home from gatherings. The butler at the residence helps me get him into the house."

"What about the ambassador's wife?"

The driver pretended not to hear the question. "Here ahead you can see the Tiergarten Park woods. We're almost at the embassy. Herr Ingason is waiting to meet you."

"Counselor Ingason? Not the ambassador?"

"No, the ambassador is at home. Herr Ingason deals with everything at the embassy on his behalf. He's a very solid and reliable gentleman. The ambassador would be lost without him."

He focused his attention on driving, shortly taking a right to arrive at a building complex on their left. In front of the complex stood a row of flags representing the five Nordic countries.

The driver parked at the curb, briskly got out, and opened the door for Anna. An older man standing nearby approached and greeted the passengers as they climbed out of the car.

"I am Counselor Arngrímur Ingason," he said, repeating his name as he shook hands with each of the three police officers in turn. Birkir introduced himself first, and then the others.

Sigmundur and Arngrímur exchanged perfunctory greetings—they obviously knew one another.

"Thank you for responding so quickly," Arngrímur said to the trio as they gathered their luggage. Gunnar handled the tool case for Anna, who used the opportunity to light a cigarette.

"That's our job, I guess," said Birkir, taking in the surroundings. Through a glass wall he could see an open area between the embassy buildings. The encircling copper wall was mostly hidden from this angle, but the complex looked impressive in the sunshine.

The driver said something in German to the counselor, then climbed into the car and drove off.

"He's going to get the ambassador," Arngrímur said. "We held a press conference in the Felleshus earlier this morning to inform the media about the case, and then Konrad went home for a rest. But he wanted to meet you here as soon as possible. We've booked hotel rooms for you, but I assume that you'll want to see the embassy immediately. Inspect the scene, and everything."

"Yes," Birkir said. "The sooner the better."

"Exactly. Please follow me," Arngrímur said, leading the way toward the entrance to the reception area. Anna was still smoking, so they stopped outside and waited while she finished her cigarette.

Birkir looked up. Horizontally across the entrance were long glass plates, one above the other, with the inscription "Nordic Embassies" in six languages. The bottom one was in German; the Icelandic one was fourth from the top and the Finnish was on top, but Birkir couldn't distinguish between the Danish, Norwegian, and Swedish ones—the spellings were too similar for his limited knowledge of those languages.

Sigmundur said, "I need to start by meeting with the embassy staffers. They're here in the Felleshus, aren't they?"

"Yes," Arngrímur said, and explained to Sigmundur where to find the conference room they were using. Sigmundur excused himself and disappeared into the building.

"Can you keep him occupied?" Gunnar asked. "To stop him from interfering in our business?"

"I can try," Arngrímur said, not batting an eyelid.

Anna stubbed out her cigarette, and Arngrímur showed them into the building and toward a reception window.

"Please hand over your passports and exchange them for visitors' passes," he said.

They were given white plastic cards bearing the Icelandic flag to clip on. Then they followed Arngrímur through double doors, which he opened with a pass card. They found themselves in the open plaza that linked the separate buildings.

Arngrímur said, "The building we came through is shared by all the embassies and is open to the public. We call it the Felleshus. Besides the front desk area, there are rooms designed for conferences and exhibitions. There's also a restaurant. We booked two conference rooms there today as a temporary working facility for our people. The Danish embassy building is here to the left, and then, working around clockwise, we have the Icelandic building over there in the corner—then the Norwegian, the Swedish, and finally the Finnish one here to the right."

In front of the Finnish embassy a small children's choir stood, singing.

People had come out of the buildings to listen. It was comfortably warm in the sunshine. The buildings provided shelter from the breeze, and the air outside was refreshing. The Icelanders automatically stopped to listen to the pure sound of the unaccompanied singing. As the song came to an end, the audience applauded and the conductor, a young woman, bowed in acknowledgment. Then she gave the tone for the next song, and the choir started up again. At this point Arngrímur had walked on ahead, but as the first notes reached their ears, he stopped dead in his tracks. Birkir recognized the melody and could hear that the choir was singing in Icelandic. The pronunciation was, forgivably, not perfect, but the children sang beautifully and in tune. It was a well-known Icelandic song set to a poem by Jón Sváfnisson, the poet who'd been one of the ambassador's visitors on the night of the killing. A strange coincidence, perhaps—though the song *was* very popular throughout Scandinavia as a choral arrangement.

As daylight grows longer and dreams multiply
a delicate breeze dusts your cheek, and you stir.
I question not whence it came, whereby,
nor whither its purposes were.
But you see that the springtime and freedom no slumber confer.

As mountain brooks babble and moorlands grow green,
A magic enthralls me, insistent, an ache.
I fetch you my fairest of verses
and find this the path I must take.
But I see that with springtime and freedom I slumber forsake.

As light casts new warmth upon lowland and hillside,
over lakes all a-shimmer the cloud-armies go.
I think about you and give thanks that
all things in creation are so.
But you see that the springtime and freedom no slumber bestow.

The choir sang all three verses and received enthusiastic applause at the end. Birkir looked at his companions; all were smiling and clapping. Not Arngrímur, though. He stood frozen, his face turned away from the others. As the applause died down, he glanced quickly over his shoulder before continuing toward the Icelandic embassy building. Birkir caught up to him.

"Is the embassy open today?" he asked.

Arngrímur cleared his throat twice. Finally he said, "No, we decided to keep the office closed until you're done with your work. Like I said before, the staff is working in the available Felleshus rooms. They can access our computer system from there, and phone calls are routed there. Consular services are open as usual in the Felleshus, and any visitors are directed there."

They reached the entrance to the Icelandic building and stopped to wait for the others. Birkir thought that Arngrímur's voice had seemed unsteady.

"Please enter," Arngrímur said, opening the door and showing them in. "A German police team was here yesterday to carry out the initial investigation on the scene, after which the body was taken away. We requested that they do the autopsy here in Berlin. Other than that, everything here is exactly as it was when I arrived yesterday morning."

Arngrímur's voice had regained its previous strength, and he added, "Commissar Tobias Fischer will arrive momentarily to deliver a preliminary report."

Birkir gazed out the window opposite the entrance. It overlooked a small open space between the building and the copper wall, loosely paved with black lava flagstones.

Seeing that this had caught Birkir's attention, Arngrímur said, "There's red lighting under the paving you can switch on so this looks like a fresh lava flow. When we have time, I'll show you around the whole building and explain the architecture."

They left their luggage by the front desk in the entrance hall and climbed the stairs up to the second floor.

"The ambassador's party was held here in the conference room," Arngrímur said, pointing at an open door. "He also had a brief meeting with part of the group in his office on the top floor," he added.

"Who attended that meeting?" Birkir asked.

"The ambassador will have to answer that when he comes," Arngrímur said. "He was a bit vague about it during our discussions yesterday."

"You weren't here at the embassy Sunday?"

"No, I was in Stuttgart all weekend and didn't get back to Berlin until late Sunday evening. There was a serious traffic accident Friday involving an Icelandic family—a couple with two children. The mother was killed, and the others were injured and are in the hospital. It's a horrible case. I went there to provide support until Icelandic relatives arrived to help."

"So you had a difficult weekend?"

"Yes, and it's not over yet. But this is all part of the job. Some days are more difficult than others. We don't complain."

"I see," Birkir said. He looked into the conference room, where the smell from leftover food was beginning to overpower the suggestion of stale alcohol lingering in the air.

"This is where the visitors had dinner," Arngrímur said. "I hope you'll give me permission to have the room cleaned soon."

"We'll do our best," Birkir replied.

They walked up to the next floor, and Arngrímur showed them the staff kitchenette.

Arngrímur said, "They got all the tableware and glasses from here. The liquor, on the other hand, was brought up from a storage room in the basement, and it seems like there wasn't much other activity on this floor that night."

"Where was the body?" Birkir asked.

"Upstairs, in the ambassador's office on the top floor. I found it sitting in a chair in there. It was totally shocking, of course."

"We won't go up there just yet," Birkir said. "First we need to hear from the local *polizei* about their crime-scene investigation. Anna can proceed with the forensics in light of that."

"It all must be done in an organized way, of course—I understand that." Arngrímur looked at his watch. "The German police officer should be here any minute."

Birkir looked around. "We'll need access to a room that was definitely locked and not used on the night in question. We'll make that our base."

Arngrímur nodded and said, "There's an office on the floor below. We use it for interns sometimes, but we haven't any interns at the moment. The ambassador doesn't have keys to that room, so he couldn't have let anyone in there Sunday evening."

15:45

As they walked back down to the second floor, Arngrímur's cell phone rang.

After a brief conversation, he told Gunnar, "That was the front desk of the Felleshus. The local police officer has arrived."

Gunnar said, "I'll speak to him. Is there a restaurant or something over there? I'm starving."

"My apologies—you need to eat, of course."

Birkir said, "A sandwich and some seltzer water is plenty for me. It'd be good if it could be sent here."

"A sandwich for me, too," Anna said, "and a Coke. But first I need to go out for a cigarette."

Gunnar accompanied Arngrímur across the plaza to the Felleshus, where they met Commissar Fischer from the Berlin Police, a tall man with thick gray hair and a neatly trimmed beard. His brown eyes sparkled with humor. Gunnar greeted him in German, and they immediately seemed to click. They agreed to go talk in the cafeteria on the second floor so that Gunnar could get something to eat.

"I think better on a full stomach," he said.

Gunnar got himself a double portion of Hungarian goulash with bread on the side. Fischer accepted a cup of coffee and a wedge of cake. Arngrímur signed for the bill and left, carrying sandwiches, Coke, and seltzer water for the others.

"Iceland—I've got to visit Iceland to see the mountains, the glaciers, and the hot springs," Fischer said when they'd settled into a corner table. "Next time we'll have a meeting in Reykjavík."

"For sure," Gunnar said, grinning.

From a cardboard box he'd brought, Fischer produced the murder weapon enclosed in clear plastic. He handed it to Gunnar, who examined it through its wrapper. It was a large hunting knife with leather handle, covered in blood.

"American product," Fischer said. "Nineteen-centimeter blade, overall length twenty-seven point three centimeters. Known as an SOG Super Bowie. List price two hundred sixty-two US dollars. It wasn't ever available in stores here in Germany, as far as we can ascertain. Unfortunately, blood spread along the handle after the killer let go of it. We can't find a clean area to look for finger or palm prints. The blade is completely unworn and very sharp—a knife in top condition. You could rip the thickest cowhide with a weapon like this."

He pulled a large envelope from his briefcase and extracted several color photographs. The first one showed a fat, bald man sitting hunched over in a fancy office chair. He was dressed in a dark-gray suit and a white open-necked shirt. A gaping wound split the man's abdomen, and the knife stuck out from its lower end. The blade had sliced through his clothing, and internal pressure had forced the wound open to fifteen centimeters at its widest.

Fischer said, "The killer plunged the knife deep into the victim's abdomen halfway between the sternum and the navel, probably using his right hand, since the incision slants marginally to the left. He then pushed the knife downward with considerable force, slitting the abdomen all the way down to the pubic bone. At that point he would have let go of the weapon, and blood, guts and stomach contents would have gushed from the wound and over the knife handle. Very likely over the killer's hand and arm, too. The victim would have passed out within a few seconds from shock and blood loss. Death probably occurred soon after."

"Wouldn't he have called for help or screamed as he was attacked?" Gunnar asked.

"Sure, but the sound wouldn't have carried two floors down to where the party was apparently being held. We can assist you in éxperimenting with that if you like. And the killer could have muzzled the victim with his free hand. The autopsy may reveal signs of that."

"At what stage is your investigation?" Gunnar asked.

Fischer took out a notebook. "We received a message from our Foreign Ministry at 10:27 yesterday morning. We were asked to come to the embassy and carry out a regular examination of the body at the crime scene prior to arranging for its removal and transportation to the pathology laboratory here in Berlin. Our procedure included marking out and detailed photography of the scene. Also preliminary medical examination, thermometry and taking some tissue samples. Transportation of the body and its detached parts was carried out by specialist removers. Our orders from the ministry were to comply with the senior embassy official's instructions. Following the body's removal, we were to do nothing more here, so no further forensic investigation was carried out at the scene. No interrogation took place, either. The Foreign Ministry was adamant that the investigation was the responsibility of the Icelandic state, and that we were only to provide such assistance as Iceland requested. The embassy is out of our jurisdiction."

"Goddamned mindless bureautwats. They've succeeded in delaying the investigation by twenty-four hours," Gunnar said. "I hope you didn't comply?"

Fischer smiled apologetically. "There wasn't much else we could do."

He pulled a wallet wrapped in plastic from his bag. "Here are the deceased's personal effects," he said, handing the packet to Gunnar. "This is what he had with him."

"Anything specific?"

"No. Cash, credit cards, business cards, a key."

"A key. You mean a key ring?"

"No key ring. Just a single key in a wallet compartment. Probably to some kind of safe."

"I see," Gunnar said. "Anything else?"

"Yes, actually," Fischer replied. "I did a search for the man's name in our database. Just to see if he had been involved in anything."

"And?"

"We have for some time been increasing our surveillance of German citizens who frequent Asian countries and are suspected of committing sexual crimes against children. We're trying to make it easier to implement laws sanctioning prosecution of such individuals here in Germany, as happens in many other European countries. We also inform the relevant Asian authorities of our suspicions so they can take measures against traffickers and child abusers at the source. Some things we do in these countries are slightly dubious according to our procedures and laws, but we take the view that these matters are so serious that the end justifies the means. Herr Eiríksson's name appeared on a list from one of our informers in Indonesia. Eiríksson is known there by the pseudonym Tenderloin, and he is very active in this field. These guys keep their real names as secret as possible, of course, but our man followed Eiríksson for two days and eventually managed to bribe his way to a copy of a hotel bill. I don't suppose that Anton Eiríksson is a very common name, so there's no doubt about this. Unfortunately we haven't yet established clear working rules on how to deal with information on citizens of other countries, so nothing has been done so far in this individual's case."

"How did Eiríksson attract your attention?" Gunnar asked.

"He was a frequent visitor to some kind of a 'rest and relaxation' hotel that has an extremely bad reputation. Very young children, boys and girls, are hired there for service jobs, but it seems that this includes some very serious sexual abuse. These children come from poor families of the lowest social orders of society, and it is very difficult to eradicate this business."

"I see," Gunnar said. He glanced at a picture of the corpse. "This guy was a serious piece of shit. He probably won't be missed."

"Probably not," Fischer said. "And it was a brutal attack. Somebody paid him back with interest."

"What would the next stage of your investigation have involved?" Gunnar asked.

"A thorough forensic investigation of the whole floor. Fingerprints, hair and biological specimens. If you'd like assistance, I can call our specialists in. Your forensic officer can oversee things and make sure the investigation is satisfactory. We can provide secure storage for any biological specimens. All this will certainly speed things up."

"Good idea and good offer," Gunnar said. He took out his cell phone and called Birkir. After a short discussion he nodded.

"Yes, please. My colleagues and the ambassador are grateful for your help."

Now it was Fischer's turn to make a call. "They'll be here shortly," he said as he hung up. "The Foreign Ministry did ask us to assist you as much as possible."

Having finished his second bowl of soup, Gunnar was wiping his mouth with the sleeve of his jacket when a man in his fifties approached their table.

"Guten appetit," the newcomer said. "I am Wolf. I'm a security guard, and I was on duty the night before last. Herr Ingason asked me to update you on the investigations we have carried out at the guard post." He was dressed in a plain uniform with an ID card hanging around his neck. He carried a laptop under his arm.

Gunnar and Fischer stood up and shook hands with Wolf as they introduced themselves. Gunnar called the waitress over and asked for more coffee and an extra cup.

"We've checked all the security systems relevant to what happened over the weekend," Wolf said. "We will make a detailed report, but I can tell you where we're at so far."

"Thanks," Gunnar said. "That'll be very useful."

Wolf opened the laptop and switched it on. He fished some printed notes out of his pocket and placed them on the table. "According to the automatic computer log, the Icelandic embassy security system was switched on at five thirty last Friday afternoon, when the last staff member left the building at the end of the workday," he read from a sheet of paper. "This is a comprehensive system with automatic door sensors at all entrances and several motion sensors on each floor. No signals were detected from any sensor until the ambassador opened the main door of the building Sunday at 18:10 and deactivated the system at the control board in the entrance lobby. The building was unquestionably empty at that point."

Wolf opened a program on his laptop to show footage from the security cameras, and Gunnar and Fischer saw an image of the plaza between the embassy buildings; a few people came into the picture, walking toward the Icelandic embassy.

Wolf said, "We have footage from the cameras monitoring the plaza, and they show us seven individuals accompanying the ambassador into the embassy building. You'll get copies of all these recordings on disc, by the way, along with our written report. Next thing we see is that at 19:40 the ambassador emerges and crosses to the main entrance of the Felleshus to accept his food delivery. At 22:55, a female arrived at the Felleshus entrance by cab and introduced herself as the Icelandic ambassador's wife. She called her husband herself, and he came over to the reception desk and checked her in as a guest. At that time, the ambassador told the guard that the meeting would soon be over, but for whatever reason that didn't turn out to be the case. At 02:25, the ambassador called the security guard and asked him to call three cabs. At 02:41, two men came out of the Icelandic building, walked across to the Felleshus, and exchanged their guest passes for their passports."

Wolf consulted his notes. "According to the guard's log, these two were Herr Gíslason and Herr Mathieu. Ten minutes later, six people came out of the Icelandic building and crossed to the Felleshus. These were Ambassador Björnsson and his wife, Herr Sváfnisson, Herr Sigrídarson, Herr Kárason, and Herr Bjarnason."

A moving image appeared on the screen: One man supported the woman, who was barefoot and carrying one shoe in her hand; another, a tall man in his shirtsleeves, performed some clumsy dance steps and waved his arms about; a third man carried a jacket that probably belonged to the dancer he was trying to steer toward the exit; the fourth was obviously limping; and the fifth was bent over, clutching his stomach. The group moved across the plaza and disappeared out of camera range.

"Herr Sváfnisson had lost his guest pass, and Ambassador Björnsson signed for the return of his passport on behalf of the embassy. The ambassador and his wife went straight to one of the waiting cabs and drove away. The other four men climbed into the second car. The guard kept an eye on them, as Herr

Sváfnisson was somewhat restless and noisy. In the end, the cab-driver refused to drive them. He got out of the car and was about to call the police, at which point the security guard came out and settled matters—Herr Sváfnisson moved into the backseat and the other three undertook to keep him under control. Herr Kárason tipped the cab driver an extra one hundred euros, and he agreed to take them to their hotel. This disturbance was the reason the guard didn't pick up on the fact that one of the visitors hadn't presented himself to reclaim his passport. When he eventually noticed, he immediately called me—I was on call and asleep in the security-section bunk room. I got up at once, and we started searching the outside area. We didn't find anybody, but we could see from our control desk that the ambassador hadn't reactivated the security system in the Icelandic building. The regulations prevent us from entering any embassy unless the alarm system gives a signal or circumstances specifically demand it. That wasn't the case, and I decided to call Herr Ingason, who lives nearby. He supervises all communications between the Icelandic embassy and the security guards, so that seemed the obvious thing to do. Herr Ingason arrived here at 03:27 by cab and proceeded alone into the Icelandic building.

"At 03:43, he returned to our guard post and said he'd found the visitor dead. I asked if he was sure the man was dead, or if we should call an ambulance. Herr Ingason said he was very sure that he was dead. I then asked if he had any instructions for us. He said he needed to consult with the Icelandic authorities immediately and that he would do this by telephone from the embassy. He asked me to reserve a conference room in the Felleshus and direct the Icelandic embassy staffers there as they showed up for work. The only thing to add is that we examined the CCTV footage monitoring the entrance to the embassy from the basement parking area, but it shows no movement from Friday until the body was removed after lunch yesterday. This tallies with the door sensor, which logged no openings during the period."

Gunnar asked, "Is the sensor active when the alarm system is off?"

"Yes. It logs the time whenever the door is opened but gives no alarm signal if the security system is not activated. There is no such entry in the log."

"Would a professional be able to open the door without the sensor picking it up?"

Wolf shook his head. "I'm almost sure that's impossible. The manufacturer says it can't be done."

"How about the other embassy buildings? Were they empty that evening?"

"There were some comings and goings during the evening, but nobody approached the entrance to the Icelandic building. It's set away from the other buildings. We've got recordings from two cameras covering the entrance, and only the people I've mentioned were spotted there."

Gunnar said, "The murder weapon is a large knife." He passed the box to the guard. "Don't you have measures to prevent this kind of weapon from being taken into the embassies?"

Wolf replied, "The weapons-inspection levels vary in severity. There are three degrees of alert status. The highest is activated when there is political tension and threats have been issued, as when some Scandinavian newspaper published a cartoon of the prophet Mohamed. At that level, we have recourse to a Berlin-based security firm for backup, and all our security measures are augmented—the search for weapons is as rigorous as in airport security. But most of the time the alert status is low, which it was on Sunday. There's a metal detector in the double entrance door from the Felleshus into the plaza. Coins or cell phones in people's pockets don't trigger it, but larger objects—which would include guns and large knives—do. If it gives a signal, the inner door won't open and the person in question is asked to step back. The security guard will then carry out a regular body search. I assume a knife like that would activate the alarm, but we can test it later."

"We'll do that," Gunnar said. "But everything seems to indicate that the killer was one of the eight in the party."

"Yes," Wolf said. "Anything else is very unlikely."

Gunnar turned to Fischer. "If you had been instructed to investigate the case, you would've brought all eight of them in for interviews yesterday morning. And you'd have isolated them and questioned them individually—correct?"

"Yes," Fischer replied. "It might have taken a while getting qualified interpreters to assist us, but we would have tried to get a good handle on the course of events right away."

"Exactly," Gunnar said. "But instead the witnesses scatter in all directions and get plenty of time to synchronize their stories. The killer is at large and capable of doing anything."

"That's right," Fischer said, nodding.

16:00

Birkir and Anna were eating their sandwiches in an office on the second floor when Konrad arrived at the embassy. The ambassador was a shortish, stout man with thin, gray hair, combed straight back and smoothed down with gel. He had a slight limp, taking noticeably shorter steps with his right foot.

"*Guten appetit,*" he said, and waved Birkir away when the latter started to put down his sandwich in order to greet him. "Don't let me interrupt your meal," he said with a weary smile and sat down in an unoccupied chair.

While he finished his snack, Birkir studied the ambassador. He'd seen his type before. Here was a man suffering the consequences of excessive alcohol the night before, who was so used to this malaise that it was more or less natural to him. His face was puffed and etched with deep wrinkles. Though his eyes were clear and awake, they were bloodshot, with bags under them.

Birkir's cell phone rang. It was Gunnar, telling him about the commissar's offer to help with the forensics. Anna was hugely relieved to hear this. She had been anticipating many days' work alone in the building. When Birkir explained to him that otherwise the office would be closed for several days, the ambassador also voiced his approval.

Anna put down her half-eaten sandwich and went out for a cigarette. Birkir took a recorder from his pocket and looked at the ambassador. "Do you mind if I tape our conversation on this?" he asked. "It's important for me to get all the details straight."

"Of course that's OK," the ambassador said.

"Tell me about Sunday," Birkir said, after dictating the usual preliminaries about place, time, and persons present.

"Where should I start?"

"When did you arrive at the embassy that day? What was the occasion?"

"I arrived at the Felleshus around two thirty. The reading of works by my friend Jón—the Sun Poet—was scheduled for three o'clock in the main auditorium. A translation of his poetry anthology was recently published in Germany, and he's here to promote it."

"Was this event only for an invited audience?"

"No, not at all. The reading was open to the public, and had been promoted in the cultural sections of some of the local newspapers. Also in a group mail to Icelanders living in Berlin, and a number of German Icelandophiles. Then I specifically invited a few visiting Icelanders I know, and some folks also accompanied Jón, or were invited by him. Around sixty people in total. It began with a half-hour reading of the translations by a German actor. Then, after a short intermission, Jón himself read the Icelandic originals for another half hour or so." Konrad grimaced. "A terribly tedious program, to be honest, but there are things you have to endure in this job. We diplomats need a strong bladder and high boredom threshold to survive."

The ambassador briefly grinned, until he saw that Birkir was not amused. "During the intermission, I mingled with those I know among the group, and invited them to drinks after the readings. About thirty people, I guess. They waited with me outside the auditorium while the Sun Poet signed books, and then we went upstairs to the second floor, where there were light refreshments. Gradually people began to leave, and there were just eight of us left by six o'clock, which marked the end of the Felleshus caterers' scheduled time. I still had some personal things to discuss with some of the group, so I invited them over to the embassy building. You have the guest list, don't you?"

Birkir nodded.

"Soon folks got hungry, so I ordered delivery from a Chinese restaurant, and we ate in the conference room."

"Why didn't you invite them over to your residence?"

Konrad smiled weakly. "Under normal circumstances I would have, but my in-laws are visiting me right now. I hate to say it, but they are so insufferably fussy that I couldn't inflict them on my guests."

"That bad?"

"It's mainly that they don't like being around folks who are drinking alcohol," Konrad admitted. "And I can't just send them to bed when we have guests."

Birkir frowned. "But couldn't you go to a restaurant?"

The ambassador patiently replied, "That would have been a good idea if it hadn't been for my friend, the Sun Poet Jón Sváfnisson. He insists on reciting poetry to everybody, and often gets up on a chair or even a table to do so. I've twice been asked to leave a restaurant when dining with that fellow. No, it was a logical decision to use this room in the embassy for our dinner. All it should have involved was cleaning a single conference room afterward. We have people to take care of that sort of thing."

"But you didn't just stick to that part of the building, did you?"

"No. As I told you, I needed to meet privately with certain individuals in the group, which I did in my office on the fourth floor. I also went up to the third floor to fetch utensils and glasses from the kitchenette. And some people went to the restrooms on the upper floors when they found the nearest one occupied."

"What were these meetings that you needed to have?"

"First of all there was Helgi Kárason, the pottery artist—and his exhibition manager, Lúdvík Bjarnason. They have booked some weeks in the Felleshus's main gallery in the new year, and were checking it out. Our meeting was just a confirmation of the embassy participation in the exhibition, as my staff will be dealing with the practical issues. Counselor Arngrímur is in charge of that, and he should have attended this meeting, but, because of other duties, he was unable to."

"Why was this meeting held on a Sunday?"

"It was a convenient arrangement, as they'd planned to attend the reading anyway. We scheduled our meeting some time in advance."

"What about the other meetings? Were they also planned ahead?"

"No. They were really just chats after the reception. I spoke with Jón and his companion about the Frankfurt Book Fair. They wanted me to go there and attend a reception to celebrate his anthology's publication. They were probably hoping I'd offer to pay for the refreshments, too. And finally there was a brief meeting for me to introduce Anton to David, the fashion designer. Anton had some extremely good connections in Asia that have been very useful for our clothing manufacturers. He sources good quality and very cheap producers, which is valuable at this time, when capital is scarce everywhere. Starkadur, David's partner, was also at our meeting."

"Did Anton stay in your office?"

"I left the three of them there so they could exchange information, but they all came back downstairs shortly afterward. Anton ate with us. I don't know when he went back upstairs—he asked me two or three times if he could use my office phone, and may have gone up more times than that. A new workday had started in the part of the world where he's got projects, I guess. The last time he went was probably a little while before we left the building."

"So you don't know who would have been the last person with him in your office?"

"No, damn it. I've gone over it again and again over the past twenty-four hours, but the picture doesn't get any clearer."

"How come you didn't notice Anton was still in the building when you left the embassy?"

"One really shouldn't speak ill of one's wife, but—in confidence—my dear Hulda kind of made herself the center of attention when she joined us. She sometimes gets goddamned cranky with me for wanting to enjoy myself in good company. When it was time for the guests to leave, I had security call three taxis. I thought Anton went in the first cab, and I wasn't aware of anything unusual when my wife and I left the embassy—we were the last ones to go. I have a feeling somebody said that Anton had left, but I can't remember who. Four of the guests were with us when Hulda and I checked out of the Felleshus."

"Are you sure you don't know who said that Anton had left? That could be really important."

Konrad shook his head. "I know it's important, but I'm not sure that anybody did mention it. Maybe I just thought I'd seen him leave with David and Starkadur."

"And the security guards didn't notice that one of the visitors was missing when you left?"

"No, but there was a reason. Jón was making a ruckus—he'd lost his guest pass, and I had to vouch for him so he could get his passport back. Then he offended the cab driver, and the security guard had to handle things because Hulda and I had already gone in the second cab. The head of security told me all this yesterday."

"How did you know Anton?"

"He's been a political supporter of mine for thirty years, and he's a good buddy. His roots were in my constituency, and he was a useful ward heeler back in the day. Then he started up this foreign business, after which he was just a contributor to party funds. I sometimes introduced him to potential customers. Our friendship helped his credibility."

"What was his business?"

"He was very familiar with the Asian scene. Early on he started going there to check out various kinds of factories. He was particularly good at finding manufacturers who could deliver high-quality but cost-effective products. Lots of entrepreneurs have used his services as a go-between."

"Entrepreneurs?"

"Yes—hardworking innovators with good ideas. They can use a guy with good connections and who knows the culture. At one point there was talk of making Anton Icelandic ambassador to East Asia, but the minister demurred on account of some gossip."

"Gossip?"

"It's not something that I can repeat."

"Did Anton have any family?"

"He was unmarried, and had no children."

"Was he in this business by himself?"

"Yes, but he had an assistant who traveled with him."

"So the assistant wasn't with him here at the embassy on Sunday?"

"No. Anton came on his own—after the reading, in fact."

"Have you heard from this assistant?"

"Yes, he contacted us yesterday when Anton didn't show up at their hotel. Arngrímur informed him of Anton's death and took the guy's information. The man also agreed to wait for our police to contact him at the hotel. Arngrímur has his name and cell phone number."

"Who knew that Anton would be visiting here?"

"I have no idea. I only found out myself shortly before the reading, when he called to invite me out to dinner. He said he was in Berlin unexpectedly for one night and wanted to see me. I told him to come to the embassy, which he did."

"So the killer must have had some other way of finding out that Anton was expected at the embassy?"

The ambassador hesitated. "Yes, if he actually did have that information in advance."

"He must have known it, since he brought his weapon with him. He couldn't have found the knife here in the building, could he?"

"No." Konrad shook his head. "I understand it was some kind of hunting knife."

"Which one of your guests is most likely to carry a knife like that?"

"I have no idea."

"You're certain you didn't keep such a knife in your office desk?"

"Absolutely certain."

Arngrímur, Gunnar, and Commissar Fischer met the German forensic team's van outside the Felleshus. Arngrímur directed them to the basement parking lot's entrance beneath the plaza, and opened it with a remote control. The van drove cautiously down the ramp, with the three of them following on foot. Arngrímur pointed out where the entrance to the Icelandic embassy was, at the far end of the basement. It was quicker to move the equipment this way than to carry it through the Felleshus and across the plaza. This was the same route taken when the body was removed from the crime scene twenty-four hours earlier.

Fischer said, "I assume the security people will have all the entrance systems here professionally tested."

"I'll look into that," Arngrímur replied, opening the door to the embassy basement.

Four forensic specialists clad in white coveralls had climbed out of the van and were fishing out bags of equipment. In the meantime, Fischer was writing something in a notebook. Finally he tore the page from the book and handed it to Gunnar. "For form's sake, here are the names of these four colleagues of mine," he said.

Gunnar took the piece of paper and shook hands with the men. "Thank you for your help," he said.

They all took the elevator up to the fourth floor, where Anna was waiting for them, also dressed in white coveralls.

"Hello," she said, coughing.

Gunnar heard the youngest German whisper to his buddy, "He brought his grandma with him."

Fischer evidently heard this, too, because he grabbed the guy's arm and said quietly, "You better show these people some respect. They are your colleagues."

The young man blushed. "Sorry, sir," he whispered.

Gunnar introduced Anna to the team. "She will be overseeing your work and countersigning all samples. I'll be available to do any necessary interpreting."

Tobias Fischer turned to Gunnar and said, "Well, it looks like I'm finished here for the day. Please contact me if you need my help."

He wrote a telephone number on a business card and gave it to Gunnar. "Here are all my details and also my personal cell phone number."

"Thanks very much for all your help," Gunnar said.

Fischer smiled. "Will you be doing anything here in Berlin other than working on this investigation?"

"Um, I'm going to go to the zoo."

"The zoo? Any particular reason?"

"I've never seen an elephant."

Fischer laughed. "I see. My daughter works at the aquarium there. I sometimes pick her up after work, so I happen to know that today is the last day of summer hours. It's open till six thirty, so you may get there this evening, but you would only have time to see the elephant. Tomorrow, the zoo is open from nine to five thirty."

Gunnar looked at his watch and said, "Then I'll wait until tomorrow. But tonight I'm going to treat myself to a good Wiener schnitzel. Is there anyplace you recommend?"

"Good idea," Fischer said. "The Mövenpick restaurant in the Europa Center does an excellent schnitzel. The place is very easy to find. There's a great view from the window tables over the square and the Kurfürstendamm."

Gunnar escorted Fischer down to the embassy's entrance lobby, where they parted.

"Let me know when you've found the killer," Fischer said as they shook hands.

"Sure thing," said Gunnar. He closed the door after Fischer and turned to Birkir, who was just coming down the stairs. It was time to compare notes on what they'd learned so far.

From Arngrímur, Birkir had gotten Anton's traveling companion's name and cell phone number, and after the briefing with Gunnar he called the number. The man answered instantly, and they set up a meeting. Birkir got the embassy driver to take him to the hotel where the guy was staying. It wasn't far from the embassy, but in the heavy afternoon traffic the trip took ten minutes, with most of that time spent waiting at stoplights.

Entering the lobby, Birkir called the number again and said, "This is Birkir Li Hinriksson. I'm at the hotel."

"I see you," came the reply.

A stocky, muscular man in his thirties got up from a sofa in the hotel bar and walked over.

"You're from the Icelandic detective division?" he asked, his deep voice betraying slight surprise. His head was clean-shaven, his features stern.

"Yes, I am," Birkir replied and introduced himself again.

"Hi, I'm Búi Rútsson," the other said, and looked searchingly at Birkir. "China?" he asked.

"Vietnam," Birkir replied.

"But of Chinese origin?"

"Probably."

"Aha."

Birkir asked, "Do you have a key to Anton's room?"

"Yeah, we got adjoining rooms. I've a key to the connecting door."

"Let's go up, then. When we're done here, I'll take Anton's luggage with me."

"OK."

Búi led the way to an elevator and pressed the button. On arrival at the fourth floor, they walked along a long corridor and stopped at one of the doors, which Búi opened with his key card. They entered a luxurious hotel room, where Búi opened the connecting door and led them through to another.

"This is Anton's room," Búi said.

An open suitcase containing clothing lay on the made-up bed. Next to it was a briefcase, also open, full of papers.

Búi said, "I've already packed. I'm just about to leave, so I'm glad you're going to deal with Anton's belongings. That means I don't have to take them with me."

Birkir gestured toward two armchairs next to a low table, and they sat down. Birkir fished his voice recorder out of a pocket and switched it on. "What was your connection to Anton Eiríksson?" he asked, after dictating the usual preliminaries into the machine.

"I was an employee of his."

"What was your job?"

"Bodyguard."

"Nothing else?"

Búi hesitated before replying, "Taking responsibility for the security of a businessman who travels as widely as Anton is more than enough of a job for one person."

Birkir frowned. "No other tasks?"

Búi shrugged. "Occasionally, if the hotel we were staying at had satisfactory security arrangements. Then, if Anton was busy, I would take his calls for him. Sometimes I booked flights and hotels. Dealt with hotel staff. Had clothes washed and dry-cleaned. Practical matters that need taking care of on long trips.

Other than that, I was on twenty-four hour duty when he was on business trips."

"Did Anton consider himself to be in danger?"

"He traveled widely and visited places that were not safe."

"Where is his home?"

"In England. He rents a furnished apartment in London."

Búi took a business card from his pocket and handed it to Birkir. "Here. His company is registered at the same address."

Birkir got up and went over to the bed. He examined the briefcase's contents. On a chain fastened to the bottom of the case was a key ring containing a number of keys.

"Did he also have a home in Iceland?" Birkir asked.

"I don't think so. I never accompanied him to Iceland. He always gave me time off when he went there. I think he probably stayed in a hotel when he was in Reykjavík."

"Where do you live?"

"I have an apartment in Spain where I go when I'm not working. I have a flight booked to Barcelona tomorrow. I'm probably looking at a long vacation."

"Do you have a key to Anton's London apartment?"

"Yes."

Birkir held out his hand. "I'm going to have to ask you to hand that key over to me."

Búi reached into his jacket pocket for his key ring. "I have some clothes and other personal belongings there, but I can get them later," he said, detaching a key and handing it to Birkir.

"When did you start working for Anton?" Birkir asked.

"Three years ago."

"What did you do before that?"

"I was in the Reykjavík police force for two years, and then I went to a bodyguard-training school in America. After that I worked for a firm that provides security personnel all over the world. Then Anton offered me a permanent position. It was an improvement over Iraq and Afghanistan."

"Do you know of anyone who might have wanted to harm Anton?"

Búi shrugged. "He was a tricky devil and treated many people he had dealings with badly, but I didn't think there was anyone who might tail him here to Berlin. Maybe that was a bad call."

"You said you were with him twenty-four hours a day when he was traveling. Why weren't you with him Sunday evening?"

Búi hesitated. He obviously found the question uncomfortable. "I sometimes get time off when Anton is visiting a secure house," he said. "We assumed that the embassy was safe. That was obviously a mistake. Bad for my résumé."

"So what did you do on Sunday?"

"I accompanied Anton to the embassy in a cab. I had the cab wait while I escorted him inside, and I left him at the front desk."

"What did you do after that?"

"I visited a brothel."

Búi's frankness surprised Birkir. "Can anyone verify that?" he asked.

Búi grinned coldly. "I have no idea where I went. I just told the cab driver what I was looking for and he drove me someplace. When I had finished my business, I had the doorman call me a cab, and I went back to the hotel. Finding the place could be tough—I didn't pay any attention to where we went."

"Who knew that Anton was planning to go to the embassy?"

"Nobody knew. It was a spontaneous thing."

"What do you mean?"

"We arrived in Berlin from Jakarta late Saturday night and planned to fly to Hamburg at two o'clock on Sunday. At eleven o'clock on Sunday morning we got a message that the Hamburg meeting had been called off. Anton asked me to cancel the flight, and then spent the next few hours fielding phone calls. Then he had the idea of inviting the ambassador out to dinner that evening. Konrad usually does whatever Anton wants, but he happened to be busy at the embassy and suggested that Anton go there. That was when Anton decided to go to the embassy, and we booked the taxi."

"So nobody knew that he was here in Berlin?"

"I don't think so. Anton was in the habit of keeping his travel plans secret. Sometimes even I didn't know where we were going until we booked the flight."

"What did Anton plan to do on Monday?"

"Fly to the next meeting. Paris or London, I think. Either he hadn't decided or he didn't tell me."

"Would Anton have gone with the ambassador to a restaurant alone?"

"No, he would have called me and I would have escorted them. I keep my cell phone switched on even when I'm not on call. Some of the better restaurants here in the city are used to their guests being escorted by their bodyguards. They have places that are easy to monitor. The headwaiters are paid well for taking care of that."

"Do you pack a weapon on the job?"

"That's a professional secret, but I do have certain licenses."

"Does Anton have family in Iceland?"

"No. His parents are dead, he has no siblings, and he had nothing good to say about his other relatives. He has a will made out."

"Will you inherit anything?"

Búi grinned. "No. Anton made it perfectly clear to me that I wouldn't get as much as a cent if he got killed. He said that I might become less focused on the job if I was expecting an inheritance."

"Was he right?"

"Who knows?"

"Do you know who benefits from Anton's will?"

Búi shrugged. "He mentioned once or twice that his assets were to go to Indonesian orphans."

"That was kind of him," Birkir said warily.

Búi gave a dull smile and said, "You could say that Anton was fond of children."

"We know Anton was a pedophile. Where did he buy access to juveniles?"

Birkir asked this as though it was a natural progression from what had been said before, and for a moment Búi seemed to be about to answer, but then he suddenly froze.

"I don't know what you're talking about."

"You can answer this. The guy is dead. You have no more confidentiality obligations toward him."

Búi remained silent.

"Maybe you're one, too?" Birkir asked. "Do we need to look into that?"

"I only buy adult women who know what they're doing. That's all I'm interested in. Prostitution is a legal profession here in Berlin."

"That may well be true. But do you think it's possible that Anton's compulsion has anything to do with how he died?"

Búi shook his head. "I don't have any idea what you're talking about. This conversation is over." He got up and went through to the other room, closing and locking the door.

17:15

Back in the Icelandic embassy, the focus was on the fourth floor—specifically the hallway, the washroom, and the ambassador's office—and on the stairs down to the third floor, along with the elevator cab. The German CSI specialists went straight to work, dusting fingerprint powder on all surfaces that might have been touched—dark powder on light surfaces, light powder on dark surfaces. They photographed all the prints they found, and then lifted them with clear tape and stuck them to index cards. They checked all surfaces with a UV lamp to highlight any possible bloodstains. They methodically vacuumed all the floors and furniture to recover any loose material, using specialized filters they systematically filed away into labeled boxes.

The ambassador had confirmed that all the guests had visited the top floor at some point during the evening. Their fingerprints wouldn't prove or disprove anything specific, but it might be possible to use their location and appearance to piece together a chain of events. Most prints would, however, probably belong to embassy staff or other visitors, making it difficult to create an overall picture. But they wouldn't get a second chance, so it was vital to be painstaking in this forensic investigation. They would figure out later whether the evidence they'd collected was of any use.

Anna's job was relatively cushy. She oversaw the Germans' work, initialed all the sample labels, and regularly went out for a smoke.

The ambassador's office was of primary interest. The large office chair had been displaced when the body was removed, but there were white chalk marks on the floor indicating the chair's position when the body was discovered. Chalk marks also showed where the victim's feet had rested on the pale parquet. A brown crust indicated the outlines of a pool of blood; the people who'd removed the body had scraped up all the parts that had spilled out, but they had, correctly, not cleaned the floor. A labeled white paper bag lay on the desk. It contained a large cigar that had been lit but only partly smoked. Also on the desk was a telephone, its receiver dangling toward the floor.

The head of the forensic team checked the desk and chair meticulously. He found a variety of fingerprint sets, but finally concentrated on a very particular handprint on the edge of the desk, facing the chair. He demonstrated to Anna how someone might have stood at one end of the desk and supported himself on this edge while lunging at the guy in the chair with his right hand. His colleague photographed him in that position. The handprint they got off the table was very clear—good enough for comparison.

At the other end of the room there were a sofa and two chairs with a low table between them. On the table stood two large candlesticks, at least fifty centimeters tall, Anna estimated. The candle in one of them had burned down a long way before being extinguished. The other candle had been lit but snuffed out soon after—its wick was black but the wax was hardly melted.

Anna watched the forensic specialist dust powder onto the candlesticks with a soft brush. Some coins on the table attracted her attention, along with fragments of white material that looked more like plaster of paris than fired clay. The German pointed at them, and she nodded. He carefully picked the coins up with pliers and put them into a paper envelope. He wrote something on the envelope with a marker, and Anna added her initials, "AT." The plaster bits went into another envelope.

The glaze on the candlesticks was covered in a mass of handprints, but the technician had trouble finding anything recoverable. In the end he shrugged at Anna, and she nodded. This would be of no use and was of doubtful relevance.

With a gloved hand she grasped the candlestick with the burned-down candle and carefully lifted it up. Looking at its underside, she could see that the initials "HK" had been scratched, in large, crude letters, on its plaster-like filling.

"Hello," she said, to attract the attention of the German, who'd turned to other things. When he looked toward her, she gestured with her free hand as if taking a photograph. The man nodded, and took a few pictures of the candlestick as Anna turned it this way and that. Finally she placed it back onto the table and picked up the other one. When she looked underneath it, she saw that the plaster filling had been broken and that there was a large internal cavity inside the candlestick.

"That's interesting," she said.

"*Bitte?*"

Anna smiled and shook her head. She pointed at a measuring tape in the technician's bag, and put her finger into the hole in the bottom of the candlestick.

Understanding her mime, the technician took out the tape and inserted the end of it into the candlestick as far as it would go. They both read the number—thirty-one centimeters.

Anna fetched Gunnar and the ambassador from the second floor to have them take a look at the candlesticks.

Konrad explained their presence on the table. "These objects are supposed to be featured in the exhibition in the new year, and Helgi mailed them here for us to use for promotional purposes.

The box arrived two weeks ago, and we unpacked the candlesticks right away. They've been here ever since. The exhibition manager photographed Helgi and me with them last Sunday. He was going to send an announcement to the Icelandic papers."

Anna showed them the candlestick with the open end. "Could someone have hidden the knife in there? There's plenty of room."

"Why in the world would they do that?" Konrad asked.

"To be available for the killer to use."

"Yes, but nobody knew that Anton was going to come here," Konrad said.

Gunnar said, "Someone must have known it."

Anna showed them the coins and the bits of plaster the technician had bagged, and explained what the table had looked like. "If these coins were stacked up on the table, it would have been easy to break the candlestick's bottom by banging it down onto them."

"Helgi must be able to explain this," Konrad said. "There wasn't anything on the table other than the candlesticks when we were sitting here."

"We'll take them back to Iceland with us," Gunnar said. "Helgi is probably on his way there, and we'll talk to him when we get back."

Konrad shrugged. "The packaging is down in the basement. It was a handmade case. We kept it so we could ship them back."

When the embassy driver had delivered Birkir to his meeting with Búi, he went to fetch the ambassador's wife from the residence and take her to the embassy. The ambassador had gone over to the temporary office in the Felleshus, so it was Arngrímur who introduced her to Gunnar.

"Mrs. Hulda Björnsson," he announced.

"Hello, I'm Gunnar Maríuson," the detective said, standing up.

The woman briefly sized him up before approaching him with a smile.

"Ooh, an Icelandic cop. How cute," she said and extended her hand.

Like her husband, she was short. In fact, she was also very similar to him in shape, being quite large around the middle. Gunnar reflected that, if she weren't obviously in her sixties, a person could be forgiven for thinking she was several months pregnant.

"Darling, are you going to cross-examine me?" she asked Gunnar as they shook hands.

She seemed to be in the habit of getting up close to people she was greeting, and then leaning her head back to make eye contact when they were taller than she was herself. Her face was round and pink, her blond hair elegantly coiffed.

"I need to hear your account of Sunday evening," Gunnar said, his chin disappearing into thick folds of flesh as he craned his head down to see his interviewee's face.

"Darling, I can't remember anything. One's always meeting all sorts of people, and one forgets everything immediately."

Gunnar's neck ached from looking down like this. He retreated carefully from the woman and plopped back down into his chair.

"Please take a seat," he said, pointing to a chair at the opposite end of the table.

She sat down and turned to the counselor. "Arngrímur, dear. Please have a caffe latte brought here for me—and one for the police officer, too."

She turned back to Gunnar. "You'll have a latte, won't you, darling?"

Gunnar sensed that there was no point in declining. He looked at Arngrímur, shrugged, and said, "And a couple of sandwiches as well, please."

Arngrímur nodded. "I'll call the Felleshus right away and have someone bring us coffee and sandwiches."

"Excellent," Hulda said, "and the policeman and I don't want to be disturbed here."

Arngrímur didn't reveal in any way what he thought of this exchange. He disappeared into the corridor and shut the door behind him.

"Sometimes I find he sticks his nose in things too much," Hulda whispered.

Gunnar switched on his voice recorder and dictated the usual identifying preliminaries.

"No need to be so formal, darling," Hulda said, gesturing with her hand.

"You are married to Ambassador Konrad Björnsson, correct?" Gunnar asked.

"Yes, that's right. Since I was eighteen. That's life, I suppose."

"Tell me about Sunday. Were you present at the reading?"

"Yes. My parents are visiting for a few weeks, and they came, too. Afterward, I took them straight home because they were tired. They're nearly ninety, after all."

"But you returned to the embassy later that evening?"

"Yes, after a dinner party at the residence with two old friends of mine from home and their husbands—and, of course, my parents. Naturally, Konrad was supposed to come home in time for dinner, but then he called with some excuse or other. Of course, I found *that* inexcusable. We had to eat without him."

"Why did you go back to the embassy?"

"I wanted to have it out with him over his rude behavior. I called a cab after my visitors had left and my parents had gone to bed."

"Did you talk to the ambassador's guests at all?"

"Yes, it's important to have some manners even if your husband is lacking in that respect. At the first opportunity, I pulled him aside and told him what was in store for him. After that I just focused on the guests. There were two really cute gays there, and I enjoyed talking to them. Those guys know so much about fashion."

"What was in store for him?" Gunnar asked.

"Excuse me?" Hulda didn't understand the question.

"I mean, what did you say to your husband?"

"Oh, that," Hulda smiled. "I have ways of making my husband's life miserable if he treats me badly. You don't need to hear about that."

"Did you see the deceased, Anton?"

"Yes, he said hello, of course. Why wouldn't he? We've known him since my husband first ran for a seat in parliament."

"Did you know that he went up to your husband's office?"

"Yes, he went up there a few times to make calls. I was actually surprised at how long he stayed here, considering how unpleasant the other guests were to him."

"Was anyone in particular hostile toward him?"

"The gays wouldn't talk to him at all. Jón the Sun Poet made fun of him, calling him 'the slave driver.' Jón's artist friend didn't speak to anyone—he has some illness or other. Only Helgi chatted to Anton. Helgi is such a gentleman—he's world famous, you know."

"World famous?"

"Yes, his ceramic work is unique. Art galleries all over the world have been buying his work. People are really looking forward to his exhibition here in Berlin."

"Did you see anybody else disappear from the party when Anton went to make his last phone call?"

"No, darling. I was otherwise engaged."

"Engaged?"

"Yes—I'd slipped my shoes off while I was chatting to the gays, because the left one was pinching my heel. Somebody kicked one of them away somewhere, and when it was time to leave, I couldn't find it. I tried to get Konrad to help me look, but he was too drunk by then. I totally lost it. The guests fled the room while I talked to him. Chickens, all of them. But then Helgi came back and comforted me. He is so polite and nice. He understands women—well, he's been married three times, I'm told. But we couldn't find the shoe, so I had to walk to the taxi barefoot."

"That can't have been comfortable?"

"Helgi let me lean on him. He's such a gentleman. He even offered to carry me, but that wasn't necessary."

21:00

The German CSI technicians had finished their work and were gathering up their equipment. Anna had packed all the items of evidence into a cardboard box (once containing champagne) that Arngrímur had found for her, and with his help she stowed the two candlesticks in their special case, which was made of water-proofed plywood lined with custom-cut foam rubber and closed with sturdy wood screws.

Arngrímur had undertaken the task of sending all this to Iceland with the express courier company the embassy usually dealt with. Also Anton's luggage, which Birkir had brought from his hotel room. The delivery would take two days at most.

Anna's final task had been to take finger and palm prints from all the embassy staff, as well as from the ambassador and his wife. Now Anna could return to Iceland, and one of the staff had booked her a flight via Copenhagen the following morning.

The ambassador and his wife had gone home, and the embassy staff had also closed its operations for the day. The Germans having departed, only Arngrímur remained.

Birkir now turned his attention to the conference room where the dinner had taken place. There was no reason to ask the Germans to search it unless his examination turned up something that warranted closer investigation. He crawled around the floor looking for blood or other traces the killer might have carried with him from the murder scene, but without success. He did, on the other hand, find the Sun Poet's guest pass at the bottom of an almost empty case of red wine bottles under the table. And under a chair he discovered a box that had contained a brandy bottle, and into which someone had stuffed a woman's shoe.

Finally Birkir used Anna's camera to systematically photograph the whole room. That done, he told Arngrímur that it would be OK to clean in there. Arngrímur had arranged for special cleaners to be on standby that evening. He wanted the whole place clean and ready for business the following morning.

Anna confirmed that the fourth floor was also ready to be cleaned. They needed, however, to call a plumber. The German forensic team had opened up the sink trap in the washroom and poured its contents into a plastic screw-top container. It was bloodstained water, showing that somebody had used the sink to wash blood from their hands. The technicians said they weren't allowed to fix the plumbing themselves—that required a certified tradesman. Arngrímur wrote "Out of order" on a piece of paper and stuck it on the washroom door. This could wait.

The three sandwiches Gunnar had eaten after talking to Hulda had done little to assuage his hunger. "Now let's go eat," he said to Anna and Birkir as they collected their luggage.

Arngrímur asked if they had any particular requests.

"Wiener schnitzel at the Mövenpick restaurant in the Europa Center," said Gunnar without consulting the others.

Arngrímur smiled. "That's a very safe bet," he said. "And it's open late, so you'll be well looked after. You can stop by the hotel with your luggage. It's on the way."

Arngrímur called them a cab and escorted them out to the street. He said to Anna, "The embassy chauffeur will pick you up from the hotel tomorrow morning and transfer you to the airport."

The taxi arrived, and they climbed in. Gunnar took the front seat, and when the driver had arranged their bags in the trunk, he gave him the hotel's name. It was a four-minute ride, and as the cab stopped by the entrance, a uniformed doorman came out with a trolley.

Gunnar got out and said a few words to the doorman, who nodded and helped him empty the trunk.

"Europa Center, Mövenpick," Gunnar instructed the driver as he got back in. He then turned to Birkir and Anna and said, "The doorman's taking all the bags up to my room."

Less than ten minutes later, the driver stopped the car again. Birkir paid the fare and they got out. No question, they were in the center of a major city, with heavily trafficked boulevards stretching along two sides of a large plaza. But the great number of cars didn't attract their attention as much as the ruin of an old church that stood, brightly floodlit, in the middle of the plaza. The bombed-out remains were like an evocation from another era, a constant reminder of the worst years this great city had endured. On one side of the church was a modern pentagonal tower, less tall than the ruin; on the other side was a smaller hexagonal building, with blue stained-glass windows lit from within.

"The *Gedächtniskirche*—the Kaiser Wilhelm Memorial Church, with its clock tower and chapel," Gunnar said reverently.

"I've seen pictures of these buildings," Anna said, lighting a cigarette. "Very imposing."

Birkir nodded. "You really sense here how loaded this city is with history," he said. "It's too bad we have to work. It would have been nice to spend a few days to look around."

"I'm hungry," Gunnar said and looked toward the Europa Center dominating the far end of the plaza. It seemed not a very interesting building—a soulless box even—but the restaurant was there, on the second floor.

The waiter was unfazed by Gunnar's request for a double portion of Wiener schnitzel and two large beers. Birkir and Anna both opted for a chicken breast and soda water.

When they had ordered, Birkir asked, "So, after today, what do we know about this killing?"

Anna replied, "We have a very interesting palm print on the desk. And the murder weapon could have been brought into the embassy in a hollow candlestick. If that turns out to be the case, it's a big step forward in the investigation. Apart from that, the forensic examination didn't turn up anything. Let's hope the guests' testimonies give us enough material to piece together a chain of events."

Gunnar said, "Before he left, the commissar and I experimented with carrying the knife through the exit from the Felleshus into the plaza. The metal detector instantly let out a beep, and the inner door refused to open. But the security guard did say it might have been different on Sunday. The whole area was closed, so the ambassador let his guests in with his pass card. There was no guard manning the door, and even though the metal detector may have beeped, it's not loud and it stops if the door is opened with a card. A security guard on duty at the front desk wouldn't notice, and there's no computer log of exceptions like that."

"I don't think the ambassador would have started searching his guests if the door gear was making noises," Birkir said. "So let's keep that possibility open."

Gunnar continued, "We figured out that the killer is probably right-handed; hopefully there'll be some left-handers in the group we can eliminate. That would include the ambassador's wife—or at least she holds her coffee cup in her left hand."

Birkir said, "The ambassador is right-handed."

"Then he's still on the list," Gunnar said. "We'll have to take a much closer look at the footage from the security cameras. Especially the footage of the guests leaving the building at the end of the night. There are also six witnesses we haven't yet spoken to—we'll need to get prints from all of them."

Birkir nodded and said, "What bothers me most is the evidence that Anton hadn't decided to visit the embassy until noon on Sunday. The murderer had a very short time window to find himself a weapon, which is totally inconsistent with the knife being hidden in that candlestick."

"How can we possibly make sense of that?" Gunnar asked.

"I don't think this was premeditated," Birkir said. "My theory is that the knife was there for a different purpose, but it came in handy when the killer decided Anton's time was up."

"You think the murderer had his sights on a different victim?" Gunnar asked.

"Yes. Or maybe he mistook him for someone else."

"So who was the intended victim?"

"The ambassador, perhaps." Birkir said. "It all happened in his office—and he and Anton actually have similar builds."

"That means the ambassador could be in danger. What could the motive be?"

"He is controversial. Maybe he knows something that's bad for someone else. There was talk about him writing his autobiography."

"Shouldn't we warn him, in that case?" Gunnar asked.

Birkir replied, "I'll call Sigmundur, the ministry official, tonight and suggest that Konrad stay in the residence until he leaves for Iceland."

Gunnar said, "If the knife was in the candlestick, then Helgi, the artist, is top of the list. Should we bring him in when we get back?"

"No, let's pretend that the candlestick didn't attract our attention at all. I don't think that Helgi will go into hiding, and if he needed to destroy evidence he must have done it already."

The waiter brought the drinks and put them on the table.

Gunnar raised one of his beer glasses and said, "This working day is herewith officially over. Cheers—prosit."

WEDNESDAY, OCTOBER 14

09:30

After allowing himself a generous amount of time to enjoy breakfast in the hotel's first-floor restaurant, Birkir took a taxi to the embassy.

Arngrímur met him at the front desk of the Felleshus. "You on your own today?"

"Yes."

"Is Gunnar working somewhere else in the city?"

"He went to the zoo," Birkir replied.

Arngrímur smiled. "Good idea," he said. "It's a beautiful day, even if the weather's getting chilly."

Birkir remained expressionless. "Yes, well," he said. "We're mostly finished here, anyway. We just need your help finding Jón Sváfnisson and his friend. We're flying to Frankfurt later today to track them down. Then we head back to Iceland in the morning."

"The Sun Poet, right. Well, the Book Fair started this morning, and Jón shares a corner of booth H251 on the first floor of building number six. Our embassy representative is attending the fair today, and we heard from him this morning that Jón had arrived."

After noting down the details, Birkir said, "I would also appreciate it if you could show me a little more of the layout here. It helps to have a clear picture of the crime scene in our heads."

"Of course, and I'll arrange for the embassy chauffeur to take you to the airport later," Arngrímur said. He looked around, deciding where to begin. "So, this here is the common entrance for all the embassies, and also for the main functions of the Felleshus. Farther along on this south side there's a separate entrance for the consuls of the five nations."

"So there's no other way of getting to the embassies?"

"Yes, through the underground parking lot, but access is very restricted, as you saw yesterday."

Arngrímur moved across to the door opposite the main entrance. "This is the largest room in the building," he said, opening the way for Birkir to look in. It was an auditorium, with stadium seating and a high ceiling. The walls were clad in dark red panels, similar in shape to the green copper plates covering the outer wall of the whole complex, and the seats were upholstered in the same red color.

"This must be where the Sun Poet held his reading," Arngrímur said. "There's seating here for just over a hundred—it's ideal for concerts, readings, and conferences."

"Is the Sun Poet widely known here in Germany?" Birkir asked.

Arngrímur hesitated. "Have you read his poems?"

"Yes. Some of them are excellent."

"Yes, they are well written, and well known in Iceland. Especially those that have been set to music. But that doesn't work here in Germany, which is a shame."

"But his anthology's being published here."

"Yes, but not on the open market. A German eccentric, who has visited Iceland every year for twenty years to learn the language, decided to translate a selection of Jón's poems. Not particularly well, to be honest, but Jón became obsessed with bringing out a book of them here in Germany, and started pestering the ambassador about it. Eventually, Konrad asked me to see about getting it taken care of. My only option was to approach a vanity publishing house. Jón is quite wealthy, and Konrad got the necessary money from him by calling it 'commission' or 'promotion costs.' Jón believes, or he likes to believe, that this is a proper publication."

"Is the book available in stores?"

"There's been some limited distribution to a few bookshops that the publishing company has a deal with, but hardly any sales. Actually, the reason I knew about the company is that I had compiled a booklet of short quotations about diplomats and their profession that I'd collected and translated into Icelandic over the years. It's called *Diplomacy*. I hired these publishers to create the book, but it's not for sale—I just use it for occasional gifts. I'd be happy if you'd be kind enough to accept a copy when we get to my office."

"Thank you very much," Birkir said.

They turned away from the auditorium, and Arngrímur closed the door.

He led Birkir up an open steel staircase in the building's central atrium. When they arrived at the next floor Arngrímur said, "This exhibition space is where Helgi Kárason will be showing his artwork. At the moment there is a display of glass art from Finland. There's a similar space on the next floor above us."

"Is this where the ambassador offered refreshments after the poetry reading?" Birkir asked.

"Yes, it's an ideal area for a cocktail party. Guests can look at the artwork while they relax."

"Are you aware of the ambassador having any enemies who might want to harm him?"

Birkir's sudden change of tack surprised Arngrímur. "Do you mean hurt him or . . . ?"

"Possibly."

Arngrímur shook his head. "No. I think that both his political allies and his opponents were relieved when he withdrew from politics. After that he was harmless."

"But what about his present job?"

"He is carefully monitored to make sure he doesn't cause problems."

"But he jumped directly into the office of ambassador. That surely must have roiled some people. What about you?"

"In this business we're used to ex-politicians moving straight into ambassadorial posts. They usually bring experience and vision that make them excellent diplomats."

"Is that the case with Konrad?"

"He has certain assets that have been valuable in this post. Anything he lacks is easily covered by an efficient embassy staff."

"He's writing his autobiography. Could he expose something that would be to someone's disadvantage?"

"Hardly," Arngrímur said. "I have no doubt that Konrad knows some secrets, but betraying his previous comrades would reflect very badly on him. He has a sense for things like that. I also think that the progress on this autobiography of his is somewhat exaggerated. He sometimes sits and reminisces into a Dictaphone, but he will surely need a great deal of help if it's ever to become a book."

They continued up the stairs, past the next floor, and up to the top.

"This is our cafeteria," Arngrímur said.

Birkir saw a bright room with around twenty tables, three of them occupied.

Arngrímur continued, "There are also rooms up here that small groups can reserve ahead of time for private lunch meetings. Would you like some coffee or anything else?"

"No, thank you," Birkir said, "I had a good breakfast. When did you start using this building?"

"In 1999. With the fall of the Berlin Wall in 1989 and the subsequent reunification of the German state, the government decided to move the capital city from Bonn back to Berlin, which meant that other countries had to establish new embassies here. It's all a remarkable piece of history."

They returned to the ground floor, and at the front desk Birkir exchanged his passport for a guest pass. They walked through the double doors and out into the plaza between the embassy buildings.

Arngrímur said, "The governments of the Nordic nations decided to work together on this project. They held a competition for the design of the complex, and the winning entry featured this copper-faced wall, which encloses the area and curves around the five embassy buildings. It's unique here in the city and considered very successful. Berliners are very happy with the result, as far as I know."

He added with a smile, "The sightseeing buses that take tourists around the city pass by here and I've heard that some guides call us the IKEA embassies."

Birkir scanned the copper wall. "Could somebody have scaled the wall to get in?" he asked.

"Not a chance. It's fifteen meters tall, and the security system here is very sensitive—I understand it picks up every single bird that flies in."

They continued walking and came to an enormous block of stone that formed the end wall of the next building.

"This is the Norwegian embassy," said Arngrímur. "The granite rock was transported here in one piece from a mine in Norway. It weighs around a hundred twenty tons, so it was a huge project to get it here."

Birkir approached the wall and gazed up at the huge stone.

"Had he been here before?" he asked suddenly.

"Who?"

"Anton, the victim."

"Oh, him. No, I don't think he's ever been here before. Konrad told me yesterday that Anton had visited him a few times at the residence. He was eager to come and have a look at the embassy building when the opportunity presented itself on Sunday."

"So you hadn't met him before?"

"No. I never saw him alive."

They met a shortish older man and another, younger one coming from the direction of the Icelandic building. Arngrímur bowed, and the others returned the greeting as they passed.

"That was the Argentinean ambassador. He's the doyen at the moment," Arngrímur said when the men had disappeared into the Felleshus.

"What does that mean?"

"He's the longest-serving of all the ambassadors here in Berlin and is their spokesman or representative vis-à-vis the German government. He came by to offer Konrad his condolences on account of this tragedy we've just suffered."

"Is it an important position, being doyen?"

"It can be. Seniority is very important since it determines the ambassadors' positions in the hierarchy that governs the protocol for all ceremonial occasions."

"Does there have to be a hierarchy?"

"Oh, yes. Before that was established, seating arrangements were a major problem affecting diplomatic relations for centuries—ambassadors argued endlessly about their arrival order at official functions."

"Couldn't they go alphabetically?"

"Absolutely not. This was a major issue. Pope Julius II tried to establish a permanent hierarchy of states in 1504, headed by the Holy Roman Empire. This was pretty much the system for the next three hundred years, but at the Congress of Vienna, which was held to sort out the aftermath of the Napoleonic Wars in Europe, fighting broke out among the ambassadors' coach drivers over what they saw as their rightful order of precedence. That's when everyone agreed to place the ambassadors in the hierarchy according to their length of service. So the ambassador who has been at his post for the longest time becomes the spokesman for all the delegations in the city in question."

"Does that work well?"

"Yes, for the most part, though it can lead to bizarre situations, like when the ambassador of that awful Somoza government in Nicaragua was doyen in Washington for several years. But still, it's better than sword fights between the chauffeurs."

"Sword fights might be interesting." Birkir smiled, then asked, "Did you know any others among Konrad's guests that evening?"

"I assisted David Mathieu here in Berlin once. And Lúdvík was introduced to me when he held an exhibition in the Felleshus a few years back. The others I haven't met as far as I remember."

"Do you think that David could have killed Anton?"

"Absolutely not."

"It looks like we imported some stone, too, just like the Norwegians," Birkir said, turning toward the Icelandic embassy on their left. "What is this?" he asked, pointing at its pale-brown masonry.

"Rhyolite, from Hamarsfjördur."

"So you don't know Starkadur, David's partner?" Birkir asked, switching the subject again.

"Maybe I've been introduced to him, but I don't remember it."

"You don't know anything else about him?"

"Unfortunately not."

They approached the entrance to the Icelandic embassy.

Birkir said, "The Icelandic building is noticeably plainer in style than the others."

"Yes, I think it works very well. As you see, there is a contrast between the access and stairwell structure, which has this corrugated concrete texture, and the part containing the actual offices, with its rhyolite accent."

At the entrance, Arngrímur let them in with a pass card.

Birkir asked, "You don't know Jón the Sun Poet personally?"

"No."

"Have you ever met him?"

"Not as far as I remember."

"I see," Birkir said thoughtfully. "It's a small building, isn't it? What's the floor area?"

"Five hundred square meters in total, with office space of around eighty square meters on each story. The site itself is somewhat small and impractical, and the service area, stairs, and elevator take up a large part of the structure. But that's how it is. Just eight of us work here, so we're reasonably comfortable."

"Was this the best solution?" Birkir asked.

"Yes, all things considered. One idea that came up at the planning stage was to have the Icelandic embassy on the top floor above the Norwegian one. I'm very glad that didn't happen, and I think our embassy looks very good among the others, even if it's not very prominent."

"Have you ever met Helgi, the ceramic artist?"

It didn't seem to bother Arngrímur that Birkir kept on changing the subject, asking questions about the ambassador's guests. He replied without a pause, "We were going to have a meeting to discuss his exhibition, but I was called away. He spoke with the ambassador about it instead, so no, I've never met him."

"When was your meeting supposed to be?"

"On Sunday."

"Isn't that unusual?"

"Yes, but Helgi wasn't able to make it any other day. Apparently he has a very tight schedule. At the embassy we do sometimes have to attend meetings on weekends. That's not a problem."

"Lúdvík was here to manage Helgi's exhibition. You'd met him before, hadn't you?"

"Yes, very briefly, as I said, when he organized an exhibition in the Felleshus. He is highly professional and efficient, and they didn't need my help with that project, but I chatted with him at the exhibition's opening."

"And I guess he's no more prone to violence than the others?"

"No, there's nothing about him to suggest that."

"Fabían, the Sun Poet's companion. He's the last name on the ambassador's guest list. Do you know him?"

"No."

They walked up the stairs. On the second floor, the sound of voices could be heard through the open office doors. The work of the embassy seemed to have returned to normal.

They arrived at the fourth floor, and Arngrímur opened his office with a key.

He said, "I hope you'll let us know if we can be of any further assistance? We'll also need instructions on what to do with Anton's body."

"If no relatives come forward, it'll be up to the authorities to arrange some sort of funeral," Birkir replied. "I assume his estate can cover the expenses."

"In that case I suggest that the body be cremated here in Berlin," Arngrímur said. "The ashes can be sent to Iceland and quietly interred. That's standard procedure when an Icelandic citizen passes away on foreign ground and no relatives come forward."

Arngrímur took a small book from a shelf and handed it to Birkir.

"This is the booklet of quotations about the diplomatic profession I promised you."

Birkir took the slim paperback volume and read the Gothic lettering on its cover:

Diplomacy
Collected and translated by Arngrímur Ingason

"Thank you," Birkir said, and flipped through the first pages. He noticed mostly short excerpts, followed by author's name or other source in small lettering. The preface bore the dictionary definition: *"Diplomacy n. 1) Foreign service, especially the functions of embassies; 2) discretion, tact."*

Birkir picked out a few entries as he skimmed:

Time was when diplomats negotiated serious agreements on war and peace and royal marriage arrangements. These days it's mainly about free trade agreement quotas and sizes of shoe boxes.
                                                    —*The Diplomat*

The diplomat's first duty is not to be surprised by anything.
                                                    —Heinrich von Bülow

A diplomat is someone who can tell you to go to hell in such a way that you look forward to the journey.
                                                    —Caskie Stinnet

A diplomat is someone who never offends accidentally.
                                                    —*The Diplomat's Dictionary*

Arngrímur's cell phone rang, and after a short exchange he said to Birkir, "Your friend Gunnar is at the Felleshus front desk. I asked them to let him in."

"Good. We're actually finished here. We'd better go catch our flight to Frankfurt."

They walked back down to the ground floor and out into the plaza. They watched Gunnar approach.

Gunnar greeted them informally. He held in one hand a fat half-eaten curried sausage; in the other he held a bun.

"Did you see the elephants?" Birkir asked.

"Yes."

"And what did you make of them?"

"I thought they'd be bigger," Gunnar said, and he bit into the sausage.

14:00

On arriving in Frankfurt, Birkir and Gunnar took a taxicab from the airport terminal to the nearby hotel the embassy staff had booked for them. Birkir waited in the cab while Gunnar took their luggage inside to check in.

"All set here," Gunnar said when he came back out. "Take us to the Book Fair, please," he instructed the driver.

"Which entrance?" the man asked.

"The main one, I guess."

After driving awhile, they eventually spotted the sign "Frankfurter Buchmesse" pointing to the exhibition area. They passed several parking structures, finally reaching a tight group of large buildings dominated by a massive tower.

"Which one is the Book Fair in?" Gunnar asked the driver.

"The fair takes up all the buildings in the exhibition area," the driver replied. He stopped at a taxicab stand and pointed to a gate. "You can go in there."

Birkir paid for the ride and waited for a receipt. Then they climbed out and walked toward the gate, where they found a guard.

"Where can we buy tickets?" Gunnar asked.

"No tickets on sale today," the guard replied. "You can come on Sunday. The fair will be open to the public then."

Gunnar shook his head, "No good. We're police from Iceland, and we need to talk to a guy who happens to be here today."

The guard eyed them suspiciously. "Wait here. I'll have to check with my boss."

He turned away and had a brief conversation on his headset, and then asked Gunnar, "Where are you going to look for this person?"

Gunnar read from a piece of paper, "Booth H251, first floor of building number six."

"You got ID?"

Gunnar and Birkir produced their passports and their Reykjavík police badges. The guard examined them carefully, and then spoke again into his headset. Finally he asked, "Is there anyone who can confirm your business here?"

Gunnar presented Arngrímur Ingason's card, prominently imprinted with the Icelandic embassy's emblem. "You can call the counselor of the Icelandic embassy in Berlin. He knows all about this."

The guard spelled out Arngrímur's name into the headset and gave the phone number.

"Wait here," he said, disappearing through a door.

Ten minutes later, he reappeared bearing two plastic cards and a map of the exhibition layout.

"This will give you access for today," he said. "You'll find your guy here," he added, pointing out the place on the map.

"Thanks very much," Gunnar said, and he and Birkir used their pass cards to enter the exhibition area.

With the help of the map, and after a long walk around the concourse, they found building six. Inside, there were books everywhere they looked, and hordes of people, but it was not difficult to find booth H251—from a distance, they could see large pictures of Icelandic landscapes promoting a new book of photographs, and portraits of familiar Icelandic writers. A slim man with thin hair stood at a table arranging booklets.

"Good afternoon," Birkir said in Icelandic.

"Oh, hello, good afternoon," the man said, looking at Birkir in surprise. "Are you an Icelander?"

Birkir nodded. "We're police officers from Reykjavík, and we're looking for Jón the Sun Poet."

"Goodness. I hope you intend to arrest him."

"Is there a reason we should?"

"He's driving all of us crazy, and this is only the first day of the fair."

"How?"

"We're a few medium-sized publishers sharing this booth, and someone was dumb enough to include Jón in the group. He's been raising a ruckus all day."

"How?" Birkir repeated.

"Jón has no idea how to work book fairs like this. You can't talk to anybody here without booking a meeting weeks in advance, but he just barges into publishers' booths and demands to speak to the boss. When he's not doing that, he marches up and down the aisles bellowing out his poems as though this is some kind of performance-art venue. All readings here are tightly organized sessions. The security guards have brought him back here three times—the booth number's on his pass card. For God's sake, take him away with you."

"I can't see that we have reason to at the moment," Birkir replied.

"He's ruining Icelandic literature's reputation. Isn't that reason enough?"

"Undoubtedly, but . . ."

"And look, there he is. I'm off to a meeting. You'll have to take care of the guy and the booth while he's here. It's your responsibility."

And with that, he was gone.

Jón Sváfnisson was tall and voluminous, clad in blue overalls that were generously large even for him, with the legs turned up to reveal old leather walking boots, and so loose around his waist that they were only held up by the shoulder straps. He wore a red checkered cotton shirt, tucked into his pants. A prominent bald patch crowned his head, around which he'd tied a red cowboy neckerchief to hold back his long, dull, frizzy hair hanging down both sides. Above his unkempt beard covering the lower part of his face, a pair of piercing blue eyes gazed at the detectives.

"What do you want with me?" he bellowed once Birkir introduced himself and Gunnar.

"We're investigating the embassy murder in Berlin," Birkir replied. "Perhaps you haven't heard about it?"

"Murder, murder most foul at the embassy! Yes, somebody may well have told me about that. Some folks' sole occupation is spreading rumors. And then they pretend to be selling literature." He underlined every word with an exaggerated gesture.

Birkir said, "You were at the embassy that evening."

"Is that a fact?"

"Yes, it happened at a party after your reading on Sunday."

"Ah, yes. The fat gate-crasher—that disgusting slave driver—was bumped off. Someone did humanity a great favor that evening. I don't think it was me, though. I would probably remember it. Although that's not certain. When does a man kill a man?"

"How do you know who was killed?" Birkir asked.

"The Holy Spirit appeared before me," Jón replied, raising his hands to heaven.

Birkir and Gunnar looked at one another.

"One of the girls at the embassy told me this morning," Jón guffawed. "It *was* that windbag Anton, wasn't it?"

"Yes, his name was Anton," Birkir replied.

"So we agree on that, then. How about we just get on with selling literature? Time is precious, and I've got so many people I need to talk to today."

Birkir said, "Anton went up to the ambassador's office several times that evening to make phone calls. Were you with him any of those times?"

"No . . . yeah . . . no, how the hell am I supposed to remember that, I was totally wasted!"

Birkir glanced uncertainly at Gunnar, who grinned broadly.

"Your friend Fabían—is he here with you?" Birkir asked.

Jón looked around theatrically. "No, he doesn't appear to be here," he said, affecting a surprised expression.

"Where can we find him?" Birkir asked patiently.

"Fabían! Fabían! Faaaabían!" Jón shouted in crescendo.

Visitors at nearby booths looked curiously in their direction, and when Jón saw that he had their attention, he held up his book and shouted, "Poetry! Icelandic poetry for sale! Come and have a look, dear friends."

His audience looked away, and some walked off elsewhere.

"I need to get an agent," the poet said, laughing.

Birkir was about to say something, but Gunnar put a hand on his shoulder, "Go get yourself a cup of tea. I think the Sun Poet and I need to have a little conversation."

Birkir shrugged and said, "See you in a half hour."

Birkir took off, and Gunnar pointed at a small refrigerator in the back of the booth. "You got any liquor here for your guests?"

Jón's interest was aroused, and he crouched down and opened the mini-fridge to reveal bottles of beer and Icelandic firewater. Gunnar grabbed a couple of beers and flipped off their caps with an opener he found on top of the fridge. He passed one of them to Jón and took a slug from the other.

"Didn't Fabían come here with you?" he asked.

Jón downed half a bottle in one gulp before replying, "Ah, this was a very good idea. You're not totally dumb."

Gunnar repeated the question.

Jón took another swig before replying, "Fabían, no, he didn't come with me. He's very ill, poor thing. He'd had enough of this goddamned trip. Flew back to Iceland on Monday. I should have gone with him."

Gunnar sat down, and indicated to Jón to do the same. They drank without speaking, then took out two more bottles when they'd finished the first ones.

Finally Gunnar asked, "How well do you know the guys who were at the embassy Sunday evening?"

"Everybody knows me, and I know everyone who can be bothered to drink with me," Jón said. "What's your name?" he added, evidently having forgotten Birkir's introduction—if he'd heard it at all. Gunnar told him his name and asked, "Were they buddies of yours from Reykjavík?"

"Buddies! Konrad and I often have a drink together both at home and abroad. He doesn't get poetry, but he likes to hear limericks—especially if they're smutty. I know some good ones. Wanna hear them?"

"Later. How do you know Fabían?"

"Fabían is my foster son."

"Your foster son?"

"Yeah, or foster brother or maybe foster father, even. I took him under my wing when he was a kid, and he's lived with me since—when he's not in the hospital. He's probably more mature than me. He sometimes gives me good advice. I certainly need it."

"Why has he been hospitalized?"

"He was in the loony bin. At the beginning he suffered from some extremely peculiar type of depression—a mental narcosis—that's what Doctor Psycho said. He was away with the fairies and didn't look after himself at all, then he became totally helpless. He had to be fed and have his butt wiped. Then things got better. He came back to earth and was reasonably with it, but then he got cancer. He's been fighting that goddamned monster for some years now."

Jón raised his empty bottle. Gunnar reached for another one from the icebox, opened it, and handed it over.

"Did you know Anton?" Gunnar asked.

"I'd heard of him."

"Were you on speaking terms?"

"No."

"Do you think that Fabían was alone with Anton at any point that night?"

"You mean do I think that Fabían killed Anton?"

"You could put it like that."

"I don't think so. How was he killed?"

Gunnar didn't answer the question, asking instead, "Did Fabían know Anton at all?"

"No."

"The other guests—Helgi, Lúdvík, David, and Starkadur. Did you know them in Reykjavík?"

"Everybody knows everybody in Reykjavík. It's a small place."

"Are they old buddies of yours?"

"Whether people want to admit they know me depends on the circumstances."

"Do you think that any of those guys is likely to have killed Anton?"

Jón gave a belly laugh. "I think Anton was the sort of guy who could have turned anybody into a killer. I don't know who the lucky person was who actually did it. I don't want him to be found. He did what had to be done."

"Why?"

"This business Anton was involved in. It was nothing but slave trade—human trafficking and exploitation. A maniac like that is no loss."

"How do you know that?"

"Word on the street, my friend. Word on the street."

"Does that really mean it's true?"

"No, the guy was probably just a relief worker helping the poor out there in East Asia. But why the fuck are you asking me? It wasn't my job to arrest him or mess with him or anything. He was none of my business, dead or alive."

Before Anna had headed off back to Iceland, she'd left her fingerprinting equipment with Gunnar. He now fished out the case containing this stuff and said, "I need to take your fingerprints so we can remove you from our suspect list."

"Fingerprints?" Jón sprang up and shook his fist. "In your dreams, buddy. Nobody gets anything like that from me."

"But it'll help us with our inquiries."

"I couldn't care less what will or won't help you. I'm not going to let you mess with my person. My dandruff and finger grease are nobody's business but my own."

"It's not like this is dangerous."

"It's harassment. I don't owe you anything."

"Right. Where can we get hold of you over the next few days?"

"In Iceland, for fuck's sake. There's nothing for me here. Nobody wants to talk, and Konrad canceled the reception he was going to hold. Change of plans, he said. My poems will find their readers in another place and another time. Probably not until I'm dead, though. A living poet is considered dangerous. He might tell the truth."

Gunnar got up to say good-bye.

"Get lost," the poet said, and stormed off along the aisle.

Gunnar heard him chanting at the top of his voice, "Poems, poems—Icelandic poems for sale! Dear friends, get yourselves a book of poems!"

Gunnar heard a woman in the next booth say to her colleague in German, "Oh my God. The Icelander is off again."

Birkir was not in the cafeteria, and Gunnar had to call his cell to find where he was in the exhibition. Birkir gave him the aisle number, and when Gunnar had at long last muddled his way to the right place, he found Birkir looking at books on classical music in a large display booth.

"I've got lots of publishing offers," Birkir said. "China is guest of honor at the Book Fair this year, and everybody thinks I'm one of their publishers. Maybe this is the right moment for a career change."

"I think I'm getting a cold," Gunnar said, sniffling.

"What did the Sun Poet have to say?"

Gunnar rehashed his conversation with Jón Sváfnisson. "We're not getting anywhere," he said finally, and sneezed into his sleeve. "Fucking foreign countries."

"Well, we're going home tomorrow," said Birkir. "The embassy has confirmed our booking. It's a direct flight from here."

As Gunnar and Birkir headed for the Book Fair's exit, they spotted two security guards escorting Jón, one on each side of him, toward the gate. They stopped and watched as the poet said good-bye, shaking hands with both guards before climbing into the cab they'd hailed for him. Evidently, the Sun Poet's business at the Frankfurt Book Fair was done.

THURSDAY, OCTOBER 15

17:30

Birkir wasn't as reluctant to travel abroad as Gunnar, but it certainly wasn't one of his favorite activities. The journey itself always took a whole day, or at least used all the energy Birkir had at his disposal for one day. He'd heard that the soul couldn't fly across the ocean as fast as the body, that it always took a few days for it to completely "arrive." He understood this theory well. It usually took him a week after getting home to return to biorhythmic equilibrium. The only foreign travel he really enjoyed was when he went abroad to participate in marathons; then he would travel in the company of like-minded folks and have the clear goal of running 42.2 kilometers along with several thousand fellow runners—preferably in under three hours, which he'd not yet achieved. Running filled him with a special energy that lasted for weeks, whereas sitting on a plane for a similar length of time left him completely drained for the rest of that day.

So, after the flight from Frankfurt to Reykjavík, he was cooked, but his sense of duty drove him to report immediately to the office of his superior, Magnús.

"I finished writing this on the flight home," Birkir said, putting his comprehensive Berlin-trip report on the desk.

"Where's Gunnar?" Magnús asked as he leafed through the papers.

"At home in bed. He came down with a cold yesterday and then he got lumbago."

"Lumbago? How come?"

"He sneezed violently."

"He gave himself a backache by sneezing?"

"Yes, on the plane. Those seats are much too narrow for him."

"Goddamned bag of lard."

Birkir shook his head. "He isn't just fat, he's big. That's not his fault."

"Maybe not."

"It took him a half hour to get out of the plane after we landed. I borrowed a wheelchair to help him out to the taxi. I wanted to get an ambulance, but he wouldn't let me. He also used a lot of very bad language."

"Did he now?"

"Yes, he wanted to fly Saga Class, but they wouldn't let him upgrade."

"He thought he needed Saga Class?"

"Yes—he'd flown Saga Class on the outward journey and was more comfortable in that seat. There's more room."

"How did he get the seat?"

"Our traveling companion from the embassy was kind enough to switch with him."

"Well," Magnús said. "Tell him to see the doctor and get something for his back. We need to get this case wrapped up ASAP."

"I took him to the emergency room. They gave him a couple injections and his back seemed to improve a little after that. The cold didn't get any better, though, nor did his mood."

"What an asshole. But enough about Gunnar, we've got to press on. Who were the main characters out there in Berlin?"

Birkir produced a list and read out the names. "They're all in their forties and fifties," he added. "Anton and the ambassador are the oldest."

Magnús took the paper and scrutinized the names. "The media are pissed that we didn't let them have the names right away. I'm afraid this'll start to leak out soon, and then these guys will get no peace. We've gotta fix this stat."

He paged through Birkir's report again. "What's your opinion?" he finally asked.

"There's something very strange going on here," Birkir said. "Everything seems to indicate that Anton decided at the last minute to visit the ambassador. But somehow the murderer had this knife ready."

"Couldn't there be some perfectly reasonable explanation?"

"Who would carry a weapon like that to a poetry reading and an embassy reception?"

"Not many people, I guess. No chance some other party was involved?"

"No. The security systems rule that out."

"What clues have we got?"

"We have the two candlesticks, one with its base broken open, and we have a palm print from the ambassador's desk. That's all."

"So, our priority is to get prints from everyone on the list. If we're lucky, that'll give us the solution. What's your feeling about these guys?"

"We've only spoken to the ambassador and his wife—and one of the guests, Jón Sváfnisson. It's hard to know what to make of him."

Magnús nodded and said, "I've seen him in the street. His behavior is gross, to say the least."

Birkir said, "We watched him get kicked out of the Frankfurt Book Fair yesterday for stirring up trouble. And then he was on the same flight as us today. This time he was sweet as candy—just sat and read Günter Grass's *The Tin Drum* the whole way. Didn't even have a single beer. And yet he's even bigger than Gunnar and you could see he wasn't comfortable in his seat."

"I don't think he's violent," Magnús said, "but I wish he were more conscientious on the home front. His house isn't far from where my wife and I live, and it's not exactly an asset to the neighborhood, to be honest. He inherited it from wealthy parents, a big luxury villa, but he doesn't take care of it. The yard is completely neglected and full of junk. He rents out rooms, and some of his tenants are, shall we say, unusual."

"Unusual in what way?"

"Oh, all kinds of artsy types and eccentrics. Really rowdy mob when they all get together. There are also tons of birds in the yard."

"Birds?"

"Yes, they're attracted by the food he puts out for them. The neighbors' cars get covered in droppings, and folks find the screeching very annoying. The residents' association has been trying to find ways to get the situation under control, but it's difficult because it's a private house."

"Any illegal activity in the house?" Birkir asked.

"Nothing actually illegal, no, but it's a blot on the landscape, and it could be lowering property values for the whole area."

Birkir said, "I'll take a look at it tomorrow. I need to talk to Fabían, and he's one of the tenants."

"You won't have any trouble finding the house," Magnús said. "It's got 'Jónshús' painted in large letters on the front. One of the many things that make it a dump."

20:30

Before Birkir finally went home, he finished off the paperwork from Berlin. Nobody had told him to do it right away, but he didn't want it waiting for him at the start of the next workday; there would be plenty of other things to do. Don't leave till tomorrow what you can do today—he'd learned that from old Hinrik, his foster father, when they used to tend the few sheep the old man kept in a shack by the coast on Vatnsleysuströnd, west of Reykjavík.

Birkir's home was on the second floor of a quaint building in Bergstadastræti, in the old center of town. The apartment was cramped and oddly laid out, but he had lived there for many years and was used to it. He found it cozy, and he'd made it his home.

He began by unpacking his suitcase. Dirty clothes went straight into the washing machine, everything else to its proper place in the closet. The only thing he'd added to his luggage in Germany was a small, attractively framed, black-and-white photograph of a woman playing the violin. He'd bought it in an antique shop in Frankfurt while waiting for the flight to Iceland. He walked around the apartment with the photo, trying to find a good place to hang it. The walls were covered with pictures, all devoted in one way or another to the same subject—people or figures with string instruments: violins, cellos, double basses. There was a mixture of photographs, oil paintings, watercolors, and drawings—large works and small—and, on shelves here and there, a few figurines mirroring the same theme.

His new photo and its frame looked to be at least one hundred years old; for this he had paid what he felt was a reasonable sum. Actually, the age of these artworks wasn't as important to him as the diversity of the collection.

Birkir found a good spot in the living room. He fetched a hammer and a nail, measured the position carefully, and tapped the nail into the wall. He hung the picture on the nail and stepped back to contemplate the result. He was pleased. The shape and design of string instruments gave him a kind of feeling of inner security, brought on by some vague recollection or image from his childhood. His memories from Vietnam were otherwise very fractured, and his experience at a refugee center in Malaysia is what had first brought any kind of perspective to him. By then he was an orphan being fostered in a large family.

He fed a CD into his music player, and the Andante con moto in E major from Schubert's Unfinished Symphony sounded through the apartment as he went around with a watering can, tending his twenty-seven potted plants.

FRIDAY, OCTOBER 16

09:30

Gunnar arrived at work, stiff and stuffy, supporting himself on a pair of crutches he'd kept since that time he'd slipped on the ice and broken his leg. María, his mother, had dug them out from under a bag of empty beer bottles in their storeroom. He tottered around awkwardly and very slowly.

"I can't straighten my back," Gunnar said to Birkir. "I need these to keep me from falling on my face." He banged one crutch on the floor for emphasis.

"Obviously," Birkir said. "When you lean forward like that, your center of gravity is in front of your toes."

"Get me a large cup of tea," Gunnar said. "White with sugar."

"Anything else?"

"A roll of paper towels. I need to blow my nose."

"Wouldn't you be better off in bed?"

"We've got a murder to solve, and you're not going to manage it without me. Now go and get me that stuff."

While he waited, Gunnar sat down and switched on his computer. He had already checked some Icelandic and German news sites when Birkir put a steaming hot cup and a roll of paper in front of him. Gunnar tore off two pieces of paper and blew his nose—cautiously, not wanting to aggravate his back pain.

"Anything new?" he asked.

"Yes, actually," Birkir replied. "One of the embassy guests has a criminal record. Assaults some years ago."

"Who?"

"Lúdvík Bjarnason."

"The exhibition manager?"

"Yeah. In his younger days he did some debt collecting."

"What, for loan sharks?"

"Something like that."

"How long ago?"

"The latest case was twenty years ago. After that he turned to more constructive occupations."

"So there isn't necessarily any connection there," Gunnar said. "Anything else?"

"No, nothing interesting. I'm trying to get ahold of the other guys on the list."

"How are you doing?"

"Mixed results. How did you sleep?"

"Badly."

"Your back killing you?"

"It's like a broken piece of wood. I should never have gone on that goddamned trip. My cold isn't helping, either."

"Are you seeing the doctor again?"

"No. He'll just start lecturing me about my weight," Gunnar said, gripping the edge of the table as he sneezed. "Ouch," he said, trying to straighten his back.

"But he's right, isn't he? You are too heavy, aren't you?"

"Don't you start," Gunnar said, and blew his nose again. "I'll just do indoor stuff today," he added nasally.

"OK," Birkir said. "Helgi Kárason is coming here around one o'clock, you can talk to him. I'll go see Starkadur and David in a few minutes. They said they'd be at home. After that I'll visit Fabían Sigrídarson. Evidently he's confined to bed, so it doesn't matter what time I get there. I've spoken to them all on the phone to arrange things."

"So what about Lúdvík?"

"I haven't been able to get ahold of him. I've got a cell number, but he's not replying."

"I'll try to locate him," Gunnar said. "Listen," he added. "Remember that I told Mom that we went to Egilsstadir. You've got to back me up if she asks."

"OK, and I'll tell her you got lumbago and caught a cold going there."

"Yeah, you do that, but only if she asks. You need a good memory if you're going to string my mother along—she sees through everything. I get my intuition from her."

"She would have made a good cop," Birkir said.

"Better than most," Gunnar replied.

11:30

Starkadur and David's home was the middle story of a triplex on the west side of town. Birkir rang the doorbell and waited.

A well-groomed man in his forties answered the door.

Birkir introduced himself and showed his badge. "Are you Starkadur or David?"

"I'm Starkadur," the man said. He wore a pale-brown shirt and matching pants, with a gaudy bandanna around his neck, and a light-colored sweater draped over his shoulders and tied loosely across his chest. "Please come in."

"Thanks," Birkir said and entered the apartment. The stale air bore witness that smokers lived there.

"Sorry about the mess," Starkadur said. "David's getting ready for an exhibition, and there's stuff all over the place."

Birkir looked around. It was true there were large fashion drawings hanging everywhere, with fabric samples pinned to them, but apart from that the apartment seemed homey and clean.

"Come on in and have a seat in the kitchen. Tea or coffee?"

"A glass of water would be good," Birkir said.

"Sparkling or natural?"

"Just tap water, please."

Starkadur took an elegant, tall glass from a cupboard, turned on the faucet, and tested the temperature of the water with a finger; when he was satisfied it was running cool enough, he placed the glass under the stream and filled it.

"You know why I'm here," Birkir said as he accepted the drink.

"Probably that revolting man at the embassy," Starkadur replied, filling another glass with water.

"Revolting man?" Birkir switched on his voice recorder and looked searchingly at Starkadur. "What do you mean by that?"

"Yeah, that Anton guy. Wasn't he murdered?"

Birkir recorded the formal identifiers before replying, "Yes, Anton Eiríksson was killed Sunday night at the embassy in Berlin."

"About time."

"Oh yeah?"

"He was such a disgusting pedo."

"Excuse me?"

"Pedo—a pedophile."

"You mean he abused children?"

"Yeah, it's been common knowledge for years. It's incredible that he was never indicted. Horrifying stuff." He took a pack of cigarettes from one of the cupboards and lit a smoke with a lighter that he held, as Birkir noticed, in his right hand.

"Do you know any individuals who were his victims?"

"I don't personally know any of his victims—just that everybody in the association says he's a pedophile."

"What association?" Birkir asked.

"Our Lesbian and Gay Association."

"Was Anton a member?"

"Absolutely not! They would never have approved him."

"Why not?"

"Monsters like him cause the worst discrimination against us. Some uninformed folks believe that all gays lust after kids."

"I see what you mean," Birkir said. "It must be difficult to deal with that."

"Exactly. Our relationships and sex lives are like everybody else's—based on mutual respect, love, and equality. Any abuse is utterly distasteful to us. Sexual orientation is not what makes someone an abuser."

"You met Anton at a meeting with the ambassador at the embassy, correct?"

"Yes, but only very briefly. I don't know what the ambassador thought we wanted with that man. Not surprisingly, Anton left the room as soon as we told him what we thought of him."

"What room?"

"We were in the ambassador's office."

Birkir took a sip of water. "Anton went up to the ambassador's office a number of times after that. Did you see anybody follow him?"

"No, for God's sake, I practically covered my eyes when he passed." Starkadur held his hands over his face to emphasize his words.

"Was David with you at all times?"

"Yes, of course."

"Did you go back up to the fourth floor any time later on?"

"No. There was no reason for me to go up there."

"Whom did you and David talk with during the evening?"

"Mainly the ambassador's wife. She wanted to discuss the spring fashion trends—and, being polite guests, we listened."

"But you were the first ones to leave?"

"Yes, and we should've left much earlier, but David sometimes needs the services of the embassy, so we didn't want to offend the ambassador and his wife."

"Did you consume alcohol during the evening?"

"Sure, there wasn't much else to do other than get stewed. I had an awful hangover the following day and I feel like I'm still recovering. But I know for sure that I didn't kill that monster, even if I would have liked to. Did someone smash his head in?"

"Why do you ask?"

"Just curiosity."

"I can't answer that question."

"Oh well. I guess we'll find out eventually."

"The details will probably be released when we've finished our inquiries. Tell me, what do you do for a living?"

"Computers. I'm a systems analyst. Freelance. I've got a work-space here in the basement. You should call me if you ever find yourself in trouble with your home computer, if you get a virus or something like that. I'm pretty affordable."

"Thank you, I'll keep that in mind." Birkir checked his list of notes. "Did you know the other guests?"

"I'd met most of them at some point."

"Did any one of them seem more likely than the others to commit murder, in your opinion?"

"No, definitely not. These were not people given to violence." Starkadur laughed, and was still laughing when they heard someone open the front door and enter the apartment. "Come in, love," he cried out. "There's a cop here telling jokes."

"Good morning," David Mathieu said. He was a man of exceptional beauty, although, being just over forty, not in the first flush of youth. His Mediterranean complexion and brown eyes contrasted with his silver-gray hair—still very thick—and neat, somewhat darker, mustache. His mouth was well shaped, his teeth white and straight, his nose delicate. He was slim, erect, and graceful of movement.

"I was asking your friend here about your visit to Berlin," Birkir said.

"You mean my husband," David said.

"Yes, Starkadur," Birkir said, looking from one to the other.

"Starkadur is my husband," David said firmly. "We are married."

"Got it. Starkadur, your husband, told me that you met with Anton Eiríksson at the embassy on the evening he died."

"Yes, the ambassador had the idea I could make use of his connections for the manufacture of my fashion line."

"Did that not work out?"

"No, it was out of the question."

"Why?"

"Anton was an out-and-out slave trader. His specialty was finding manufacturing companies and offering to seek out cheaper production facilities for them. He boasted that there was nothing that he couldn't get made for half its current cost."

"Is that unreasonable in the global market?"

"Oh, absolutely. Anton sought out the poorest areas of Asia where there's no control over child slavery or employment rights generally. He used to visit well-known fashion designers with complete garments—exact copies of their own lines, same materials, same finish. Even identical labels. He would offer the copies to them at half the price they were paying their own producers. He'd tell them that, whether they liked it or not, these products would be out there in the market. Most people threw him out, of course, but some opportunists may have made deals with him."

"Did he specialize in clothing?"

"No. He dabbled in everything. He sought out factories where the working conditions were good and people were paid proper wages. He'd find out what they were producing and have the same stuff made in one of his slave bins. Then he'd show up at the company whose merchandise it was, and offer his version of the product at half the price. He didn't need many deals like that to earn serious money."

"How do you know this?"

"Everybody in my line of work knows this. Word gets around fast. Anton represented the very worst in this game. He was totally unscrupulous. His death is no loss to the world."

"Do you know anything that might help us in our investigation?"

"No, and even if I had witnessed something, I would've been quick to forget it. I'm not in favor of killing people, not even when they're the personification of evil. But since it's over and done with, I just want to stop thinking about it. Just forget it, immediately."

"How come you were visiting the embassy that day?"

"The ambassador knew we were in town, and he invited us to attend the reading. Then he asked us to stay afterward for a chat. Turned out he wanted to introduce Anton to us. Naturally, Konrad didn't know that we knew about this guy. But by that time it was too late to escape. We had to attend the party."

"Were you and Starkadur together all the time at the embassy?"

"Yes. We sat together the whole evening."

"No trips to the restroom, separately?"

"No, always together."

Starkadur nodded in agreement.

"I'll need to take your finger and palm prints for the investigation. Are you OK with my doing that?"

Starkadur and David looked at one another and then shook their heads.

David said, "We won't agree to anything of the sort without consulting our lawyer. We haven't had good experiences with police."

13:00

It had taken Birkir considerable effort to track down Helgi Kárason. In the National Register his address was given as being in the eastern town of Seydisfjördur, and it wasn't clear where he lived in Reykjavík. Birkir had eventually managed to get him on the phone and ask him to come to police headquarters to be interviewed, to which he readily agreed.

Gunnar met him at the front desk of the police station and escorted him over to the violent crime division. He was now able to move reasonably fast on his crutches. He was getting used to them.

"You got a bad back?" Helgi asked sympathetically.

"Yeah," Gunnar replied, "and I also have a stinking cold. But a murder investigation is a murder investigation, and we need to solve this case however bad I'm feeling."

"I guess so," Helgi said. His darkly tanned face was gaunt, his forehead lined with deep wrinkles and cheeks peppered with old pockmarks. Though reasonably fit, he looked like someone who at some stage in his life had abused his body. He was dressed in a brown suit cut in a quaint, old-fashioned style, and wore a thick tweed cap. He seemed polite, low-key.

Gunnar led the way to an interview room and gestured for him to sit down. On the table between them were Gunnar's open laptop and the two candlesticks the detectives had brought back from the embassy.

"Those were supposed to be in Berlin," Helgi said as he sat down and removed his cap. "I called them Sunna's candlesticks back in the day."

Gunnar nodded. "You're right. They were in the ambassador's office when the murder was committed. We needed to examine them more closely here."

Helgi frowned. "Really? I can't see what for. I hope you'll be able to send them back before the exhibition. They represent a particular era of mine in ceramic, and there are only a few such examples in circulation."

"Hopefully this will all be over quickly. You were a guest at the ambassador's party—can you describe the evening's events for me?"

"There's not much to tell. Lúdvík and I were in Berlin to prepare for my exhibition that's scheduled for the beginning of next year. We looked at the space and were planning the setup. We'd also booked a meeting with the embassy counselor that Sunday, but he was called away unexpectedly, and the ambassador decided to talk with us himself. He invited us to the Felleshus to attend Jón Sun Poet's reading before our meeting. That proved helpful, because the exhibition space is directly above the auditorium, and during the interval the visitors went up there to look at the Finnish glass art exhibition that's currently showing there. It's always good to look at spaces when there's a crowd milling around. It makes it easier to work out the best way of arranging the exhibits so they come alive. We took photos and noted down how people moved about."

"But you stuck around afterward, didn't you?"

"Yes, it was always the plan to go across to the embassy after the reading. Lúdvík wanted to take a photo of me and the ambassador with the candlesticks. Then we were going to meet with the counselor to talk money and things like that, but he couldn't come, like I said."

"Why the photograph?"

"It was for the promotional campaign. I guess that's on the back burner now."

"Are all these photos available?"

"Yes—I even took the trouble of bringing them with me. Lúdvík was busy with his camera that evening, and I suspected you'd want to see them."

He fished a thumb drive from his pocket. "I'd appreciate having it back when you've downloaded the pictures."

"I'll do it as we speak," Gunnar said. He plugged the drive into the laptop in front of him and clicked on "Copy." He went on, "And you stayed behind at the embassy after the meeting?"

"Yes, Konrad invited us to dinner. He ordered food from a nearby restaurant."

"Did you know the other guests?"

"Everybody of my generation knows the Sun Poet," Helgi grinned. "Jón and I were good friends in our youth, but I don't see him much these days. I've met David and Starkadur a few times."

"Did you know Anton Eiríksson?"

"No. I had never seen him before."

"Did you speak to him that evening?"

"Yes, a bit. He didn't seem to have too many friends there, so I chatted with him a little, just to be polite."

"What did you talk about?"

"Mainly it was me listening to him droning on about business opportunities in Asia. He offered to help me get cheap reproductions of my artwork. No way I want to do that, of course, but I let him talk. It was actually interesting to hear how people like that operate."

Gunnar picked up one of the candlesticks and showed it to Helgi. "The bottom of this one has been broken open. The bits were lying on the table in the ambassador's office."

Helgi frowned. "That's strange. But no harm done—it's easy to fix. The bottom is made of unfired plaster of paris. You just need to mix up a dollop and stick it into the hole. Then you smooth it with a spatula. Might need two rounds."

"Why do you do it like that?"

"No reason, really. Sometimes I fill such things with clean, dry sand to make them heavier and more stable. You don't need to do that with these big candlesticks, because they're already so heavy—but if the bottom is sealed, no dirt gets in. I can also sign them by scratching 'HK' into the plaster before it hardens completely."

"When was this candlestick made?"

"Probably about twelve years ago."

"Could someone have opened up the bottom, put a knife inside, and then closed it again with plaster of paris?"

Helgi looked at Gunnar in surprise. "What in the world for?" he asked.

"In order to smuggle a knife into the embassy."

Helgi shook his head. "No, that's impossible. How would that have happened?"

"Maybe you'd like to think about that for us. Tell me who owns these objects."

"I do. I've kept them as examples of that period of my career. But I know nothing about a knife."

"Who packed the candlesticks for shipping to Berlin?"

"Lúdvík looks after all that kind of stuff for me."

"Lúdvík Bjarnason hasn't answered my calls. He came back to Iceland with you, didn't he?"

"Lúdvík? No, what gave you that idea?"

"Information we had from the embassy."

"That's a misunderstanding. Lúdvík was planning to stay in Europe awhile to see an exhibition. I don't know when he was planning to come home."

"Can you try calling him for us?"

"The best thing to do is text him. His number's in the phone book. But he usually has his cell switched off when he's traveling."

"OK. I'll try texting. Do you have a clear memory of the party at the embassy?"

"Yes, of course. It was only a few days ago."

"It seems that some of the guests were quite drunk. Were you sober?"

"I stopped using alcohol and other substances fifteen years ago. So yes, I was sober that evening, as usual."

"So can you tell me about it?"

"Yes, but I can't help you with the murder. The last time I saw Anton was when everyone was about to leave. The ambassador was going to call for taxis, but then his wife started freaking out—she'd lost one of her shoes and seemed pretty unhappy about it. I tried to calm her down while the others scoured the place for her shoe. It was kind of an embarrassing scene, and it held us up for quite a while."

"Can you remember who was involved in the search, and whether anybody else disappeared at the same time as Anton?"

"No. I escorted madam down to the first floor and tried to pacify her. She was a bit noisy and used offensive language. Not very ladylike, if I may say so."

"What happened next?"

"David and Starkadur came down and said the cabs had arrived. At that point Hulda ran back upstairs. I followed her into the room we'd had dinner in, where she sat down and said she wouldn't be moved until the shoe had been found."

"But she didn't stick to that?"

"No. I gave up, and said good night to her. Jón also wanted to leave, and the four of us decided to share a cab—me, Jón, Fabían, and Lúdvík. But then madam came out and wanted to go home, too, without her shoe if that was the only option."

"By that time Anton must have disappeared. Did you notice that?"

"Yes, I did. The six of us, that is the four of us and Konrad and Hulda, were the last to leave. Anton wasn't with us, so I assumed that he'd gone in the first cab with Starkadur and David. The ambassador seemed to think so, too."

"So the six of you left together. All in one group?"

"Yes. And then another thing happened with the night guard because the Sun Poet had lost his guest pass. The ambassador had to fill out some kind of form so that Jón could get his passport back."

"Then you parted company, right?"

"Yeah, the ambassador and his wife were going in a different direction from us four, so they took one of the cabs, and we took the other."

"What happened then?"

"Jón got into the front seat and wanted to shake hands with the driver. The driver didn't understand what he was trying to do, so Jón got physical with him. The guy was startled, of course, and got out of the car. He wanted us all out and threatened to call the cops. The night guard came out, and between us we managed to get the driver to agree to take us to the hotel. I gave him one hundred euros extra and switched seats with the Sun Poet. Jón had gotten tired and realized it was in his own best interest to behave himself. We got to the hotel without any further trouble."

"Were you all staying in the same hotel?

"Yeah. The embassy booked our rooms for us, all in the same place."

"You said you didn't notice if anyone had disappeared from the party with Anton. But when you were all leaving, did you notice anything unusual about any of the other guests?"

"Most of them were pretty drunk, but other than that I can't remember anything in particular."

"You say most of them. Was someone else sober?"

"Fabían is an invalid and on medication. He didn't drink any alcohol that evening, he just smoked a few joints. It helps him when he feels nauseous."

"Had you met him before?"

"Yes, I know him well. Fabían is an artist, and we've exhibited together. He doesn't take to everybody, but we have a good relationship."

"Did you notice any interaction between him and Anton?"

"Fabían kept to himself that evening. He wasn't feeling well."

"What's the matter with him?"

"Cancer. He's on medication that slows its progress, but apparently they've run out of other options."

"You mean he's dying?"

"Yeah, he doesn't have long. All his friends can do is hope he gets a few more months in reasonable health."

Gunnar turned to his laptop, which had finished copying Helgi's photos. He unplugged the thumb drive and handed it back to Helgi, and then opened the first image file. "What's this?"

"This is the exhibition space in the Felleshus. Most of the photos are from there."

Gunnar scanned the pictures one by one. The first photos showed people in the public space looking at various exhibits, but then the scene changed to show Helgi and the ambassador sitting together in Konrad's office. The two candlesticks on a table between them held large unused candles. "These pictures were going to be included in our promotional materials," Helgi said.

"You didn't light the candles?"

"No. We didn't have anything to light them with. And anyway, Lúdvík didn't want them lit—the photo showed off the candlesticks better that way."

"They were lit later in the evening. Who might have carried matches or a lighter? Any smokers?"

"Anton smoked cigars. I remember he had a lighter. David and Starkadur smoked cigarettes. I can't remember if anybody else was smoking. Fabían had his grass, of course."

"Did the ambassador allow smoking in the embassy?"

"I don't recall anybody asking."

Gunnar continued clicking through the photos, slowing down for a sequence taken during dinner. Might do well to remember that people eating don't look good in photographs, he reflected. The last picture showed the Sun Poet standing on a chair, presumably reciting a poem.

"That's the last one Lúdvík took that evening," Helgi said. "After the ambassador brought out the brandy, things got kind of rowdy. There was no point in taking pictures anymore."

"Toward the end of the party, would you have heard anybody shouting from the upper floors?"

"No, the ambassador loaded a disc of German *schlager* music into the sound system and turned up the volume. By the third time through, it had gotten really irritating."

Gunnar smiled. "One final thing. I need to ask you to let me take your finger and palm prints for the investigation."

"Have the other guests agreed to this?"

"We haven't spoken with everybody yet."

"I want to consult a lawyer about my status before I agree to that."

"You have the legal status of a witness," Gunnar said, "so you can refuse. We'll let you know if the situation changes."

"In that case, let's wait."

"OK, but we'll probably need to talk with you again."

"I'll be at your disposal."

Helgi stood up, said good-bye, and left. Gunnar stayed in his chair, contemplating the candlesticks. Then he picked up a receiver and dialed Anna's extension. Soon, she joined him in the interview room. Gunnar pointed at the table and said, "I carefully wiped the tabletop before inviting Helgi in here. His prints are all over. Can you see if you can get something useful? But don't record it formally. This is just between us."

14:45

Birkir parked his unmarked squad car in an open spot and walked the last few meters toward the house where Jón the Sun Poet and Fabían Sigrídarson lived. It was on a quiet road in a long-established neighborhood just west of the Landspítali University Hospital. The road was narrow, one-way, with parking spaces on both sides. The houses on its south side were close together, with only the sidewalk separating them from the road. On the north side, though, they were widely spaced, with generous front yards. These were spacious villas—two floors with basements and attics—and one of them, sticking out like a sore thumb among its nicely maintained neighbors, was the poet's house.

The rusty gate's hinges squealed as Birkir pushed it open, startling a flock of snow buntings from the stately line of tall poplar trees in front of the house. Birkir paused and considered the yard. It was mostly filled with dense trees and bushes; aspens, rowans, and birches intertwined chaotically over low-growing bushes—perhaps red currants, he thought. Amid the trees were sculptures made of various materials, and little rivulets of water trickling into small ponds. Against the wall of the house was an old bench that looked like it might have once belonged to a bus stop.

In the driveway sat an old American car; judging by its completely flat tires and rusted fenders, it had been there a long time. Birkir peered in through a half-open window. The car's interior was covered in bird droppings, and between the front seats was a small abandoned nest.

"The wagtail nests there every summer," a woman's voice said behind Birkir.

Birkir spun round.

"There were four eggs this year." The speaker was a tiny old woman snugly wrapped in a thick parka, hood up, and with a green parrot sitting atop her head. "They all hatched chicks," she added, beaming. "I'm taking Konstantín for a walk," she said by way of explanation, noticing Birkir looking at the bird. "Bye, then." She turned abruptly and walked away. The parrot flapped its wings to maintain balance, but stood firm as they disappeared beyond the surrounding wall.

Birkir turned back to take a better look at the house. It was in sore need of maintenance: In several places, the dark roughcast finish had come away from the walls, and somebody had done a slapdash job of patching the worst bits with pale-colored cement, which looked particularly bad against the original facade. A sheet of plywood replaced a broken windowpane in the basement. It bore the house's name, "Jónshús," crudely painted in black lettering. Three cooing pigeons sat on the awning above the front door.

Birkir pressed the doorbell and heard it ringing inside the house. After a short while, the door was opened by a woman in her fifties wearing no makeup, and with thick, grayish hair gathered into two braids. She wore faded jeans and a flamboyant T-shirt that reached halfway down to her knees.

Birkir introduced himself and asked for Fabían.

"Yes, he is expecting you. Please come in." Her voice was slightly hoarse, almost a whisper.

Birkir heard someone playing jazz on the piano in the living room.

"Fabían's room is upstairs," the woman said, and pointed Birkir toward the staircase in the hall. Birkir went ahead and she followed. Everywhere works of art decorated the walls, and Birkir paused on a step to take a closer look.

"Jón's lodgers sometimes pay their rent with pictures," the woman said. "And he always hangs them up."

"Is Jón at home?" Birkir asked.

"No, he went downtown with a friend."

They moved on up the stairs and entered a hallway that stretched the full length of the house. A man lay asleep, fully dressed, on a narrow couch next to the wall.

The woman whispered, "This is a homeless guy I let rest here sometimes when things are bad for him. Fabían's room is over here, second on the left." She slipped past him and opened the door. "Please come in."

"Thank you," Birkir said and walked in. The room was empty, but Birkir saw a half-open door to the right and light behind it.

"Fabían, dear, you've got a visitor," the woman called out.

"Just a moment," came a voice from the other room.

The woman gave Birkir a smile and said, "He's coming." She went out, leaving the door ajar.

Birkir looked around. This was the bedroom of a chronically ill patient. Despite the open window, the air was heavy with smells of medicines and disinfectants—and also with the odor of some kind of incense, Birkir thought. Or maybe cannabis.

The bed was large and robust with an adjustable frame, and above it a bar to help the patient pull himself up. On the comforter nestled a cordless phone; within reach by the side of the bed was a DVD player and sound system, and at its foot a wall-mounted television. Classical music wafted quietly from speakers. Birkir recognized the orchestral version of Pachelbel's *Canon*.

There were shelves stuffed full of magazines and books. The large bedside table held medicine bottles, tubes of ointment, a thermometer, a banana, and a water bottle. Next to the bed stood two chairs, and in the middle of the room was a wheelchair.

Birkir heard someone flushing a toilet and washing their hands at a sink. There was a cough, and then the door to the little bathroom opened wide and Fabían entered the bedroom.

"Good afternoon," Birkir said. He introduced himself.

"Hi," Fabían said. He was dressed in blue cotton pajamas and woolen socks. His snowy-white hair was still as thick as a young boy's, cut in a fringe across his forehead and long enough to cover his ears. He had a neat nose, large eyes, a delicate chin, and a small mouth—his pale lips were almost invisible. Although tired and drawn, it was an extraordinarily childlike face that seemed to have grown older in step with the body, yet never matured. Like a being from another world, Birkir thought.

He said, "Thank you for seeing me. I hope this is not a bad time for you?"

"No, I'm all right at the moment," Fabían replied.

Though Birkir was only five foot five, Fabían was considerably smaller, and his emaciated body was almost lost in his too-big pajamas. He took a thick dressing gown from its hook and wrapped it around himself. Then he switched off the music. "I'm always cold," he said, offering Birkir a seat. He sat down in the other chair. "The Berlin trip was too much for me. I've been in bed since I got home." His voice was quiet and gentle.

Birkir set up his voice recorder, dictated the formalities, and asked Fabían to consent to his recording their conversation.

Fabían nodded, listlessly.

Birkir spoke into the recorder, "Fabían indicates his consent with a nod."

There was a momentary silence while Birkir set the machine on the table, and then he continued, "The object of this interview is to go over incidents that took place at the Icelandic embassy in Berlin the evening of Sunday, October eleventh, and early morning of Monday, October twelfth. You were present, were you not?"

"Yes." Fabían nodded again.

"You know why I'm asking about that evening, don't you?"

"Yes, we heard on the news that one of the guests had been found dead. It's not difficult to guess which one."

"Why were you at this party?"

"My friend Jón the Sun Poet asked me to go with him on this reading trip to Berlin."

"When did you arrive in Berlin?"

"October ninth, that Friday. We had planned to stay just over a week."

"Why did that plan change?"

Fabían reached out for the water bottle and took a swig. He gagged briefly, but managed to keep things down. "Can I do anything for you?" Birkir asked.

Fabían shook his head. He took some time to recover before replying, "I'm not too good. That's why the plan changed. I had a relapse. After two days in Berlin I'd had my fill of traveling. It's hard enough for healthy folks to keep up with my friend Jón, let alone an invalid like me. I managed to change my flight, and flew back Monday."

"Were you OK to travel alone?"

"No, I couldn't do that. The artist Helgi Kárason came with me. He looked after everything—booking my flight, check-in, everything. He took me in a wheelchair to and from the airplane. I've never been well enough to do much traveling, so I need a reliable escort. I don't speak any foreign languages either, so I'm pretty lost abroad. Helgi took wonderful care of me."

"So, you were a guest at the embassy at a time when someone died. Can you go back over what happened during the last hour or so you were there?"

"It was pretty much the same as at any cocktail party that's about to break up. People were variously sober. Or not."

"Meaning?"

"The ambassador and his wife had gotten unnecessarily argumentative, and David and Starkadur were turning all melodramatic." Fabían coughed and took a sip of water. "By this time I was totally fed up with Jón, and I was getting sick. Lúdvík had fallen asleep in the bathroom, and Helgi—who was sober—was trying to maintain order."

"And Anton?"

"He spent most of the time either in the ambassador's office making calls or in the bathroom. I guess he had an upset stomach. The food wasn't much good."

Upset? Yes, his stomach was certainly that, Birkir thought, but not because of the food. "Can you remember anyone else leaving the party to follow Anton upstairs?" he said.

"Nobody went upstairs."

"Nobody?"

"No, definitely not. Are you sure Anton didn't commit suicide?"

"What makes you say that?"

"He was always alone upstairs." Fabían reached into the nightstand's drawer and fished out a hand-rolled cigarette and matches.

"Did you notice that Anton wasn't in the group when you left the embassy?" Birkir asked.

"No. People left in dribs and drabs. I thought that Anton had gone ahead of us. I was sure the ambassador had arranged taxis for everyone," Fabían said, lighting his cigarette—which didn't smell like tobacco. "I use this to counteract the nausea from the drugs. I hope the smoke doesn't bother you."

Birkir moved his chair back a little. "I need to take finger and palm prints from you for comparison. Do you consent to that?"

"How does that work?"

"You put your fingers and your palm on a special ink pad, and then you press them onto paper."

"Ink? So it's a colorant?"

"Yes, you could say that."

"In that case I can't do it. I've got terrible skin allergies, and all colorants are very bad for me."

Fabían held out his arms and pulled up the sleeves of his nightshirt. Red patches of eczema extended down to the backs of his hands.

Birkir said, "We may have other ways of doing it. I'll need to talk to our technician."

Fabían shook his head. "I don't think we're likely to agree on this. I'm extremely wary of all chemical substances."

Birkir hesitated, then decided to change the subject. "We've been checking the security-camera footage. We studied images of all of you on your way into the embassy, and then again on your way out, so we have a good picture of how everyone was dressed. We saw that when you left the embassy you were wearing Jón's jacket and carrying your own."

"Yes."

"Why?"

"Jón's jacket was warmer. I was cold. Jón is never cold."

"Can I see your jacket, please?"

"No, I'm sorry. I left it behind in the hotel in Berlin, hanging in the closet. Very careless of me, but I guess it doesn't matter, since I won't have much need of my clothes in the future. It was no great loss."

"I'll get the embassy to chase it down at the hotel," Birkir said.

"That's very kind of you. I guess they'll send it to me, then."

"You'll get it back after we've given it a thorough examination. Were you wearing a shirt?"

"Yes."

"Where is it?"

"All my clothes went to the laundry as soon as I got back. Rakel took care of that."

"Rakel?"

"She let you in here. She lives with us and looks after me when she's not on duty at the hospital. She's a nurse. I am very fortunate to have such good friends."

"Did you know the other guests at the embassy?"

"I've known Jón since I was a kid. I also know Helgi well. I didn't know the others. I don't know many people."

"Had you met Anton before?"

Fabían didn't reply immediately. His stomach seemed to be hurting, and he grimaced. "No," he finally said. "Not that I know of."

"Did you talk to him at all that evening?"

"Yes, I wanted to sketch him."

"How did he respond to that?"

"Pretty well, to start with."

"What happened then?"

"He asked me why I wanted to draw his picture."

"How did you respond?"

"I said I'd never seen a face before that looked like a pig's ass."

Heavy footsteps approached the room. A voice thundered, "What's going on here?" as the door flew open and Jón stormed in.

Birkir was startled, but Fabían raised both hands. "Just a polite chat," he said. "I don't often have visitors."

Jón looked from Birkir to Fabían and back again, but decided to let things lie.

"Fabían is an invalid," he said to Birkir. "We really don't want him disturbed."

"The occasional disturbance can be good," Fabían said somewhat petulantly.

"We're done," said Birkir, and packed away the recorder. He stood up.

"No need to run away," Jón said, abashed.

"That's OK," Birkir said. "You can show me out."

He turned back to Fabían. "Thanks for talking with me. I may need to speak to you again."

Fabían replied, "It's a pleasure. Why don't you stop by tonight? I'm at my best in the evening. And you have a good presence."

"I'll try to come by," Birkir said. Fabían aroused his curiosity, and he thought it might be interesting to talk to him informally.

"I'd like that," Fabían said.

Birkir went into the hall and down the stairs.

Birkir stopped a moment in the foyer and turned to Jón, who'd followed him down. "Have you thought of anything that might help us in our investigation? Something in addition to what you told us in Frankfurt?"

"Come into the living room," Jón said.

It was a large room containing a miscellany of unmatched furniture. At one end was a full-size grand piano, at which sat a young man wearing thick glasses.

"This is Jörundur," Jón said. "He is a composer."

As if to confirm this, Jörundur struck two chords on the instrument and then took up a pencil and wrote something down on a piece of staff paper. The parrot Birkir had encountered on his arrival was now perched in a large cage next to the piano. It screeched when the composer played a couple more chords. "Sometimes he comes up with useful suggestions," Jón said, pointing at the bird.

"Hardly ever happens," Jörundur countered. "It's just noise."

"Is there anything you can tell me about Berlin?" Birkir asked again.

"I've thought about it a lot," Jón said, "and I'm positive that guy was alone upstairs during the latter part of the evening. Wasn't it just suicide?"

"You're sure there was nobody with him?"

"I remember Lúdvík falling asleep in the john. Some folks who needed the bathroom tried knocking on the door, but gave up and just went upstairs. I was reciting poetry for the company, and everyone was having a damned good time. I always paused when anybody left the room. Except, of course, for Anton, since he was upstairs most of the time. I waited ages when Lúdvík went out, until Helgi went to check up on him and said he was sick and had probably fallen asleep in there. Konrad offered to go look for a key, but Helgi said it was probably best to leave him in peace for a while."

"Jón, Jón!" The small woman who'd had the parrot on her head came scurrying into the room. "There's a cat in the garden!"

Jón reacted immediately and rushed out, returning with a handsome bow and arrow. He hurried over to look out the large window the woman had opened.

"Over there," the woman said, pointing.

Jón drew the bow and tried to take aim. "Where, where?" he asked frantically.

"Don't worry," said a voice at Birkir's shoulder, "he always misses." It was Rakel. "And anyway, the arrow has a harmless rubber tip," she added.

Jón fired the arrow and said, "Did I get him?"

"No," said the small woman. "But the cat ran away."

"Cats always do," Rakel said. "The birds know they're safe in this yard."

Gunnar, Birkir, and Magnús held a progress meeting back at the station.

Gunnar was eating a Danish and drinking coffee from a large mug. "Amazing how hungry you get when you're not feeling well," he said with his mouth full.

"You're *always* hungry," Birkir said.

"Not this hungry," Gunnar said. "D'you want a bite?"

"No, thank you."

Gunnar wiped his mouth on his sleeve. "Strange how these guys are all standing together, refusing to let us take their prints," he said, reaching for the last piece of the pastry.

Magnús replied, "I've asked for a warrant. We'll get the papers tomorrow, and then we can go take them one by one. It won't be a problem. Dóra and Anna will deal with it."

Birkir nodded. This was an excellent plan. Dóra would handle it with diplomacy and sensitivity. Birkir held her in high esteem. She had joined the violent crime unit when she was recovering from some sort of car accident while serving in the uniformed police. She turned out to have good people skills, and she was methodical and scrupulous. These were great assets in a detective, and she got the next vacancy that opened up.

Birkir had already spoken with Anna about how to take Fabían's prints. She proposed using a colored glass plate, which would avoid needing ink or other chemical substances.

"Mm, there's something very odd about this," Gunnar said, chewing energetically. "I don't like the way they're all in agreement. It's like they've decided among themselves to object. It's a very unusual reaction. Witnesses who have nothing to hide are usually keen to help us."

"They've got their rights," Birkir said.

Gunnar made a face. "This wouldn't have happened if the *Kripo* had been asked to handle the case right away in Berlin. They would have interviewed everyone individually Monday morning, so the guys wouldn't have had the chance to synchronize their stories. The perp would have stood alone with no alibi. Then we wouldn't have had to travel to Germany, and my health would be a lot better."

"We'll solve this," said Magnús. "We'll work through them one by one, comparing their palm prints with the one we got from the embassy. When we find a match, that'll be it. In what order should we collect them?"

"Should we start with Helgi?" Birkir suggested.

"No need," Gunnar said. "I actually got his palm prints today—without his knowledge or consent. I got Anna to check the table he sat at when I was interviewing him. The prints we got wouldn't be usable in court, but that doesn't matter because they didn't match. He's not our man. Neither is the ambassador, nor is his wife. We've already checked them."

"David, then," Birkir said. "And Starkadur at the same time."

Magnús looked at Gunnar, who shrugged.

Birkir said, "OK, then after that we'll visit Jón and Fabían. If it's not either of them, it has to be Lúdvík."

The meeting was over. Gunnar finished his pastry and helped himself to more coffee. Then he called Lúdvík's cell for the twentieth time. Finally he got an answer.

"Gunnar Maríuson, Reykjavík detective division. Could you spare a few minutes to answer some questions?"

"Yes," Lúdvík said. "I'm free for the next half hour."

"You've been difficult to get hold of. Where are you now?"

"Keflavík Airport. I just got back to Iceland."

"You know why I'm calling, don't you?"

"Yes, the murder at the embassy. I just talked with Helgi, and he told me about it. How awful. To think something like this could occur right under your nose without anybody noticing anything."

"Can you describe the last part of your evening at the embassy?"

"No, I'm sorry, I can't."

"Why not?"

Lúdvík said, "I was sick by then. I usually drink in moderation, but that evening I had a little too much brandy. I vomited in the restroom and fell asleep there. Helgi woke me up by banging on the door when everybody was leaving."

"Is that so?"

"Yeah, it's unpleasant to have to admit it, but I'm ashamed to say that's what I was like that evening."

"How long do you think you were sleeping?"

"At least an hour."

"And nobody else used the restroom in the meantime?"

"No, I'd locked myself in. There were other restrooms on the upper floors."

"Did you know the other guests?"

"No. I knew Helgi, of course, and I knew of Jón from the past. I didn't know any of the others personally."

"What do you mean by 'personally'?"

"Well, they're well-known guys, of course, but I'd never rubbed shoulders with them."

"Did you have any dealings with Anton that evening?"

"We spoke briefly during the party. I didn't find him very interesting."

"How so?"

"I thought he was arrogant and aggressive. He seemed to think he was the guest of honor, but Jón the Sun Poet made it clear to him that this wasn't the case, and after that he mostly stayed upstairs."

"Where upstairs?"

"In the ambassador's office, making calls—courtesy of the Icelandic state."

"Did you go up there at all?"

"Helgi and I briefly met with the ambassador in his office. We took photographs and shook hands on a deal about a promotional campaign. I also went upstairs at one point later in the evening."

"Was Anton there then?"

"I don't think so. I went up to use the bathroom because the downstairs one was occupied."

"What was your business in Berlin?"

"I set up exhibitions for artists. Helgi and I have worked together in the past, and he asked me again this time. I installed an exhibition of paintings at the embassy three years ago, so I was familiar with the space, but we needed to go to Berlin to take a look at it together. Ceramics need a different approach than paintings."

"Do you arrange shipping for the exhibits?"

"Yes, usually. I get a specialist carpenter to make the crates— under my supervision."

"Did you send the two candlesticks that were in the ambassador's office?"

"Yes, I arranged that."

"Did you see them there?"

"Yes, I took a photograph of Helgi and the ambassador with the candlesticks between them."

"Were they all right?"

"Yes, of course. Did something happen to them?"

"No."

"Phew, that's a relief. Those are priceless objects. Helgi doesn't do that particular style anymore."

"Tell me in detail how you arranged their shipping."

"How are the candlesticks relevant to your investigation?"

"Maybe they're not, but it may turn up something useful."

"OK. In consultation with me, Helgi has been collating a list of artifacts that are to be displayed in his exhibition. He decided to send the candlesticks ahead for use in the promotional materials, and asked me to arrange the shipping, as usual. I went to his studio and measured them. The crate was made in my workshop with waterproofed plywood and lined with foam rubber cut to fit the candlesticks precisely. I transported the crate to Helgi's studio, packed the candlesticks, and personally screwed the crate closed. It's my usual procedure, and ensures that the contents are one-hundred percent secure. A shipping company then picked up the case for delivery to Berlin."

"Did you have a good look at the candlesticks before you packed them?"

"Yes, of course."

"What sort of bases did they have?"

"The usual kind—the same Helgi always uses for such things. He closes them off with plaster of paris and inscribes his initials, HK."

"So there was nothing unusual about them?"

"No, nothing unusual."

Gunnar mulled things over. "OK," he said, finally. "That's all for now. I'll need you to come to police headquarters so we can take your fingerprints and palm prints for comparison."

"Fingerprints? Is that necessary?"

"Yes, please, as soon as possible."

"Yeah, well, I'll bear that in mind as soon as I get a chance."

As promised, Birkir went to visit Fabían. He had no other plans, and anyway, his mind was completely occupied by this murder case. Maybe Fabían had something to say that would throw light on the embassy guests' circumstances during that fateful night.

He'd started his evening with a ten-kilometer run around the west part of town, and then, after eating leftover vegetable soup and a slice of homemade bread, he'd sat down with a mug of lemon tea for a half hour to listen to some music. Now, donning suitable clothing to protect against the rapidly cooling evening air, he headed out. He didn't have far to go, so he decided to take a detour up a street lined with little artisan shops, in whose windows he enjoyed studying the displays of handicrafts and all kinds of artwork. There was a sort of contentment in these little shops. Birkir was friendly with an old man who was a goldsmith and ran a small workshop in a back lot behind one of the main houses. He'd been robbed some time back, and Birkir had been instrumental in solving the case. Since then he would occasionally stop by the shop for a chat and to check that the security system was working. There was a real community feel to the neighborhood.

When he got to Jónshús, once again Rakel opened the door; she seemed to be expecting him. "Fabían is in the kitchen," she said, showing him the way.

"Welcome," Fabían said. He was alone, standing at the kitchen table and slicing an apple. He was dressed in a thick cotton sweater with a hood that he'd pulled over his head. His pants were made of the same material, thick and somewhat too large for him, and he wore fur-lined leather boots.

"Please sit down," he said, nodding toward a chair next to the table. "I'm just preparing breakfast for our birds. Úlfheidur usually does it, but she's otherwise occupied tonight. She's a fortune-teller and she knits sweaters. A good combination."

"Is she a good fortune-teller?" Birkir asked.

"It varies, but when she hits the mark, it really works. Two years before the banking crash she told Jón to get rid of all the shares he'd inherited from his parents, and buy euros and dollars instead. That was after she dreamed that they'd moved the Art Academy into the Central Bank building—not a bad idea, actually."

He laughed quietly, which turned into a coughing fit.

"Did Jón follow her advice?" Birkir asked.

"Yes," Fabían answered once he'd recovered. "And our household greatly benefited from it. Our annual accounts here usually show a deficit, so it's great to have access to a reliable reserve fund. Jón is very generous to us."

He lined up the apple slices on a wooden board and cut out the centers with a corer. "The holes are so I can hang the rings from the trees," he said.

Then he fetched a glass bowl from the refrigerator. "Jörundur cooked meat broth yesterday, and I skimmed off the fat from the leftovers at lunch today. I'll dip some bread in it, it's good for the thrushes." He put the bowl into the microwave, and set it for one minute.

"Tell me about yourself," Birkir said.

"Myself?"

"Yes, where were you born? Where have you lived?"

"Why do you want to know about that?"

"Just curiosity, I guess. I hope you don't mind."

"No, I'm just surprised—folks aren't usually interested in my life story. But, since you ask, I'm from the Northwest, born in Ísafjördur in the spring of 1961."

"Did you grow up in Ísafjördur?"

"To start with, but after a few years I became homeless."

"Tell me about it."

Fabían paused to think before he started his account. "I lost my father before I was even born. When my mother was six months pregnant, he decided the relationship wasn't working for him. I've never met him."

"Why are you called Fabían? It's not a common name."

"I'm fond of my name. It's the only thing I've got left from my mother. My mom loved music. She named me after Fabian, an American singer she idolized—he was very popular, and his songs were always being played on the radio in the fifties and sixties."

"Did something happen to your mother?"

"Yes. She got sick and died."

"Tell me about it."

The microwave beeped, and Fabían took out the bowl. "Mom coped really well during her first years as a single mother. She had a job in fish processing, and she always provided for me. She was lucky with day care, because she found me a woman who had three kids of her own and took in five others during the day. I was an easy kid, so it was never a problem for me to stay there into the evening if they had to do overtime at the freezing plant. Sometimes I'd fall asleep in bed with one of the other kids, and then they just left me until morning. Mom would swing by and give me a kiss before going back to our little apartment on her own. So my early childhood was good, but when I was seven, my mom fell ill with a neurological disorder and could no longer work. Of course I was in school by then, but outside of that I just fended for myself. Mom stayed at home for a few months, but after that she couldn't even look after herself and was sent to a sanatorium here in Reykjavík. A year later she was dead."

As he talked, Fabían soaked slices of bread in the hot fat. "When Mom couldn't live on her own anymore, I was sent to a farm to be looked after by a couple who fostered boys in welfare. It was a small place, isolated in the far corner of the fjord, mostly sheep, but also seven cows. It wasn't altogether bad, but there was no love at all. There were five of us little guys, all different ages, scared to death of the husband, who ruled with terror and tongue-lashing. I don't actually remember him beating us, but somehow that was always the hidden threat. I was unusually small for my age and kind of puny. My mother's death had been a great shock to me, and no one helped me deal with that. My poor little soul was in a bad way."

Fabían took his tray of fat-soaked bread and put it in the refrigerator. "We'll let this harden a moment before we take it outside." He sat down at the table. "Can I offer you anything?"

Birkir shook his head. "Go on with your story," he said.

"One fall, I got very sick and was sent away to the district hospital. It was partly an infection and partly malnutrition because of the poor appetite I'd always had. I was also psychologically blocked—I never initiated conversation, and personal hygiene was a problem. The folks at the hospital decided that I had some kind of developmental disability, and when the farmer refused to have me back after my hospitalization, I was placed in a home for mentally handicapped people. I was not unhappy there and, since I wasn't as challenging to deal with as most of the others, I was left in peace. They didn't do much to develop our abilities. Every day was more or less the same, and I spent most of my time sitting by the window, looking out at the yard. Somebody had the idea to give me paper and pencil, and I began to draw what I could see outside. It was crude stuff to start with, but gradually I developed a pretty good freehand technique. I always destroyed my drawings as soon as I'd finished them, though, because I didn't want to attract undue attention to myself. I was comfortable being left to my own devices, and I stayed there for the next few years."

Fabían stood up and took out two plastic containers, which he filled with grains from two sacks in the adjoining pantry. "This one is a mixture of wheat and grits for the snow buntings," he said, placing the containers on the table in front of Birkir, "and this one is sunflower seeds for the redpolls."

"How did you meet Jón the Sun Poet?" Birkir asked.

"That's a story in itself. One spring, a young poetry-writing hippie from Reykjavík took a summer job at the home where I was kept. This was Jón Sváfnisson, who later became known as the Sun Poet. His behavior was sometimes a bit over the top, but he was sensitive to his surroundings and to other people. One time, he caught me reading a magazine when I thought I was unobserved. The other inmates were all illiterate, so this was out of the ordinary, but he didn't tell the staff, he just started chatting to me about this and that, and didn't seem to mind that I didn't respond. Also working there that same summer was Sunna, a girl from a nearby village. Nicknamed "Sun," she was a kitchen assistant and cleaner, and whenever she had a free moment she sang and played the guitar. I was entranced by the beautiful sounds she made, and one day I abandoned my safe place by the window, moved closer, and started drawing her as she played. The finished sketch was really good, I thought, and I couldn't bear to destroy it like the others, so I slipped it into her guitar case when no one was looking. There was pandemonium when they discovered it. Nobody figured out that it was the idiot by the window who'd produced this masterpiece—except of course for Jón, but he didn't say a word. Sunna loved the poems Jón had written, and set some of them to music. She and Jón ended up as an item and went together to Reykjavík at the end of the summer."

Fabían fetched the bread pieces from the refrigerator, picked up the board with the apple rings, and signaled for Birkir to pick up the grain and seed containers. "All this needs to go out," he said. Then, stopping only to put on a thick parka in the hallway, he led the way into the yard.

Despite the overhanging trees, there was a fair amount of light out there, cast by the streetlamps and spilling out from the living room windows. There was a full moon, too, shining down from a northern sky. The only sound they could hear in the stillness was the trickle of a tiny brook that flowed between two small ornamental ponds.

Birkir stared at the water in surprise.

"There's a neat little device that pumps the water through a pipe back up to the upper pond," Fabían said. "And some of the outflow from the mains hot water gets added to it, that's why it's not frozen. There's always fresh water for the birds."

Birkir took a closer look. The ponds' edges had been painstakingly constructed with flat stones, and mosses had rooted themselves at water level.

Fabían nodded toward a folding stepladder lying beneath the trees. "Would you mind putting that up for me? I want to hang up the apples in the rowan." He pointed at the trees, which had lost most of their leaves in the previous week's wind. "The thrushes have been eating the rowanberries, and there aren't many left, so it makes sense to give them apples and fat now. Then they'll remember where they can find food in the winter when there are no more berries and frosts are harder. I'm convinced that the same birds come here year after year."

Birkir set up the stepladder where Fabían pointed. "Can you support it while I climb up, please?" Fabían asked. "And can you hold the board for me? We have to put the food as high as possible, because of all the neighborhood cats. We keep shooing them away, but they always come sneaking back."

With Birkir holding on to the stepladder, Fabían climbed unsteadily up. Then he held out his hand for the apple pieces. "We've cut back some of the smaller branches here to make hooks to hang the food from," he said as he threaded the apple rings one by one onto the protruding stumps. He repeated the process with the bread slices.

"Now it's ready for them when they come out of their sleeping places in the morning," Fabían said as he stepped carefully back down to earth. "The thrushes and the starlings will fight over it. Sometimes the odd blackbird, too."

He stood awhile, collecting himself. "I just need a moment," he said. "Climbing makes me dizzy."

Birkir waited for him to recover before asking, "What happened to you after Jón finished working in the home?"

"I got sick again and spent most of that winter in the hospital. They had a lot of interesting books there, and I stopped bothering to hide the fact that I could read. A teacher regularly came to the hospital to tutor a girl who was chronically sick. He took an interest in me and had me join in the classes. I learned a lot in a very short time, and people realized I was maybe not so retarded after all. Still, when I'd gotten better, they sent me back to the previous place while they considered other solutions. In the spring, Jón and Sun came to visit in an old Russian jeep. When they heard about the problems finding somewhere for me to live, they offered me the chance to come and do farm work for them, as they were about to move out into the country down south. I was worried about having to do heavy work, as I was physically very feeble, but Jón promised that wouldn't happen. He stood by his word—I never had to overexert myself while living with them."

He turned away from Birkir and moved over to the tallest aspens. He pointed to where horizontal wooden boards were firmly attached to the branches three meters above them.

"Would you mind scattering the grain for the snow buntings up there for me, please?" he said. "I'll support the ladder."

Birkir repositioned the stepladder and clambered up.

"The buntings arrived unusually early this fall," Fabían said. "They came straight after that cold spell at the beginning of the month."

Birkir sprinkled the contents of the plastic container onto the boards and climbed back down.

"This should be enough for our morning visitors," Fabían said. "Úlfheidur will feed them again at noon tomorrow. It's easier to do this in daylight."

"So you moved south—how was that?" Birkir asked.

Fabían coughed. "Yes, I left with Jón and Sun, and we went to Fljótshlíd in the Southeast, where they set up a small commune with another couple, Helgi Kárason and Rakel Árnadóttir. Helgi was with Jón and me in Berlin, as you know, and you've met Rakel here."

"What was the farm?" Birkir asked.

"Jón's father had inherited a small plot of land with an old house on it, far up the river valley. A remote place, called Sandgil. Jón was one of those typical anarchist hippies rebelling against their wealthy parents, and he and his friends decided to squat on the land. His father avoided confrontation by pretending he didn't know Jón had taken over the farm. For me, things were better than they'd ever been since I'd lost my mother and my home. My housemates were extremely kind to me, and we had a great life. Other good people came and lived with us from time to time, but only the five of us lived there permanently the whole time."

Fabían walked around the corner of the house and pointed to a shelf attached to a sheltered corner on the west side of the house.

"That's where we put the food for the redpolls. Would you mind?"

Birkir set up the stepladder where he could reach the shelf, and climbed up. He scattered the seeds around and climbed back down.

"What did you live off of out there in the country?" he asked.

Fabían replied, "Housekeeping was actually a bit of a struggle because we had very little income. The idea was to earn money selling handicrafts, ceramics, candles, and my drawings. Jón would sell pamphlets of his verse, and Sun would sing her songs. But none of this brought in enough money, so Jón expanded our cottage industry into growing cannabis in the attic. There was a perfect space up there, once they'd brought in lights. Jón and Helgi had learned how to do this on their travels in Europe. I became just as good at horticulture as I was at drawing. For nearly a year, this all worked quite well, but then the authorities got suspicious and busted Jón, Helgi, and Rakel on a sales trip near Reykjavík."

"What happened to you?"

Fabían coughed several times, and his voice cracked as he continued, "The same evening my friends were arrested, our house burned down, and Sun died in the fire. I managed to escape. I was found the next morning, wandering aimlessly. I'd suffered some kind of mental breakdown, and they sent me to a psychiatric institution."

Fabían coughed again more violently, and he suddenly vomited. He continued gagging for a while, and when he looked up, Birkir saw that he had a nosebleed.

"I'm sorry," Fabían mumbled. "I'm having a relapse."

"Let me help you in," Birkir said, helping Fabían upright and supporting him as they made their way back through the yard. As they approached the steps to the house, Fabían fell to his knees. Birkir bent down and gathered him up. It surprised him how light his load was.

"Can you carry him inside?" Rakel had appeared on the porch and was holding the front door open.

"Yes," Birkir said, and walked up the steps carrying Fabían in his arms.

"And up to his room?"

"Yes." Inside, he continued up the stairs and carried the patient into the room on the second floor, laying him down on the bed.

"Thank you," Rakel said, "I'll take over now."

"Do you mind if I stay awhile to see how he's doing?" Birkir asked.

"Don't worry, I'll give him an injection and he'll fall asleep. You can come back tomorrow."

After a generous evening meal at home with his mother, María, followed by a half-hour nap, Gunnar decided to round off the day with a visit to his regular bar on Smidjustígur, in the hope that a couple shots of bitters would alleviate the misery of his head cold. The bar was walking distance away, but, although he could move around reasonably well with the aid of his crutches, his back hurt like hell. He called a cab.

As he entered the bar, Gunnar signaled to the bartender, then paused to scan the room for a seat. He didn't think he could cope with standing or sitting at the counter. There were no free tables, but he saw an empty chair by a table for two, at which sat a familiar figure—a slim, sharp-nosed man with grayish, wavy hair parted in the center, and a neatly trimmed goatee. He was writing something on a piece of paper, but looked up through his thick spectacles as Gunnar sat down next to him.

"Emil Edilon. Good to see you, Maestro," Gunnar said.

"By all that is holy! If it isn't the Germanic Giant, back from the dead," Emil said, eyeing the crutches Gunnar had leaned against the table. "Are you trying for a disability pension? I know a doctor who's good at forging certificates."

Gunnar pretended he hadn't heard this and asked, "How's the writing going?"

Emil sadly looked at the paper in front of him. "I think too much. One shouldn't think. One should just write gibberish. That's what readers like best. But you wouldn't understand—you have no more feeling for literature than for any other nonedible pleasures."

A waiter came to the table and set before Gunnar a Holsten beer and a small square bottle of Jägermeister bitters.

"Where on earth did you learn to drink that stuff?" Emil asked.

"From my mom. She likes bitters."

The bar owner stocked these brands specially for Gunnar, who was the only customer who ordered them.

"OK," Emil said. "Now go and bother someone else. I'm working."

Gunnar looked around but couldn't see any free seats. "Hey," he said, "do you know Jón the Sun Poet?"

Emil looked at him suspiciously. "Why do you ask?"

"I bumped into him in Germany."

"What were you doing in Germany?"

"Never mind that. Do you know the Sun Poet?"

"Yeah, I used to buy pot from him back in the days when I still enjoyed the stuff. He grew a good strain and knew how to process it."

"What about now?"

"I stopped smoking cannabis a long time ago. It's bad for people who need to use their brains—but you don't have to worry about that sort of thing."

"I mean, do you know the Sun Poet now?" Gunnar asked impatiently.

"We sometimes talk," Emil said reluctantly. "You can have an intellectual discussion with the Ogre if you catch him at a good moment. He's at his best when he's had three or four pints. After that he becomes tiresome."

"Is he a decent poet?"

"He stopped writing poetry a long time ago. He never recovered after the accident."

"What accident?"

Emil Edilon looked wearily at Gunnar and set aside his pen.

"In the early seventies, the Sun Poet was living on a hippie commune down in Fljótshlíd. That all came to an end when the house burned down. His fiancée perished in the fire. It was a terrible loss—she was a very gifted musician and a particularly sweet person. The rest of us never understood what she saw in the Ogre." Emil hesitated, struggling to remember the man's full name, but then it came. "Jón Sváfnisson. Apparently, there was a nice side to him, though he kept it to himself."

Gunnar was familiar with Emil's problem remembering people's names, and how he'd sometimes invent nicknames to help sidestep the issue. That's why he called Gunnar the Germanic Giant.

"What do you mean, he never recovered?" Gunnar asked.

"The guy was transformed. Before, he was full of ideas. He was focused and meticulous in his writing. After the fire he just got weird. You can occasionally detect a creative thought in him, but it never ends up on paper."

"Does he have any tendency toward violence?"

Emil shook his head and briefly smiled. "The Ogre is big, and he was once fit. I've seen him step in to stop a fight or two, but otherwise he can't be bothered to start throwing punches himself."

"What about Helgi Kárason?"

"The artist?"

"Yeah."

"What about him?"

"Do you know him?"

"No."

"And Lúdvík Bjarnason, do you know him?"

"I know who he is."

"What can you tell me about him?"

Emil peered into his empty glass, then picked it up and showed it to Gunnar. "It would help to have a refill."

Gunnar turned toward the counter and shouted, "Waiter! The same again for the author and another round for me, please."

The bartender acknowledged the order.

"Who is this Lúdvík?" Gunnar asked.

"The guy wanted to be an artist, but his dream was undermined by his total lack of talent. Instead, he found his niche helping out artists who did achieve success. He organizes exhibitions and that kind of thing. He may never have been able to create a work of art worth more than the materials used, but he has an eye for presentation."

"Can a person make a living doing that?"

"I think so. He handles the whole shebang, including packing the artworks and arranging their delivery, all of which can be a mammoth job if it's a big exhibition, and he only works for the artists who can afford to pay. When he's not doing that, he works in the studios, stretching canvases and so on. He even paints the backgrounds for one of the artists who does big paintings. He's got plenty to do."

Gunnar lowered his voice. "He's got a record of violence."

"I know."

"What did he do?"

"Couldn't you be bothered to read the police report?"

"I just haven't got around to it," Gunnar replied.

The bartender brought the drinks and put them on their table.

Emil waited until he had left, and then continued, "This guy—what was his name again?"

"Lúdvík."

"Oh, yes, Lúdvík. As a young man back in the seventies he was into weight lifting, which was definitely not trendy during those hippie years, but he pursued it with great enthusiasm alongside his art studies. He also liked exposing himself, but he mostly satisfied that urge by posing nude at the art school."

"So was he convicted for something connected with that?"

"Oh, no, it was for something quite different. At that time in Reykjavík, people were dealing in all sorts of dope, naturally, and although everybody always went on about love and peace, there was a need for effective and able-bodied heavies. The hippies were prone to buying stuff and paying later—sometimes forgetting to pay altogether. Our weight-lifting friend was called upon when kids owed money, and he would spook them so efficiently that they instantly got clean and found themselves jobs to pay the debts. Either that or they hit up their fathers for loans, which was probably more common."

"Is he still involved in that kind of thing?"

"Oh, no. He stopped some years ago, right after he nearly killed someone by accident."

"Do you know if he has any connection with Jón Sváfnisson?"

"No doubt he collected for the Sun Poet, the same as he did for others in that line of business."

SATURDAY, OCTOBER 17

07:00

Birkir woke to the sound of his alarm clock. This was his day off, and he had resolved to keep it that way—at least to start with.

He got up, retrieved the morning paper from the front door mailbox, and sat down to read it over a leisurely breakfast: a sip of cod liver oil, a cup of strong tea, and two pieces of toast with cheese and cucumber. Then he set about getting ready for a training run. A long one.

First he went out onto the balcony to check the weather and decide what to wear. The wind had changed directions, and there was now a stiff easterly breeze, but it wasn't raining. Back inside, he began by smearing a thick layer of Vaseline on all the usual friction points—nipples, neck, groin, and his protruding navel. He'd suffered in the past after skipping these precautions, even drawing blood on long runs, and now he was careful to avoid repeating that mistake. Then he put on tight running pants, thick socks, a thin sweater, and a light windproof jacket topped with a bright-yellow reflective vest, and tied on his Asics running shoes.

Mixing up an energy drink, he filled two small plastic flasks with it, another two with water, and then fastened the four flasks to a belt that he clipped around his waist. Finally he stuck a couple of bananas into his jacket pockets and put on a wool hat, thick gloves, and running goggles with yellow lenses. He picked up his bag containing clean clothes, toiletries, and swimming gear, and headed out to his Toyota Yaris, parked in his reserved spot behind the house.

At ten minutes to nine, he swung into the parking lot outside the West Reykjavík public swimming pool, parked the car, and joined the group of five men and two women gathered in the entrance lobby, all clad in gear similar to his. After a brief discussion, they agreed to take the same route as last time, and at precisely nine o'clock they headed out, running in a southerly direction down to the sea, where they turned east into the breeze. The runners took turns setting the pace against the wind, holding a rate of about five minutes per kilometer. They passed the airfield and the heated waters of Nauthólsvík Bay, and crossed the highway via the footbridge, heading toward the Ellida River valley. Before long, there was more shelter from the headwind and the runners were able to increase their speed to four and a half minutes per kilometer, maintaining this rate until they reached the valley, whose steep slopes slowed them down again. Eventually they reached their approximate halfway point, the Árbær swimming pool, where they stopped briefly to use the bathrooms and refill their water bottles, before retracing their route westward. With a short detour around the hot-water tanks at Öskjuhlíd, by the time they returned to their starting point, they had covered exactly thirty kilometers.

It was now eleven thirty, and they were tired and sweaty. After twenty minutes of stretching exercises, and having showered, the group gathered in one of the hot pools for a discussion about training schedules and targets, and proposed distance runs in Iceland and abroad. They caught up on news of absent running mates and swapped lively reminiscences of runs from all over the world. By the time he stood fully dressed outside the swimming pool at twelve thirty, Birkir realized he hadn't given a moment's thought to unsolved murders all morning.

He drove back home, put his running gear away, had lunch—orange juice, rye bread with herring, a boiled egg, and yogurt—and then headed out to walk to Jónshús—this time taking the direct route.

There were three of them outside in the yard. The small woman, whom Birkir now knew to be Úlfheidur, stood on top of the stepladder adding bird feed to the boards in the aspen. Around her fluttered a cluster of snow buntings, pecking at the grains almost the moment they left her hand. Fabían and Rakel sat on a bench against the side of the house, enjoying the brief rays of sunshine that had broken through the early afternoon clouds.

Birkir greeted them.

Rakel stood up and offered him a seat. "I guess I've got to go do some food shopping," she said, and left.

Birkir sat down. "How are you, Fabían?" he said.

"I'm feeling better than yesterday," Fabían replied, lighting up a joint. "I need to be careful not to overdo, though."

"Would you mind continuing with the story you were telling me yesterday?"

"Where had we gotten to?"

"You told me the house in the country burned down and your friend died in the fire."

"Yes, but I'd rather not talk any more about that."

165

"That's OK," Birkir said. "But what about you? How did things go for you afterward?"

"The incident affected me really badly, and I was committed to the Kleppur mental hospital. I had an acute nervous breakdown and retreated into deep depression, a real dark night of the soul. I just sat by the window staring out, seeing nothing, hearing nothing, saying nothing. I suffered severe dissociation—couldn't feed myself, didn't care about my personal hygiene. When things hadn't improved after several months, I was diagnosed as a chronic mental patient and they gave me a permanent place on the quiet ward. I spent several years there."

Fabían stopped talking and stared at some starlings fighting over the apple rings he had hung in the tree the night before.

"It's funny, but all my life I've watched birds," he said. "My mom taught me their names when I was little up north, and guys who know about these things have taught me over the years to recognize the rare ones, the vagrants. I've seen waxwings here in the yard. Birds have always been a comfort to me when I'm down."

"What happened to the rest of your housemates at Sandgil?" Birkir asked.

"They were charged with producing and selling cannabis and were convicted, though I'm not sure they ever served a sentence. They were no more able to heal their grief over Sun's death than I was, and all went their own ways. Sometimes they visited me, but that was all they could do for me. I'd been witness to Sun's fate, and my little soul couldn't deal with that. My life was over."

"But then you began to recover."

"Yes, actually, much later. Twelve years passed, and a young woman came to work in the hospital. She'd just completed a postgraduate degree in clinical psychology at some foreign university. She got professionally interested in the phenomenon I'd become, and decided to try hypnosis and conversation therapy. It was a somewhat one-sided conversation for the first few months, but then, little by little, she managed to ignite a spark of life in me. I began to draw again. After two years, I was beginning to function reasonably. Jón Sun Poet visited me a couple times a year and always kept an eye on how I was doing. We were even roommates for two weeks at one point—he was admitted for treatment for mania brought on by an alcoholic binge. Life on the ward for those two weeks was definitely not boring."

He finished his smoke and stubbed it out. "That's about the time I discovered blood in my stools. I didn't have the nerve to tell anybody, so it got worse, and eventually I was bleeding from the rectum. Somebody noticed red patches on the back of my pants. At the beginning they assumed I had a ruptured hemorrhoid, but when it persisted they sent me for a checkup. The diagnosis came quickly—colon cancer. I had surgery to remove part of my bowel, then radiotherapy and chemo—the whole package. I had a colostomy and began to feel better. Oddly, when I was on the cancer ward, my mental health improved because there I was among sane folks who treated me as an equal. I didn't want to return to Kleppur at all, but I had nowhere else to go. Then Jón came to my rescue yet again. After the fire, he'd moved back to live in the basement of his parents' home, but by now they'd passed away. Jón lived in this large house and rented out rooms. He asked if I'd like to move in and said we could always discuss the rent later."

Fabían stood up and walked out onto the grass. Birkir followed.

"This house has benefited from Jón's excellent choice of lodgers," Fabían said, looking fondly at his home. "The folks here are all artistic eccentrics, men and women of different ages, and the house is really a living academy. I've stayed here ever since I got out of the mental hospital—and I've been very happy, socially."

"But how's your health been?" Birkir asked.

"The cancer has recurred twice. They managed to arrest it the first time, but now it's become chronic and it has metastasized. I'm on medication to slow its progress, but other than that the aim of the treatment is just to ameliorate the symptoms. I don't have much time left, which is sad, because I really appreciate the life I have now."

"How have you spent your time here?"

"I collect my disability pension and draw pictures. Whenever Jón brings out new editions of his verse, I do the book design in my own—some say peculiar—style, and also draw illustrations to accompany the poems."

Birkir's cell phone rang as Fabían spoke. He answered it and listened for a moment. The sun disappeared behind a cloud, and Fabían prepared to return inside.

"Can I offer you a cup of coffee or something?" he asked when Birkir had finished his call.

"No, thank you. It looks as if I have to go check out another guy. Thanks for the chat."

15:00

Birkir's call had been from Dóra. She and Anna and two uniformed cops had gone to David and Starkadur's home with a warrant to take their prints. It had taken a deal of persuasion to get the two to comply, but they succeeded. Anna immediately compared the palm prints with the print found on the ambassador's desk and got a positive result: The palm print on the desk belonged to Starkadur. Dóra arrested him then and there. She was in the process of taking him to the police station when she called Birkir.

Birkir relayed this information to Gunnar, and they decided to conduct the interview with Starkadur together. They figured it might just turn out to be a very important conversation.

Dóra and the prisoner were waiting for them in an interview room. Starkadur looked like thunder and said nothing when they greeted him. "You know why we've brought you here," Gunnar said once he'd switched on the audio and video recorder and listed those present.

"Yes, and it's harassment and illegal arrest," Starkadur replied. "My husband is arranging for a lawyer to get me out of here."

"Would you like us to suspend this interview until your lawyer arrives?" Birkir asked.

"It's all the same to me," Starkadur replied. "I have nothing to hide."

"In that case, we'll press on," Birkir said, and nodded to Gunnar, who was trying to sit up straight.

Gunnar spoke loudly and clearly for the benefit of the recording, "This is in connection with the murder at the embassy in Berlin. We have your palm print on the ambassador's desk in a position consistent with the attack on the victim. Can you explain this?"

"I told the cops who broke into my home how that might have happened," Starkadur replied.

"Would you please be kind enough to repeat that account?" Birkir asked.

"I said that I'd been in the ambassador's office once that evening for a meeting with the ambassador. When the ambassador left, Anton plopped himself down at the desk and prepared to make a phone call. As David and I left, we let him know what we thought of him and his so-called business. I may well have leaned on the desk as I told Anton in no uncertain terms what a revolting piece of shit he was. I admit that I leaned over him as I spoke. At that point he put the phone down and fled from the room. I didn't kill him then, and I didn't kill him later. I have an alibi for the whole evening—David and I were together the whole time."

Birkir had printed out stills from the embassy security-camera footage, and the photographs that Lúdvík took during the party. The CCTV images included pictures of David and Starkadur walking with the ambassador toward the embassy after the poetry reading, and again when they left the building later that night. Starkadur was dressed in a light suit and dark shirt. Though Birkir studied the images closely, he couldn't detect whether stains were visible on the jacket; the resolution wasn't good enough.

Birkir passed Starkadur the best picture he could find. "This suit you were wearing that evening—do you have it at home?"

Starkadur looked at the picture. "No, it went to the dry cleaner after we got back home. It was supposed to be ready yesterday after five o'clock, but I haven't had time to pick it up."

"What about the shirt?"

"I washed all my shirts during the week. I don't remember which one I wore that evening."

"If there is blood from the victim on your clothing, it's very likely that our forensic scientists will be able to find traces of it, even after cleaning."

"That's not something I need to worry about."

Birkir asked Starkadur the name of the dry cleaning store he had taken his suit to. As he noted down the reply, he asked, "Are you happy for the police to take these garments in for examination?"

"Yes, assuming you pay the bill and return the clothes in the same good condition you got them in," Starkadur replied.

"We'll do our best," Birkir said.

Now Gunnar took over. "Did you take a knife with you to the embassy that evening?"

"A knife! Why on earth would I do that? No way." Starkadur shook his head.

"Was any other guest carrying a knife that evening?"

Starkadur again shook his head. "No, of course not."

Birkir said, "You told me yesterday that you had met the other guests before. How well did you know them? Have you had any communication with them since the murder?"

Starkadur leaned back in his chair. "I've already said I didn't kill that guy Anton, and that's the truth. That's all you need to hear. I want to speak to my lawyer before I answer any more of your questions. This interview is going all over the place, and I'm not going to risk saying something you can misinterpret and use to get me into trouble."

"That's fine," said Gunnar. "We'll keep you in custody until we've examined all the evidence properly. It might take a day or two, and we'll try to make you comfortable meantime."

Starkadur said, "I'll sue. This time is going to be expensive for you."

"You have every right to do that, but it would help speed things up if you could make a written statement of what you have told us," Gunnar said, pushing a piece of paper across the table.

With a sigh, Starkadur picked up the pen with his right hand and began to write.

Gunnar and Birkir stood and left the room; Dóra remained with the prisoner.

When they had sat down at their desks, Birkir said, "So Starkadur is right-handed and therefore possibly our man, but we have to find more evidence if we're going to nail him."

Gunnar rummaged in his drawer for something to eat. "I think we have the right guy," he said, triumphantly contemplating a half-eaten chocolate bar he had found among the clutter of pencils and paper clips.

Birkir shook his head. "I'm not so sure."

"Why not?"

"I don't know." Birkir shrugged.

"Whatever, we need to break this thing down. There seems to be an astonishing solidarity within the group—the fact that every single one of them refused to let us take prints suggests collusion. I think they all know more than they're admitting, and if we take one of the bunch and make things a bit uncomfortable for him, it might all disintegrate. Even if he's not the right guy—or perhaps *because* he's not the right guy."

"You think that's a good idea?"

"No, of course it's a lousy idea, but it's all we've got. We have the palm print and we can use that. We'll get a custody order and try keeping Starkadur locked up for a few days."

"Isn't that misuse if that's all we've got?"

"Yeah, no, I mean it's a last resort thing. The palm print's the only thing we've got to go on. Otherwise we'd better just give up."

"I don't like it," Birkir said.

"All right," Gunnar said. "Leave it to me. We'll let him go after a couple days, and if anybody complains I'll apologize and say I wasn't thinking straight because of my cold and back pain. Which is, in a way, the truth." He blew some dust off the chocolate bar and took a bite, smiling.

Birkir said good-bye and left. He had to go find the suit Starkadur had been wearing in Berlin.

Birkir got the contact details of the manager of the dry cleaner's from the company website, and arranged to meet him at the store for the handover of one freshly pressed suit belonging to Starkadur Gíslason, which Birkir took straight to Anna in the forensic laboratory.

"If there's even the tiniest trace of blood, we'll find it," she said. "We'll get deep down into the seams, where the cleaning process can't have reached."

"I hope that won't damage the suit at all," said Birkir.

"We'll see."

"I'd prefer if it didn't."

"Listen," Anna said. "It's a murder investigation. One man's suit is not a big deal."

"Even so," Birkir said. He appreciated a nice, well-made suit cut from good material, and he fully understood that Starkadur would be unhappy if it was ruined.

"Go out for a breath of fresh air if you can't bear to watch." Anna smiled.

Birkir left—not because of what Anna was about to do to Starkadur's suit, but because he wanted to find Helgi, the ceramic artist, to ask about his past friendship with Jón. There was more linking those two than first met the eye, and Birkir needed to investigate all possible angles to the case. He stopped by a small downtown gallery whose owner he knew; after making a few phone calls, the guy was able to give him the address he was looking for.

Located on the second floor of what had once been a net-maker's workshop on Reykjavík's west harbor, Helgi's studio was a room of considerable size—necessarily so, since over the years he had progressed from making small items, such as candlesticks and tableware, to creating large-scale works like sculptures and murals. Finished and half-finished works by him more or less filled the space.

Birkir knocked on the door. There was no response, so he tried the handle, and when the door proved to be unlocked, he let himself in. The place reverberated with loud music from massive speakers. Birkir recognized Janis Joplin, a genuine rock classic from the seventies, though he rarely listened to this type of music. *Perhaps too rarely*, he thought in awe, as Janis thundered, "Cry-y-y baaaby."

Helgi stood before a three-meter-long triptych, fitting a small piece into position; the pieces were made of fired clay of various colors, and as the artist set them in place within the picture, expressive figures emerged.

"Good afternoon," Birkir yelled, holding up his police badge. "I'm from the detective division."

"You what?" Helgi looked up, cupping a hand to his ear.

"From the detective division. I need to ask you a few questions."

Helgi went over to the sound system and turned the music down so it became barely audible. "Right," he said.

"Is that OK?" Birkir asked.

"What do you want to ask about?"

"I'm investigating the Berlin murder. There are some things we need explained."

"I've already given a statement."

"Yes, but we need further information. You can expect a few interruptions like this over the next few days, I'm afraid. It's unavoidable."

"Oh, all right." Helgi put aside the piece he had been working on.

Birkir said, "I know that you were living with Jón, Fabían, and others in a commune in the early seventies. Can you tell me a bit about your friendship?"

"You mean my friendship with Jón and Fabían?"

"Yes."

"What business is it of yours?"

"It's relevant to the murder case. I'm trying to form a picture of the connections within the group that visited the embassy Sunday evening."

"Oh, well, that story is no secret. Lots of people know about it, so you'll have no problem sniffing it out somewhere, and it's probably best I explain it myself so there won't be any misunderstanding."

"Exactly."

"Where shall I start? It was a long period of time."

"Start at the beginning. I'll listen." He held up the recorder for Helgi to see, and the artist expressed no objection to it.

"OK, listen carefully. I'll carry on working while I tell you about it. It's a long story and I need to use my time well, so if you have any questions, please keep them until after."

Birkir nodded. "I understand," he said. "I'll keep quiet."

"Let's see now—Jón and I met in our teens, and we hung out together all the time until our paths parted after the fire out in Fljótshlíd. We originally got to know each other when we were in the same class at high school. I'd had a difficult childhood; I was unsettled, and only just scraped through the eighth-grade exams.

We got along well—we were both very rebellious and challenged everything around us. After one year at high school we decided to ditch the petty bourgeois world of Reykjavík, and headed off for Europe. That was the summer of 1969, and for the next three years we dropped out, broke and crazy, mainly in Copenhagen, Amsterdam, and Spain. We either hitchhiked or conned our way onto trains. All we had were a few clothes in a duffel bag, but it was amazingly easy to get around by begging or even stealing, if necessary. The beginnings of the hippie culture were everywhere, and these groups would always share their food with you provided your hair was long enough. Sometimes we managed to get into a commune and stay there until they got tired of us. We experimented with everything that was offered, every substance. The effects were variable, but this was a chemistry class we enrolled in wholeheartedly.

"We spent summers down by the Mediterranean, sleeping on the beach, never indoors, and when we were in Spain, we got to know some guys who grew cannabis, and we agreed to sell it for them. We'd mess around in the beach bars by day and the clubs at night. Kids with money to spend flocked south in the summer, and we made a good profit. Our system was perfect. I had all the gear wrapped in a towel and lay there sunning myself while Jón looked for buyers. Because the cops sometimes raided the beach, he never carried much stuff with him. When he'd done a deal, he'd sit down nearby me and light a cigarette. While he smoked, he dug the cash into the sand while I buried the merchandise next to where I was. Then we got up and changed places, I dug out the cash, and he collected the stuff. We did this right under the cops' noses, but nobody spotted the pattern. Everyone on the beach knew Jón as the Weed Man, but nobody knew me or about our connection. We used a similar system in the clubs at night.

"We also learned how to grow cannabis, which came in handy later when we were living on the farm at Sandgil. But in Spain we didn't just sell the stuff, we also smoked it, a hell of a lot of it. Most of our commission went to fund our own consumption, but then getting rich was never the idea. Our European adventure was more or less a total mess, apart from a couple of things that significantly benefited both of us. I met two girls who made pottery that they sold at the hippie markets, and they taught me to work with clay; and one summer Jón met an Icelandic high school teacher, who spent three weeks on the beach teaching him prosody in return for some very good grass. Then Jón started writing poetry, all correctly metrical—he definitely wasn't into modernist verse styles—and produced some really good poems there, some of which are classics today. But in the end we got bored of traveling, and as soon as we had enough money for the tickets, we came home.

"We decided we'd better get some cash together before our next trip, which was to be to the United States. Jón went up north and began working at a home for handicapped people—I'm sure he was a lively addition to the staff. But while there he met Sunna, and that put our trip on hold. She had hardly even been to Reykjavík and had no urge to go to America with a couple of penniless crazies. She loved Jón, but she wanted to keep both feet on the ground.

"Then, in the spring of 1973, Jón had this brilliant idea of moving to Fljótshlíd and squatting in the house at Sandgil. It had been deserted for two years, but his father, who owned it and rented out the hayfields for horse grazing, intended to use it as a summer house. Jón didn't ask permission, he just stole the keys off his old man and off we went, inspired by the squatters movement that had spread out from London in the late sixties.

Based on homeless people occupying unused buildings and living together in peace and happiness, it had become part of the hippie culture, and we had encountered it as part of many of the communes we stayed in on our travels around Europe.

"Jón's father pretended he knew nothing about the squat, and I think the truth is he was petrified of his son at that time. But he did stop paying for the electricity, so in the end we were cut off and had to scrape together the cash to pay the bill, and Jón made a deal with the utility company. Otherwise, we managed well enough initially, even though the money we had at the start soon began to run out. We kept a few chickens, and we had a small, fenced-off vegetable patch. Horses grazed in the field next to the house, so we couldn't make hay or keep other animals—not that we would have known how to go about it. We were all busy making various kinds of art. I'd acquired an old rough-and-ready ceramic kiln that was good enough for the simple hippie artifacts I was producing at that time, the things I'd learned how to make in Europe. The kiln went in an outbuilding, where there was also space for me to do the rough work on my pieces. Otherwise, we all worked together in the living room of the farmhouse—Jón wrote his poems, Rakel was writing a novel, Fabían practiced his drawing, Sun composed music and made candles, I did my pottery. We were going to make a living of this.

"On Friday afternoons, we gathered outside the cooperative store at Hvolsvöllur and tried to sell our products. Sunna played her guitar and sang, and the rest of us offered our pieces for sale. We hardly sold anything, but people would throw coins into Sun's guitar case and feel good about themselves. They didn't realize what they were hearing. By pure chance, a recording has survived that the Icelandic Radio made at a June seventeenth National Day celebration in the village, with Sun singing three of the songs she composed to Jón's poems. They're all classics of their kind now, especially "Spring Wakes." The recording quality is patchy, but they're still played today and are considered a unique musical treasure. It's sad that no other recordings were made of Sun's singing.

"We were having a great time back then at Sandgil, but our income was much less than we wanted it to be. We owed money at the co-op and we had to find some way of raising cash. It was then that Jón had the idea of growing cannabis in the attic. It wasn't intended as a permanent solution, but it would do while we were trying to sort ourselves out financially.

"The start-up costs were considerable. We needed greenhouse lamps and some seeds, so we borrowed from a loan shark in Reykjavík; most of what we made selling the crop went toward paying off the loan, so it had to be a big operation if we were going to have enough to live on. It was a spacious attic, and we had plants at all stages of cultivation. We dug up topsoil from the hayfield, and mixed it with horse manure and sand from the riverbank. Irrigation was precision work, and this was where Fabían came into his own; you have to let the plants dry a certain amount between waterings, and he had an instinct for it. We suspended the lamps at the correct height above the plants, and put up aluminum foil all around to make the most of the light. Harvesting was also tricky because you had to make sure to do it at a time when the active compounds were at their strongest concentration. Jón and I had learned how to do this in Spain, so we were producing high-quality stuff that sold well in Reykjavík.

"Before long the cops got interested in us. We used a similar system as the one we'd had going in Spain. A young girlfriend of ours in Reykjavík followed us into the clubs; she kept the supplies, Jón and I did the dealing, and Rakel transferred the stuff between us. The cops searched us a few times, but only ever found small quantities, just enough for personal use, and they didn't consider it worth their while to charge us. But the authorities became increasingly suspicious, and eventually ambushed us one Friday afternoon as we were approaching the outskirts of Reykjavík. It was a massive police operation, lots of squad cars and a huge commotion. All the stuff in our car was confiscated and Jón, Rakel, and I were arrested.

"We were kept in solitary, and nobody said a word to us for three days. Then the prison chaplain came to speak to each of us, one by one. Sun was dead. She'd been burned alive the night we were arrested.

"I can't even begin to describe to you how this affected us. We were released after a week in custody, and then we got suspended sentences on most charges, with the rest canceled out by the time already served. It felt as if the system was embarrassed about something.

"I went on a drug-and-alcohol binge, and was wasted for the next twenty years—it was the only way I could get through each day. Rakel and I broke up a few weeks after the fire. Our memories of Sun were so intertwined with our relationship that we just couldn't deal with it. I went to Amsterdam, where I stayed for most of those two decades. It was the easiest place to get weed, and I funded my own use by pushing stronger stuff; for a good few years, I supplied a large part of the hard drugs that came onto the Icelandic market. But hophead though I was, I still managed to function on some level, because I attended classes at various open arts academies, where I succeeded in developing a distinct style of pottery that got noticed. I was able to work two or three hours a day around noon, enough to produce the odd piece. They became sought after, and I made so few that the price skyrocketed. It was just as well, since tougher guys than I muscled me out of the drugs market. I was done with that scene, burned out. I'd burned my candle at both ends, too, and lost my creative ability. By then I was heavily into heroin and I ended up on the street. News reached Iceland, and one day Jón and Rakel turned up. They pulled me out of the gutter, literally, and they straightened me out. They began by finding me my next fix and getting me off the street and into a bath. Then the detox began. Rakel had abandoned her novel when Sun perished in the fire, but she got through her grief by throwing herself into nursing studies, and after graduation she worked in a treatment center for alcoholics and junkies, so she knew all about tough love. After three weeks, I was well enough to travel, and the three of us flew back to Iceland. For the next twelve months I lived with them at Jónshús, and I've been clean ever since, and able to practice my art. I go to AA meetings most days and I'm grateful to God for every moment I'm allowed to live and work on my projects. That's how I get my rush today. I'm lucky to be alive. Heroin can kill you any time."

Janis Joplin had provided a quiet backing to this account, but now Helgi increased the volume and listened in silence:

"And that'll be the end of the road, babe, I know you got more tears to share, babe."

The track ended, and he turned the volume down again and asked, "Do you know how Janis Joplin died?"

"No." Birkir shook his head.

"Her heroin dealer wasn't a user himself, and he always needed to get a regular addict to try any new batch to assess its strength, because you never knew for sure how strong the stuff was that you got from the middlemen. The dealer got a new delivery, and this time his guinea pig wasn't around, but he distributed the stuff anyway, and Janis got a fifty-dollar fix. She shot up alone in her hotel room, and then went down to the lobby to change a five-dollar bill so she could buy fifty-cents' worth of cigarettes from a vending machine. She was back in her room when the heroin hit her. It was eight times stronger than what she usually had, and eighteen hours later they found her dead, clutching four dollars and fifty cents. Eight users died that weekend after injecting stuff from that consignment."

Helgi was silent for a moment before adding, "I could have ended up the same way every time I shot up."

"Tell me about the Sun Poet," Birkir asked. "What has his life been like?"

Helgi smiled listlessly. "My friend Jón has not written one single line of poetry since his ray of sunshine died. People began to call him the Sun Poet because the songs Sun composed to some of his poems had become popular standards in Iceland. The original poems have been republished, but there are no new ones. He recites them whenever he gets the opportunity, but his spirit died with Sun. After the Sandgil fire, his parents let him move into their basement, and they provided for him while they were still alive.

"He couldn't work, and would probably have ended up in an institution if they hadn't taken him in. When they died, he inherited the house and various other assets. He lives mainly by renting out rooms, but he's a bit haphazard about collecting the rent. You could say he's created the beginnings of the commune he dreamed about having at Sandgil. Rakel looks after any practical issues. His choice of lodgers isn't based on their ability to pay the rent, but rather on whether they can add something to the culture of the house. Life is never dull in Jónshús—it's an academy of free thought and rampant creativity in the most unpredictable fields. A tiny legacy of the hippie culture is alive there in a protected workplace. Jón keeps a watchful eye over everything, and although he produces nothing himself, he gets satisfaction in helping others with their artistic undertakings.

"He drinks more than is good for him, but not so much as to be life threatening, and he doesn't use any other stuff. In fact, if he's immersed in his literary studies, weeks can go by without his remembering to have a drink—but then an old buddy shows up and drags him off to the bar. That can end with him going on a real bender, especially if he's in a manic phase, and sometimes that's resulted in a few days on the psychiatric ward. Rakel deals with that, like she deals with everything to do with Jónshús."

Helgi stood up. "That was the story of Jón the Sun Poet and me, and now I'd appreciate it if you'd leave me in peace to get on with my work."

He turned up the volume of the music to indicate that the conversation was over.

Birkir returned to the police station to upload the voice recordings from his visits to Fabían and Helgi. Then he called Gunnar to tell him about his day's success, or lack of it.

"I don't think we're on the right track in this case," he concluded.

"What do you mean?"

"We definitely have the wrong guy in custody."

"Sure, but it'll stir things up some. I'm convinced of that."

"This is not correct procedure," Birkir insisted.

"Hey," Gunnar said petulantly. "Go home and press your pants—or whatever you do to help you relax. We'll talk about this tomorrow."

21:20

Gunnar knew exactly how *he* wanted to finish the day: at the bar where he spent most evenings. He did try to take a good break from alcohol now and again—to allow his body to recover—but today he had plenty of excuses for having a drink.

The first person Gunnar saw as he hobbled into the bar was Konrad, the ambassador, sitting at a table all by himself reading *Der Spiegel*, a whisky on the rocks in front of him. Gunnar signaled to the waiter to bring his usual and, without pausing to ask permission, plumped himself down opposite the ambassador.

"Hello again," he said, putting aside his crutches.

It took Konrad a moment or two to realize who this guy was, but then he greeted him cheerfully.

"The Germans are writing about the murder at the embassy," he said, pointing at the magazine. "And they've got it absolutely goddamned on the nail. They report exactly what happened, and what we knew at the time of writing. No speculation, just facts. This is what I like so much about German reporting."

Gunnar could see that Konrad was not on his first glass of the evening. He asked, "Any chance you've thought of something new about that evening, something you haven't already told us?"

"It's clearly a conspiracy," Konrad said. "A goddamned conspiracy to get me into trouble. And they succeeded—the foreign minister has reshuffled some postings, I'm getting a desk here in Reykjavík, and I have to look after a few negro states in Africa out of a suitcase. Pardon my language."

"So will the counselor, Arngrímur, take over your post in Berlin?"

"Arngrímur!" Konrad snorted with laughter. "No, Arngrímur Ingason will never be an ambassador."

"Why not? Isn't he a very skillful diplomat?"

"Skillful diplomat! Oh yes, he is, the asshole, but an ambassador he will never be."

"Why not?"

"That's just how it is. Some embedded rule at the ministry, no one knows from where."

"What do you mean?"

Konrad leaned over toward Gunnar and lowered his voice. "Every time a new minister takes office, the chief secretary, among a load of other practical concerns, reviews a list of various foreign policy matters, and I happen to know that the list includes a declaration that Arngrímur Ingason will never be appointed Icelandic ambassador. Never! No explanation. On the other hand, he gets certain perks, like he doesn't have to work here in Iceland and he can spend as long as he chooses in each posting. So he hasn't had to move around as much as others. He's a very handy assistant to any ambassador, of course, because he drives himself hard in his duties. He's so goddamned boring, though. Doesn't even drink."

Konrad took another sip of whisky and, although his glass was still half full, he waved to the bartender to bring him another one.

"Can I offer you something?" he asked Gunnar.

Gunnar had finished his beer and bitters, and pointed at the glasses in front of him. "Same again, please. So what's this rule on Arngrímur all about?"

"That's the big question. Arngrímur's father was Ólafur Ingi Esjar, a member of parliament and big-time wholesaler—in his time, he was Iceland's most powerful man behind the scenes. Arngrímur was born with a silver spoon in his mouth. He completed his law qualification with top marks and was made sheriff at Hvolsvöllur before he was thirty. That was in 1972. In the Register of Lawyers from that time he's down as Arngrímur Esjar, but he changed his name to Ingason when he started working for the Foreign Ministry in 1975."

"Any idea why he changed his name?"

"No."

"Was there some malpractice when he was sheriff?"

"If so, it's been covered up."

"Well, anyone who's interested should be able to dig that up. But I don't see that it has anything to do with our case, so it's none of my business."

The waiter brought Gunnar another Holsten and Jägermeister and, for Konrad, a whisky on the rocks. Konrad took a sip from the glass he already had, poured what was left into the new glass, and passed the empty one to the waiter along with a fifty-euro note. "Keep the change, my friend," he said, and then turning to Gunnar added, "Not a good idea to have too many glasses in front of you. People might think you're on the sauce."

Gunnar said, "We found out there were more connections between the guests at the embassy than they were willing to admit at first. Jón and Helgi are childhood friends and went on to live together in a commune in Fljótshlíd, on a farm called Sandgil. Fabían lived with them there, too. Jón's fiancée died when their house burned down in 1975."

"I remember that," Konrad said. "Jón didn't improve with the loss of his sweetheart, poor guy."

"So three of the embassy guests are linked to this fire."

Konrad was about to take a sip from his glass, but put it down. "No," he said. "Four."

"Really?"

"One of that gay couple is the brother of the girl who died."

"Which one?"

"Starkadur, I think his name was."

"How do you know that?"

"It came out at the party that night. There was some drama around it."

"In what way?'

"When Jón recited his poem 'Spring Wakes,' Starkadur burst into tears. Helgi tried to calm him down, and I heard them talk about how the girl was his sister."

Gunnar pondered this news. "Is it possible Anton Eiríksson was linked to the fire in some way?" he finally asked.

"No, I don't think that's possible, I can't see it. He was living in a different part of the country at that time. We were comrades in arms in politics."

"Oh, well, that's that, then. Must have been a coincidence."

"Probably," Konrad said, taking a large sip of whisky. "But there is another angle. Arngrímur was the local sheriff at the time and must have been involved in the case somehow."

"Were there any irregularities?"

"Definitely not. Arngrímur always does everything by the book. That's what's so irritating about him."

"And he wasn't even at the embassy the night Anton was killed," Gunnar said.

"Alas not. He had that meeting scheduled, but was called away to handle another matter. I would be ambassador in Berlin tonight if he had been present. He always makes sure everything goes like clockwork. Anton would not have been killed on his watch, goddammit."

He emptied his glass in one gulp.

22:30

"Go home and press your pants," Gunnar had said to Birkir, and that was exactly what Birkir did. In the center of his living room stood a large heavy ironing board that was his refuge when he needed to think. He began with the pants he'd worn that day, pressing them and hanging them up. Next, he turned his attention to the nine shirts he had washed the previous week; he had not had time to deal with them since, but now set about ironing them with his customary efficiency, bestowing on each shirt the same methodical attention to detail. First sleeves, then back. He did not rush the job—if the occasion demanded, this was a task he could complete in no time at all, but he preferred to wait until he had the leisure to enjoy the process and leave his shirts looking like new.

Tchaikovsky wafted over from the music system: "Elégie" from his Serenade for Strings, played by a chamber orchestra. This was the type of music Birkir almost always listened to, slow classical pieces; he had a sense of having had sounds like this in his environment when he was very young, but he couldn't link it to other memories, nor did he usually try to. It wasn't important.

He was thinking about the men who had been the ambassador's guests in Berlin on the night of the murder. They were all unusual characters, and it was worth getting to know them properly. He'd already gotten a fair picture of these guys, but he needed to keep going, to delve into the past, if necessary. He was convinced that would lead them to the last visitor to enter the ambassador's office that night.

He decided to drive out to Fljótshlíd the following day to take a look at the place where a young woman had lost her life so many years before.

SUNDAY, OCTOBER 18

01:20

Gunnar had drunk enough. After having bought several rounds, Konrad said the bar had gotten too rowdy and he was going to move on elsewhere. But Gunnar decided to go home, and asked the bartender to call him a taxi. He tottered out to the sidewalk, leaning on his crutches, and the cab soon arrived. It was a short drive back, and having paid the fare, Gunnar got the driver to open the door for him and take the crutches, before easing himself out of his seat. "It's my back," he explained. "Lumbago."

"Get well soon, then, and take care," the driver said as he climbed back in and drove off.

Gunnar had to support himself on one crutch while holding the other with the same hand as he fumbled for his house keys in his jacket pocket. This took all his attention, and he didn't notice the shadowy figure sneaking up behind him.

Suddenly someone kicked the crutch out from under him. He landed on all fours on the sidewalk, where he received a vicious blow to his side.

"Shit!" Gunnar yelled as he rolled to avoid the next kick.

"Not so cocky now, fucking niggerlicker," said a shrill voice that Gunnar recognized.

"Oh, they let you out, huh?" Gunnar said, trying to shield himself from the next blow.

"You didn't know that, you fucking fag?"

"Fag? You coming on to me?" Gunnar winced as a kick struck his brow.

"Don't try to be clever with me," said the blond pyromaniac Gunnar had interrogated the previous Monday morning. He looked for a good spot to aim his next kick, but Gunnar defended himself with his arm.

"How did you find me?" he said.

"You're in the National Register, asshole. Think I don't know how to use a computer? I've been waiting here all night."

"Ah, the National Register. Yes, of course," Gunnar said. "Hey, I'm not up for a fight with you tonight. Go home—ouch!" The blond psycho interrupted his speech with a heavy kick to Gunnar's chest.

"Who's going home? Eh?" he said triumphantly.

"You," said a harsh female voice from the doorway. "You to go home or now I do shoot."

The blond guy looked up and straight down the barrel of a rifle aimed between his eyes. He took a few steps back, and then turned and ran as fast as his legs would carry him.

"Thanks, Mom," Gunnar said, digging out his cell and dialing.

"Emergency," said the voice at the other end.

Gunnar gave his name and address. "I need an ambulance right away. I think I have a cracked rib, and my back is really sore. Never mind that I have a cold, too."

Birkir found Gunnar in the emergency room, lying on his side in a hospital bed and eating crushed chocolate raisins from a crumpled plastic bag. A large bandage covered his swollen right eye.

"Found this in my pocket," Gunnar explained. "They don't give you anything to eat here."

"Your mom called," Birkir said. "She said someone tried to kill you."

"Yeah, it was that blond freak—the pyromaniac we brought in on Monday. Jumped me from behind."

Birkir took out his cell. "I'll have him picked up immediately."

Gunnar snatched his hand. "No, don't do that."

"Why not?"

"They'll put him away anyway because of the arson," Gunnar said. "It'll only boost his status with his fellow prisoners if he's charged with roughing me up. Let's not indulge him."

"Is this the right thing to do?"

"Yeah. He'll make a big noise about beating me up, but if there's no charge, people will stop believing him and laugh at his story. That's much worse punishment for a lowlife like him. I'll settle up with him later."

"OK. Your call," Birkir said. "How are you feeling?"

"The doctor says there's nothing broken. I'm badly bruised, but in reasonable shape other than that. A small cut and a black eye. They'll give me an injection for my back later, and I'll sleep here tonight. You can tell Mom that."

Birkir smiled. "I will. Your mom never wants you to go to Egilsstadir again. She says you've been in really bad shape since you went there."

"She's dead right. Did she ask questions about the trip?"

"She started to, but I said I was in a hurry to get here to talk with you."

"Great. We need to synchronize our stories. We'll go over it later."

"Fine." Birkir smiled again.

"You know what?" Gunnar said. "My old mom just saved me from that guy."

"She did?" Birkir frowned. "She didn't tell me that."

"She was still awake when I came back in the taxi. She heard the car and looked out the window. She was worried about me because of my back. She saw when the asshole went for me. Got out my rifle and staggered downstairs. The guy ran off as soon as he saw the gun."

"That was a piece of luck," Birkir said. "But don't we have to file a special report on this use of a firearm?"

"The hell we do. I'm not bringing charges for the attack, and nobody mentions the old lady threatened someone with a rifle. OK?"

"Yes."

"The rifle wasn't even loaded."

"That's good."

"Yeah. In other news, I ran into Ambassador Konrad earlier this evening."

"You did?"

"Yeah, and we talked a lot about that hippie business down in Fljótshlíd those years ago. He's a great guy, Konrad. Generous and friendly."

"I imagine he's a good drinking companion."

"Hey, that's not the only thing. He came up with some interesting tips." Gunnar ran back over his conversation with Konrad about the folks living at Sandgil and the sheriff in Hvolsvöllur.

"There seem to be more and more threads leading eastward to Fljótshlíd," Birkir said when Gunnar had finished his account.

"Yes," Gunnar said, popping the last chocolate raisin into his mouth. "Why don't you take a look at the evidence on that fire?"

"I'll do that."

"And see if you can find anything for me to eat."

When Gunnar's mother, María, had called at twenty to two that morning to tell him what had happened to her son, Birkir had been asleep for about two and a half hours. After spending an hour at the hospital, he'd returned home and tried to get back to sleep, with limited success. By seven o'clock he was wide awake, but lay in bed for an hour thinking about things before getting up, eating breakfast, and heading off to Fljótshlíd in his car.

All was quiet at the police station in the little town of Hvolsvöllur, and the cop on duty, a chubby guy in his forties, decided to drive with Birkir out to the Fljótshlíd district and show him Sandgil, the place where Jón the Sun Poet's hippie commune had operated from 1973 through 1975.

The sky was clear and the air cold and pure. The view that lay before them justified this trip in itself, never mind anything else. The majestic Eyjafjallajökull glacier rose against the sky in the southeast, and sunshine intensified the fall colors of the slopes to the left as they drove into Fljótshlíd.

Birkir asked whether the Thórsmörk National Park was visible from the road, but the cop said it was too far away. You needed to go much farther up the valley, on a dirt road, to see the trees of Thórsmörk on the far side of the river.

Birkir was picturing Húsadalur, the finishing point of the Laugavegur run, a grueling fifty-five kilometer cross-country race over the highlands from Landmannalaugar down to Thórsmörk. He'd competed in the race the previous summer, coming in fifty-eighth out of three hundred twenty participants, in six hours and three minutes. Next summer he intended to do the run in less than six hours. That was the plan, at least.

They drove a good distance along a narrow road, paved to start with but later turning into dirt. There was a scattering of farmsteads and summer houses on both sides as they went farther up the valley, and finally the policeman stopped the vehicle by a beautiful forest grove, far from the nearest habitation.

They got out and scanned the scene.

"The ruins from the fire were cleared away very soon after the incident, or so I'm told," the policeman said. "And then the plot was fenced off and given over to grazing, and this grove was planted. I understand Jón Sváfnisson still owns the land, but he never comes here."

They climbed over a fence and waded through frozen, withered grass to get to where the old farmhouse had stood. The place was not visible from the road—all that was left of it was the concrete floor. Tufts of grass had seeded themselves through cracks in its surface, most of which was carpeted with green moss. A symbol had been cut into the concrete: a circle, nearly two meters across, with a cross inside. The grooves of the pattern were around ten centimeters wide and two centimeters deep; someone had expended considerable effort to make it.

"The sun cross," Birkir said.

"I know of people who come here to pray in times of need," said the cop. "They say you should stand in the middle of the cross at midday with outstretched arms and look toward the sun. Then your shadow falls over the cross, forming another cross."

"Who are you supposed to pray to?" Birkir asked. "This is a heathen symbol."

"That's right," the cop replied, "but it doesn't matter who you pray to, be it Christ, God, the Holy Spirit, Allah, Buddha, Odin,

Thor, or even that old Viking—Gunnar of Hlídarendi—who lived nearby. There's a direct line from this place to whatever Almighty there may be. It listens to your prayer without bothering about the name it gets called, or what language is used. It's enough that you focus on what's on your mind. Just so long as it's not frivolous."

"Sounds to me like you've tried it."

The cop blushed. "My son was very ill one time. I came here then."

"I hope he got better."

The policeman nodded.

Birkir checked his watch and saw that it was nearly noon. He stepped into the center of the cross, his back to the sun, and stretched out his arms. His shadow formed a cross superimposed upon the carved symbol.

"Are you going to pray?" the cop asked.

Birkir shook his head. "No, I've nothing to pray for except frivolity. Either that or world peace and happiness, but the Almighty is hardly able to grant that as long as we humans keep devoting ourselves to the opposite. It's good to know this place exists, though."

Birkir meant what he said. This space felt kind of sacred; he had a rare feeling of peace, and promised himself he'd visit here in summertime.

They drove back to Hvolsvöllur and had coffee and sandwiches at the police station.

"Can I see the evidence about the fire at Sandgil?" Birkir asked.

"Not today, I'm afraid. The archive is locked and the sheriff has the keys. I'll photocopy it for you tomorrow and send it."

"Thanks very much."

"But you might be able to take a shortcut. Your boss at the violent crime division—isn't that Magnús Magnússon?

"Yes?"

"He was a police officer here at Hvolsvöllur during that time. He didn't move to Reykjavík until after the accident. I think he was called to the scene of that fire and wrote up the report on it."

15:00

As he drove back toward Reykjavík, Birkir called his boss.

"We need to talk," Birkir said. "About the fire at Sandgil."

"Is it really necessary to open that up again? It happened decades ago."

"Yes, and I'm not happy about having to go all the way to Fljótshlíd to discover that you were involved in that investigation."

"It's no concern of yours, as far as I can see," Magnús snapped.

Birkir replied patiently, "All the main characters in the Berlin murder investigation are in some way connected with it. Of course it's my concern. I need all available information about this case."

"Oh, all right. Drop by my house when you get back to town."

Magnús lived with his wife in a handsome old villa on a street just north of Jónshús. Birkir's apartment was in the same district, but much farther west. It was a quiet part of town but conveniently close to the city center, so parking spaces were sometimes difficult to find; Birkir therefore drove straight back home, left the car in his reserved spot, and walked over to his boss's place.

"You've managed to take advantage of the good weather," Magnús said as he greeted Birkir at the door and ushered him into his hobby room. This was his sanctuary, where he did his fly tying—that and trout fishing in the summer were his two main interests. The walls of the room were hung with stuffed freshwater fish, pictures of anglers fishing in lakes and streams, and individually labeled frames displaying colorful fishing flies; books about trout fishing and distinguished anglers lay on the table and lined the shelves.

Magnús offered Birkir a seat and took his place at his work-table. Secured by a little clip beneath a magnifying glass was a small fishhook onto which he had already bound the first feather. Above the worktable was a rack with transparent plastic drawers containing the raw materials for tying flies.

"Tell me about this incident at Sandgil," Birkir said. "How were you and Sheriff Arngrímur involved?"

Magnús squinted through the magnifying glass. "OK," he said. "I'll rehash it, but there are several reports about the case, written at the time, and you should have a look at them if this is so important. I'm not sure I can remember the details accurately."

"I'll do that," Birkir said. "I'll be getting the reports tomorrow."

Magnús started his account tentatively. "I'll begin with the background, my working relationship with Arngrímur at the time. You'd better hear the whole story since you're digging this up now, though I can't imagine how it's going to help you in any way in your investigation."

"Let's just see what comes up," Birkir said. "Please continue."

"Well, I was a police officer in the Rangárvellir district when it happened. Even though I was from there, it wasn't my dream job, because I wanted to move to Reykjavík. I'd met my wife at Lake Laugarvatn, where she was at high school and I was at the PE training college. I got myself a summer job with the police force back home, and preferred it to the teacher training course, so I didn't go back to college. My wife went on to study law after high school, and I wanted to be with her in Reykjavík. But getting a job with the city force was difficult at that time, and even more so for somebody from out of town."

As he spoke, Magnús picked up small tufts of feathers with a pair of pliers and offered them up to the fly he was working on.

"Arngrímur Esjar became district sheriff in Rangárvellir in the spring of 1972. He wasn't quite thirty, the youngest ever person to get such a post. He had a high-class law degree and had distinguished himself as an attorney at the Reykjavík Criminal Court, but even so, that in itself was not enough to get such an appointment. No, he had connections. His father, Ólafur Ingi Esjar, was a member of parliament and one of the most powerful men in the country, who would have been a cabinet minister but for his extensive and lucrative business interests. He could run his businesses and serve in parliament, but the workload involved in being a minister would have taken too much time away from his business affairs, and he chose to stay on the sidelines. But he had his fingers in every pie, and the government didn't do a thing without his knowledge and consent. Word is, Ólafur more or less totally financed his party's activities."

He paused a moment while he tied a complicated knot.

"Arngrímur and I got to know each other well during that time in the Southeast. He was single and didn't know anyone in the district, and I was on my own while my wife was at law school. So we hung out outside of work, too—we rode horses and played badminton in the gym of the local primary school."

Magnús looked up from his work and turned to Birkir.

"And now we get to your question," he said. "Soon after Arngrímur came to work out there, this very odd group moved into the little farmhouse at Sandgil, way up in Fljótshlíd. They were hippies from Reykjavík, two young men—Jón and Helgi—and two young women—Sunna and Rakel—and a boy, Fabían. Those five were the permanent residents, but they had a heap of visitors, some of them long-term."

Birkir said, "Those three men were all guests at the Icelandic embassy in Berlin last Sunday. Also Starkadur, Sunna's brother."

"Yes, but that has to be coincidence. There's no connection here."

"Nevertheless, please carry on with your story. You seem to remember it all pretty well."

"Yes, it's coming back to me. OK . . . so Jón and Sunna were a couple, as were Rakel and Helgi. Fabían was supposedly employed by Jón but was in fact a homeless, dysfunctional kid they'd taken under their wing. The house they moved into was on some rural land that had belonged to Jón's great uncle, but the uncle had died without any children, so Sváfnir, Jón's father, inherited it. I understand that Jón took over the house without asking Sváfnir's permission, but it seems the matter rested there.

"The young people were all involved in various kinds of art, which was supposed to support their rural existence. Jón wrote poems, Helgi was into ceramics, and Sunna was a musician and also made wax candles. Rakel wanted to be a writer, and Fabían was an artist. On Friday afternoons, weather permitting, they would set up outside the co-op store and try to make money. Sunna played the guitar and sang her songs, and the others offered their artwork for sale. The boys didn't sell a thing, but folks would throw coins into Sunna's guitar case. Eventually, realizing they couldn't live off their art, the hippies found another way to earn money—they grew cannabis in their attic to sell in Reykjavík. Small amounts to begin with, but then they increased their production. That was when the cultivation stopped being a secret, because the electricity company noticed the sudden surge in consumption at the cottage. Before that, Jón had always had difficulties paying the electricity bill, but now he began to pay up front, even though the bill had tripled. People passing the cottage at nighttime reported seeing strange lights shining through the cracks in the roof. It didn't take us long to put two and two together."

Magnus continued: "Fridays, they would head off to Reykjavík in an old Russian jeep and circulate round the clubs to sell packs of the stuff. We set up an operation to arrest them outside Reykjavík on one of their sales trips, and as a follow-up the sheriff and I drove down to Fljótshlíd to conduct a house search at Sandgil and arrest the two who'd stayed behind. We'd arrested Jón, Helgi, and Rakel in possession of a large quantity, but Sunna and Fabían remained at home. We were only a few kilometers away when we saw smoke and then fire at the house. We drove as fast as we could, but we got there too late. Fabían had escaped and vanished into the night, but Sunna was trapped inside—we heard her shouting for help. Arngrímur tried to rescue her, but his efforts were in vain. He was lucky to get away with his life, because he lost consciousness trying to get back out of the house, and I had to drag him to safety. The house burned to the ground before firefighters could get there. It took a search team to find Fabían, and he was completely incapable of explaining the cause of the fire. When it became clear that he was a mental and physical wreck, he was committed to an appropriate institution."

"So what was the cause of the fire?"

Magnús paused. Finally he said, "The forensic investigation of the ruins indicated that a gas stove had been in use when the fire started. A large saucepan containing traces of wax lay on the floor. Witnesses said that there had always been things for candle production—molds, coloring, wicks—in the living room. The surviving household members confirmed that candle production had taken place in the house. The investigators' conclusion was that Fabían had been melting wax in rather rudimentary conditions. The wax overheated, and fire broke out. He was able to get out through the back door, but Sunna was probably in the attic tending to the cannabis plants, unaware of the fire until it was too late. Her body was found under the collapsed roof near the small skylight she probably tried to escape through."

"So it was an accident."

"Yes, a tragic one. Sheriff Arngrímur was so traumatized by the experience that he quit his job and went to work for the foreign service. Shortly afterward I was offered a position in Reykjavík, and I tried to put the matter behind me. This experience was simply too devastating to even think about."

"Why did Arngrímur stop calling himself Esjar?"

"I don't know," Magnús said. "Maybe to keep his head down. The Esjar family name was kind of prominent, and his father made a lot of noise wherever he went."

"And instead of taking on his father's first name for his patronymic, Arngrímur used his father's second name," Birkir said. "Any idea why?"

"No," Magnús answered, impatiently. "I haven't seen Arngrímur since all of that happened. He suffered from burns and smoke inhalation, and I think it took him a long time to recover. He never went back to Hvolsvöllur."

Even though Gunnar was officially on leave, Birkir knew he wanted to be kept up to speed on the investigation, so he decided to make a sick call to his home.

María met him at the door. "Birkir Li. My favorite." She smiled, and invited him into the apartment, which smelled of cooking.

"You make sure Gunnar not go back to Egilsstadir," she whispered as she ushered him into the living room, where Gunnar sat in a comfortable chair with a stool under his feet.

"Mom is cooking meat stew," he grinned, looking at Birkir with his good eye; the left one was completely obscured by an ugly blue swelling. "Stay for dinner. There's plenty. Enough to last all week."

"How are you doing?"

"I'm great," Gunnar said. "But the doc thinks I'll be worse tomorrow when the bruising on my chest kicks in. I asked Mom to cook the stew a long time, at least two hours, because I don't want to have to chew too much."

"How did you sleep?"

"Really well. The rest of the ward needed extra sleeping pills because of my snoring. The night shift had never heard anything like it," Gunnar said triumphantly.

"You're lying," Birkir said.

"OK, I might be exaggerating, but I slept really well, thanks. The hospital gave me strong painkillers. I'm supposed to take more if I can't sleep tonight."

Birkir told Gunnar about his trip out to Fljótshlíd and his conversation with Magnús. Then they ate meat stew and watched *CSI* on television. When Gunnar had fallen asleep in his chair, Birkir went home.

MONDAY, OCTOBER 19

09:00

Birkir had hardly sat down at his desk when his phone rang; a female voice said, "Good morning, this is the Icelandic embassy in Berlin. Just connecting you with the acting ambassador—one moment, please."

After a brief pause, Birkir heard a man's voice, "Birkir Li Hinriksson?"

"Yes, speaking."

"Hello. Sigmundur here. Berlin embassy."

"Oh, yes. Good morning."

"I need your assistance," Sigmundur said. "Do you have a moment?"

"Sure. What can we do for you?"

"Our counselor, Arngrímur Ingason, went to Iceland last Friday and we haven't been able to get ahold of him since."

"Is this a police matter?"

"No—or yes, actually. Something strange is going on."

"Strange?"

"Yes. Arngrímur got a call Friday morning from the Foreign Ministry with instructions to go to Iceland for an urgent meeting with the minister. A plane ticket arrived by e-mail shortly after."

"Is there something strange about that?"

"Well, no. Unusual, perhaps, to be summoned like that, but not in itself strange. It became strange when we needed to get in touch with him during the weekend in connection with a case he's dealing with here. When he didn't pick up his cell phone, I had our secretaries contact all the hotels in the Reykjavík area, but he wasn't registered as a guest in any of them, so this morning we contacted the ministry to find out where he was. Nobody there knew anything about any summons to go to Iceland."

"You're saying the phone call was a fake?"

"It looks like it. We checked Arngrímur's e-mails and found the one that came with the ticket. It appears to come from the ministry, but the sender is not an actual employee there. The attached ticket was business class, the next flight to Iceland that same day."

"So you're saying Arngrímur was tricked into going to Iceland, and then disappeared when he got here?"

"Yes. There's something going on here that's not right."

"Do you want us to start a search?"

"No, absolutely not—I mean, not right away. Hopefully there's a reasonable explanation. But perhaps you could look into it without being conspicuous?"

"Does Arngrímur have any relatives here in Iceland?"

"None that he was in touch with. He never went to Iceland as far as I know."

"Where should we start looking?"

"I don't know. I'm not a policeman."

"Well, we can ask our computer specialists to check this e-mail. I'll have them contact you. They know how to analyze that kind of data. And we'll try to find out who paid for the ticket."

"Great. Is there anything else that can be done?"

"We may be able to check the security cameras at the airport."

"Good, very good. The chief secretary at the Foreign Ministry was going to speak with his counterpart at the Ministry of Justice, but suggested I meanwhile contact you directly to speed things up, because you're familiar with our embassy and you've met Arngrímur—which is why I'm calling. This is a priority matter, but we want to keep it under wraps in case there's a good explanation—we've had more than enough trouble recently. Hopefully, Arngrímur is just staying with friends somewhere."

The conversation over, Birkir called the police at Keflavík Airport and asked them to send him, as a matter of urgency, all the security-camera footage from the arrivals area for a period of two hours from the time the Berlin flight landed the previous Friday. Then he headed for Magnús's office to brief him about this development; they would doubtless be getting orders from above, and it would be good to be able to report that the matter was already in hand. This missing-person situation was different from the usual ones involving underage rebellious teenagers who'd gone into hiding.

Magnús seemed shocked by what Birkir had to tell him. "The embassy staff really didn't have any idea where Arngrímur might be staying here?" he asked.

"No. They seem to be completely in the dark."

Thinking aloud, Magnús said, "Let's hope he's just happily ensconced somewhere with his phone off in order to have a break from work. It wouldn't be the first time someone's done that."

Birkir was silent as he mulled things over. Finally he said, "But there's that strange knife at the embassy. As I've pointed out, whoever smuggled it in can't have planned to use it on Anton. Arngrímur was supposed to be at the embassy that day but was called away. Could the knife possibly have been intended for him?"

"Why, in heaven's name?"

"Arngrímur was involved in the Sandgil drug investigation. Maybe the three former members of the commune had some beef with him because of the fire."

Magnús shook his head vigorously. "After all these years? What makes you think that?"

"It's the only lead we have."

"Arngrímur was only at Sandgil in an assisting role as district sheriff. The investigation was a police matter under my responsibility, in collaboration with the Reykjavík force. Many individuals were more involved than Arngrímur in that investigation and the arrests. Why on earth should vengeance be focused on him after all these years? Especially as it required so much prior organization. No, there's something completely different behind this—if there's anything at all."

Birkir's telephone was ringing again when he returned from speaking with Magnús. It was the station's switchboard.

"There's a lawyer asking for somebody dealing with the Anton Eiríksson murder. Can you take the call?"

"Sure. Put them through."

Birkir introduced himself to the caller. "What can I do for you?" he asked.

"We are attorneys representing Anton Eiríksson here in Iceland," the man said.

"OK. Do you have information that can help us with the investigation into his death?"

"No, I can't say we do, but I felt it would be right to be in touch. We are going through his file just now."

"Is there anything in it we should see?"

"Not really, it's just some accounts, a tax return, and a will. There were instructions to open it a week after his death, which is why we only did it this morning."

"Isn't that unusual?"

"Is what unusual?"

"Putting off opening the will."

"It varies. Some people feel it's appropriate to wait for a few days."

"I see. So what does it say?"

"All his estate goes to orphans in Indonesia. There are names of institutions that perform relief work in that part of the world."

"Huh," Birkir said. "Carrying on the good work, then."

"Yes, well, then everything seems clear."

"I guess so. What does the estate consist of?"

"The papers list a number of bank accounts, both here and abroad. There's also a reference to liquid assets kept in a safe-deposit box."

"How much?"

"Around four hundred thousand euros."

"That's quite a sum."

"Yes. We would not have advised keeping it as cash. A sum as large as that would of course have accrued considerable interest."

"Maybe Anton didn't trust banks."

"Possibly not."

Birkir thought this over. "Where is the safe-deposit box?" he asked.

"In his apartment."

"In London?"

"No, here in Reykjavík."

"We didn't know he had an apartment here. No property was registered using his national ID."

"The apartment is in the name of a private limited company owned, in turn, by another company. It's somewhat complicated. Tax reasons."

"Where is this apartment?"

"It's in a high-rise on Austurbrún."

"We'll need to have a look at it."

"Yes, of course. I'm free on . . . let's see . . . Thursday at eleven o'clock."

"No, not Thursday. Today," Birkir said.

"I can't do that."

"We need to find a way."

There was silence on the other end. Finally the lawyer said, "I see I have a meeting just after noon that I can put off. Shall we say twelve thirty?"

"That works," Birkir said. "One of our team will be there at twelve thirty. Do you have a key?"

"No."

Birkir reached for the key ring he'd found at the Berlin hotel. It contained several keys that might fit an apartment lock. "We have some keys here we can try," he said. "If they don't work, we'll call a locksmith."

11:15

The Keflavík police responded promptly to Birkir's request. They called to say they'd uploaded a password-protected folder containing the video footage to the Reykjavík police computer network, and gave him the information he needed to access it. Then they e-mailed him details of the security-camera positions, together with the order in which to view the video files to follow the progress of passengers coming from the Berlin flight's arrival gate.

Birkir had already called Gunnar to tell him the news about Arngrímur.

"I'm coming in now," Gunnar said, ignoring Birkir's protests. Thirty minutes later, he came hobbling along the police station hallway, leaning on his crutches.

"How are you?" Birkir greeted him.

"I can't breathe right because of the bruising around my ribs, I can't sneeze or cough even though my cold is killing me, but I think I can sit at a desk and make myself useful."

"Great," Birkir said. "Then you can help me examine some pictures from the airport."

"That'll be exciting," Gunnar said, and carefully lowered himself into the chair in front of the computer. Birkir watched over his shoulder as, with a few clicks of the mouse, he set the first video in motion. Observing the time stamp in the corner of the picture, he fast-forwarded the film until they got to the confirmed arrival time of the Berlin flight.

"There he is," Gunnar said, as passengers emerged into the walkway. Birkir saw that he was right. First to disembark were the business-class travelers, and there among them was Arngrímur, carrying an overcoat on his arm and looking uncertainly from side to side. After a brief hesitation, he headed off in the wake of his fellow passengers, who clearly had a better sense of where to go next.

Birkir's cell rang. He had Gunnar stop the video, and answered. He listened a moment, thanked the caller, and returned the phone to his pocket.

"They've traced the payment for the ticket Arngrímur was sent," Birkir said. "A credit card belonging to Anton Eiríksson."

"Anton. But he's dead."

"So somebody's using his card."

Gunnar said, "There were some cards in the wallet the German police found on him."

Birkir nodded. "So he must have had more."

They turned back to the computer. "The time stamp says 14:43," Gunnar said. "Let's check the same time on the next camera so we can see where he goes."

They worked steadily through the sequence of files from the security cameras in the terminal and were able to piece together Arngrímur's progress through passport control and along the walkways to the baggage claim area, where he eventually took up a position by the carousel and waited for his suitcase.

"D'you think they've got pictures like that of us from Thursday?" Gunnar said. "When you pushed me in the wheelchair all the way through the terminal, I was goddamned furious." He fast-forwarded.

Birkir smiled. "Maybe we should get a copy to show at the annual gala dinner."

"Look, he's picking up his bag," Gunnar said, slowing down the picture again.

They watched Arngrímur walk toward the green customs gate and disappear through the doorway. The next footage was from the greeting area, packed with people waiting to meet the passengers as they emerged, one after another. Eventually Arngrímur appeared. Still holding his overcoat, he now pulled a small wheeled suitcase. He paused and looked around, and then walked straight across to a man holding up a white card; they exchanged a few words and then left the building.

"Who's that?" Gunnar asked.

"I don't know, but haven't we seen him somewhere before?"

The phone rang, and Birkir picked up. It was Dóra, who'd gone to meet the lawyer at Anton's apartment. "A couple keys on the key ring opened the main entrance and the door to the apartment," she said.

"Good," Birkir said.

"No, not good. There's a dead man in there. With a head injury."

Birkir and Anna arrived at the Austurbrún high-rise and pulled on the usual white crime-scene coveralls. In the lobby outside Anton's apartment they greeted Dóra, who was waiting for them.

"Where's the lawyer?" Birkir asked.

"Gone to a meeting," Dóra replied. "There wasn't really anything for him to do here. We left the scene when we realized what had happened."

Anna moved toward the half-open door of the apartment and sniffed. "Three days," she said.

Birkir followed Anna as she slipped carefully in; he detected a faint smell, one he had come across before—not often, but often enough. More experienced than he in this sort of thing, Anna could tell by smell alone how long ago death had occurred—if it was no more than a week, that is. After that it was just a foul stench.

Inside was parquet, an airy entrance hall with living room beyond; kitchen to the left, a bathroom, and two rooms on the right—in one of those was the body and a wall safe, wide open and completely empty. A large power drill accounted for the two holes in the safe's door where the locks had been.

The deceased lay on the floor, face turned toward the wall. He'd been wearing ear protectors, but they now lay askew across the top of his head.

"Two blows," Anna said. She pointed at the back of the head, which was covered in blood. "This was the first one. The attacker approaches from behind and strikes him hard with a blunt instrument." She indicated the metal bar lying beside the body.

"The back of the skull is the strongest part, and the blow isn't enough to knock him out. The skin is broken and he bleeds, but he backs away and turns toward his attacker, who strikes once more—this time harder, and in the center of his forehead."

She pointed at the man's crushed brow. "The skull is weaker here, and it shatters under the impact of this heavier blow. The guy loses consciousness and collapses."

Birkir nodded. This analysis seemed right. Sadly, he regarded the corpse; he had seen this man before, talked with him. Búi Rútsson, Anton Eiríksson's bodyguard, had not told Birkir the truth when he said he was leaving Berlin for Spain; he'd traveled instead to Iceland on this, his final journey. He evidently had urgent business to attend to in his employer's apartment, where this brutal attack had ended his life.

Anna turned to the drill, clamped into an impressive horizontal drill frame standing next to the safe. "He used a core drill to cut out the two locks from the door of the safe. Not a very professional method, but effective. It must have taken hours to get through this."

Birkir said, "And he was wearing ear protectors with a radio to while away the hours. That would have made it easier for the attacker to sneak up behind him."

"Yeah, although it's not as if he was actually wielding the tool by hand," Anna said. "This gear here holds the drill in place and maintains pressure on the cut. Very convenient. But a skillful professional burglar would have tackled the actual locks. It's quicker, quieter, and cleaner."

Birkir pointed out the key ring, holding dozens of keys, that lay on the floor. "That's something a professional would have, right?"

Anna looked at the keys and nodded. "Those he would have used to get into the apartment. The safe is more complicated."

Birkir was familiar with the method. The key ring contained all the most common types of house key, with the peaks of their blades filed down to small points so they could be used to open any lock matching the given type of key. You insert the key into the lock and tap it with a hammer while at the same time gently turning it. The force of the blow bounces the upper tumbler pins above the shear point, allowing the key to continue turning. Having seen this demonstrated one time, Birkir had immediately attached a bolt to his front door.

Anna said, "The attacker must have struck as soon as the safe was open."

"Maybe they were working together," Birkir said. "And one of them decided he didn't want to share the loot."

"Could be," Anna said.

More detective officers arrived at the apartment, and Birkir decided to leave them to it; he trusted that if there was anything useful to be found, Dóra and Anna would find it. He wanted to focus on something else.

Starkadur wasn't pleased to see him when Birkir greeted him in the holding cell.

"You just shut me in here and then ignore me," he said. "My attorney has already appealed to the Supreme Court."

Birkir felt guilty. He said, "We're shorthanded at the moment and other things came up."

"Right, and you just left me here to rot."

"I hope we are about to get things sorted. But right now I'd like to ask you about your sister."

"My sister? Sunna?"

"Yes."

"What's she got to do with all this? She died when I was in my teens."

"I know," Birkir said. "But I've heard that she was very special. People who knew her don't seem to be able to forget her."

"You'd understand that if you'd met my sister. She had a naturally kind soul, and her death was so incredibly unjust."

"Tell me about your relationship."

"Why would I do that?"

"You don't have to. But I will do my best to have you released directly. I can argue that your being free won't jeopardize the investigation."

"I'll get out today?"

"I'll do my best."

"But you want to know more about Sun?"

"It's not a condition for your release, but I would be grateful."

"Oh, OK then. I'll tell you about Sun. She deserves to have her memory kept alive."

"I understand," Birkir said.

"Well, there were just the two of us—me and Sun. Dad was a teacher in our village up in the Northwest, and Mom kept house. They were both kind of old-fashioned and conservative, and we weren't really close. They were nearly forty when I was born. Sun was five years older than me and always looked after me. When I was fifteen, I discovered that I had a massive crush on one of my classmates—a boy. I didn't really have a clear idea of what was happening, because the image I had of homosexual people was horrific. There was a guy in the village who was thought to be 'one of those,' and he was totally isolated. He was a drunk and he was filthy. We kids were warned not to have anything to do with him, but that just prompted us to bully him atrociously. Someone would say 'Let's get the homo!' and we'd gather outside his house and throw garbage at his windows until everything was covered in shit. I thought that was what my future would be like, and I planned to drown myself. Sun was the only person I could confide in, and she saved my life. She said I should trust my feelings and not let anybody tell me what was right or wrong in these matters. If my heart was pointing in this direction, then that was the road intended for me. No one should twist their feelings. Sun told me that there were places where people like me could live in freedom, live good lives in harmony with their surroundings. She promised to help me get there."

He teared up and sobbed as he continued, "And Sun was as good as her word, in spite of being taken from this life. Because of what she said to me, I set myself a goal to strive toward, although I did remain deep inside the closet for many more years. I didn't venture out until both my parents had died, and the one thing I regret is that I said good-bye to them while still living a lie. And the place Sun promised me did exist, but instead of me going there, it came to me. Today, Reykjavík is becoming that place, and I've done my best to help make it so."

Starkadur finished speaking and wept quietly as Birkir left.

15:20

The body had been removed from the apartment, and Anna was moving ahead with the crime-scene investigation. She had called in two specialists and sent everybody else away. Dóra was busy visiting all the other apartments in the building to find out if their occupants had seen or heard anything that could assist with the investigation.

The forensic pathologist who came and examined the body indicated that Anna's initial theory was correct. He estimated the killing had taken place the previous Friday, though he couldn't confirm that until after the autopsy. Food wrappers from the garbage suggested that Búi had spent two days in the apartment, but there was no indication he'd spent the night there. Thursday's and Friday's newspapers were in the kitchen.

The drilling of the safe had created a substantial amount of debris, but it hadn't been spread around the apartment sufficiently that footprints could be detected. The floor was, in fact, remarkably clean—someone had evidently swabbed it recently—but their examination of the area where the body had been lying revealed tiny, widespread droplets of blood. From the droplets' size and shape it might be possible to calculate the force of the blows struck, their angle of impact, and the attacker's position. Each drop was photographed alongside a centimeter scale and a position marker.

The metal bar—the murder weapon—attracted most of their attention. They could find no fingerprints on it—someone seemed to have wiped them off with a tea towel that they found discarded on the kitchen floor. The towel was stained with blood, presumably from the bar, and on the front doorknob they found a trace of blood but no prints, and they surmised that this one cloth had been used to wipe everywhere that might have had fingerprints.

The weapon itself was made of glass-smooth stainless steel, a tube five centimeters wide and eighty centimeters long. Anna regarded it for a while before she made the connection. "Of course! It's a rod from a closet."

The room where the murder had taken place had a closet, and it had just such a rod, one end of which sat in an O-shaped bracket while the other was in a U-shaped one so it was easy to remove it by lifting that end up. Anna went into the bedroom next door, where she found another closet, its sliding door half open. Inside, the brackets were identical to those in the first room, but there was no rod. Anna observed this, and then looked down. Something attracted her attention, so she fetched a powerful flashlight to see it better. A thin layer of dust covered the floor of the closet: In it she saw fresh footprints.

16:00

Gunnar didn't object when Birkir said he'd made arrangements for Starkadur to be released. Keeping him locked up was completely pointless. There wasn't a trace of blood on the guy's clothing, and they had no further evidence against him. They didn't even have any sensible questions to ask.

"OK, OK," was all Gunnar had to say. His mind was elsewhere. The man who'd met Arngrímur Ingason at Keflavík Airport had seemed familiar, but they hadn't been able to place him. Gunnar had scrutinized the video over and over, and finally he had the idea of reviewing the footage from the Berlin security cameras; that was the focus of his attention as Birkir sat down next to him.

Although the images from Berlin were far from sharp, they were clear enough to identify all the ambassador's guests as they left the embassy: Starkadur and David had left ahead of everyone else, so it was obvious which ones they were. Jón the Sun Poet was easily recognizable, of course, and Birkir was able to point out Fabían. The ambassador was short and limped, and there was his wife, leaning on Helgi's arm. The only other one was Lúdvík Bjarnason, whom they'd seen neither in the flesh, nor in the party photos Helgi had shown them—that's because he'd been behind the camera taking the pictures. But there was a fair image of him from the Berlin security camera.

Gunnar copied a frame and compared it with the Keflavík Airport footage. His hunch was correct—it looked like the same man.

"Wasn't he supposed to be abroad?" said Birkir.

"No, he was back home when I spoke with him. Or so he said."

"Call him on his cell."

Gunnar tried the number he had called before. "It's off."

"I think I'd better go have another word with Helgi Kárason," Birkir said.

Birkir took a taxi to Helgi's studio in the west end of town. He could see a light in the window, so Helgi must be working. The main door into the building was unlocked, but when Birkir knocked on the door of the second-floor studio, he got no reply. This was hardly surprising, given the earsplitting rock music he heard coming from within. He tried the door. It was locked, and he banged on it with the flat of his hand, but Cream's "White Room" at full volume overpowered everything. Birkir saw that he wouldn't be able to break down the door, but he looked around and spotted a cabinet on the wall, farther along the hallway. He went to investigate and, as he suspected, found it was the fuse box for the whole floor—an old-fashioned board with screw sockets, and packs of spare fuses lying at the bottom of the cabinet. He couldn't decipher the fuse labeling and so unscrewed the main fuse. The music stopped instantly, and the hallway was plunged into total darkness. Birkir waited until he heard someone open the door, and then reinserted the fuse.

"What the hell are you doing?" Helgi said, when the light came back on and he saw Birkir standing by the fuse box.

"We need to talk. You didn't hear when I knocked on the door."

"I'm working."

"You can keep working, no problem. But if you refuse to answer my questions, I'll have you arrested, and then you won't be able to work."

"Arrested?"

"Yes. There are plenty of reasons for doing that. Do I need to explain?"

"Yes. You do."

"A staff member from the Icelandic embassy in Berlin, Arngrímur Ingason, disappeared on arrival here in Iceland last Friday. We think his disappearance is linked to the fire in Sandgil, and I want to hear the rest of that story."

"Arngrímur Esjar has disappeared?"

"Yes. You know him?"

"He was sheriff in Hvolsvöllur."

"Have you met with him recently?"

"No. I never had any dealings with him when we were living there, I only saw him from a distance in the village, and I haven't seen him since."

"Are you, the former occupants of Sandgil, responsible for Arngrímur's disappearance?"

"Not me."

"What about the others?"

"I don't know."

"Is it a possibility?"

"You better come in," Helgi said, beckoning Birkir into the studio. He went across to a small kitchen unit at one end of the studio, picked up a thermos flask, and unscrewed the lid. "Would you like some coffee?"

"No, thanks. Just a glass of water, please."

Helgi took a glass out of a cupboard and passed it to Birkir. "The water's there," he said, pointing at a faucet over the sink. Then he poured himself some coffee.

Birkir repeated his question, "Is it possible that Jón Sváfnisson, Rakel, and Starkadur are linked to Arngrímur's disappearance?"

"Not Rakel."

"How about Jón and Starkadur?"

"I don't know."

"Do you have any reason to think it might be possible?"

"I don't know anything anymore. This is all becoming too toxic for me. My nerves can't take it."

"What do you mean?"

"I'll tell you the story, but I don't want you to record it. I don't care what happens anymore, but I don't want this recorded. No way."

"I understand," Birkir said.

Helgi sat down in a comfortable chair next to the kitchenette and offered Birkir a seat.

"I'm not in the mood for more work today," he said, sipping his coffee. Then he was silent.

Birkir was silent, too, his gaze resting on the glass of water in his hand, and a few long moments passed before Helgi seemed ready to speak. Finally he began: "When Jón and Rakel came to Amsterdam to drag me out of the gutter and my heroin-induced stupor, they had a story to tell. Fabían had languished in a mental hospital since Sun died in the fire. He'd been unable to express himself, had been in some kind of mental shock—for years he'd been awake but not there. But things changed after a young woman, a psychologist, at the hospital had, with patience and persistence, managed to get through to him using some kind of hypnotism. The first advance was when he spontaneously helped himself to a glass of water. Then he began to say the occasional word. It took a couple years to get him back to the stage he is at today, which is pretty good, mentally. But part of that proce-dure involved having him work through what happened to him in the fire. It turned out that every single fraction of a second of that evening was etched into his mind like a movie on a DVD.

He could describe the course of events and the surroundings in minute detail. He was also able to draw pictures of his experience.

"His story revealed that he and Sun had been making candles—he in the kitchen watching over the pot of wax on the stove, and she in the living room working on the molds. Our method for melting wax was quite primitive and demanded a lot of care. The correct way is to stand the pan of wax in boiling water so the wax temperature never exceeds a hundred degrees Celsius, but we were impatient and just used to melt the wax over a gas ring, watching it all the time. Then as soon as it was melted, we took it off the stove and poured it into the molds. So Fabían was standing by the stove when he heard a car come up to the house. He heard someone come in, and then the sound of the newcomer and Sun talking next door in the living room, but he didn't check what was going on because he was stuck there looking after the hot wax. The muffled conversation continued awhile, but then he heard a commotion and stomping of feet as Sun ran up the ladder into the attic, followed by the bang of the trapdoor slamming shut. Fabían could resist no longer and stuck his head around the door into the living room, where the visitor had clambered up the ladder and was banging on the trapdoor. Fabían saw the man, and the man saw him. The man jumped down to chase after him, but Fabían escaped through the back door in the pantry and hid behind the outhouse as the man searched around in the dark for him.

"Abandoning the pursuit, the man went back inside, and shortly afterward Fabían saw smoke billowing out the back door. He called out Sun's name, but the smoke was increasing, and he soon saw flames in the pantry. The wax must have ignited, and the fire spread quickly through the bone-dry timbers of the house and the highly flammable paper that covered its walls. The whole house was soon ablaze, and all Fabían could do was retreat into the darkness. Finally, he saw the little skylight fly open and Sun trying to climb out through it, but at that moment the house collapsed and she disappeared into the flames.

"This vision haunted Fabían's every waking hour for all those years. He could neither hear nor see anything else—could not free himself from what had happened. The memory overpowered everything else, until at last the hypnotism treatment tore a tiny hole in the black shroud that had enveloped his mind. The image of that visitor in the living room was still etched in his brain, and eventually he regained enough mental balance to be able to transfer that image onto paper. His artistic skills were the same as they had been before the catastrophe. The picture he drew was of a man he had never seen before that night, because he never had any business in Hvolsvöllur with the rest of us; but Jón and Rakel immediately recognized the young sheriff.

"Officially, the sheriff's version of events had been that the house was already on fire when he and the policeman got there, and that, despite their efforts to get in, they couldn't save anything or anyone. The young sheriff suffered burns in his attempt, and the story went around that the experience so discombobulated him that he didn't feel able to continue in his post, and went to work in the Foreign Ministry instead. But according to Fabían's story, there was no fire when this man first entered the house. His actions had caused Fabían to run away, abandoning the melting wax, which must have reached flash point and ignited, bringing about the conflagration. In which case, Arngrímur was obviously responsible for the fire and Sun's death. Worst thing was, as a result of the sheriff's testimony, Fabían got the blame for the fire—the inquiry determined that he failed to exercise due care while melting the wax, and that the fire was his fault. And we, his best friends, believed it."

Birkir asked, "Maybe he said all this about the sheriff specifically to escape blame?"

Helgi replied, "No. Fabían had no idea what was in the official report, nor what people in general thought about this. He simply told his story when his mental health had improved enough for him to be able to do so. It didn't matter to him what other people thought. He would never have made this story up. His drawing of the sheriff was as accurate as a photograph, even down to the coat of arms on the buttons of his uniform. And he had never seen this guy, not before and not since. Fabían just wanted to stay at home and do his thing. He never went into Hvolsvöllur with us, and the sheriff never visited the house until that evening."

Birkir shrugged. "OK, let's assume his story is true."

"It *is* true. I have no doubt Arngrímur Esjar is guilty of Sun's death. But we all saw there was no hope he would ever be brought to justice through the official legal system. Fabían was not a witness you could rely on in court, and then there was the question whether the statute of limitations meant we were too late. And even if we revealed the story, there was no guarantee anybody would believe it; there might even be a backlash against us. Our only hope was to get Arngrímur to tell the truth, and that's what we decided to do. We kept track of where he was working, first Washington, then Bonn, and finally Berlin. We figured our only option was to grab him and get him to confess his part in the crime. In writing or on tape."

"Who is the 'we' in this context?"

"It was me, Jón, Rakel, and Starkadur—Sun's younger brother."

"What did you do?"

"We made various plans over the years, all of which revolved around grabbing Arngrímur on arrival in Iceland. We waited and waited, but he never showed up. Starkadur knew a young woman who worked as a secretary in the Foreign Ministry, and he asked her to let him know if Arngrímur was coming to Iceland—told her he needed a clarification of some old record dating from the time Arngrímur was sheriff at Hvolsvöllur, a minor matter, no need to bother him in Berlin. He jogged the secretary's memory on a regular basis, but the answer was always the same: Arngrímur Ingason is not expected in Iceland."

"So you decided to go to Berlin."

"Yes. Things just started happening all of a sudden. The embassy invited me to hold an exhibition in the Felleshus, and Jón received a German translation of his poems. The new ambassador in Berlin was a personal acquaintance, and through this friendship he arranged for the poems' publication in Germany. Self-publication in disguise, actually, because Jón had to pay the costs himself. I'd previously met the ambassador's wife at an art exhibition, and I sent a message to her that it would be a good idea to invite Jón to do a reading at the embassy in connection with his visit to the Frankfurt Book Fair. The second Sunday in October, just before the fair opened, would be the perfect day for it. I contacted the embassy to say I was coming to make preliminary arrangements for my exhibition and requested a meeting with Arngrímur Ingason that same Sunday. And Starkadur got his husband, David, to go with him to Berlin the same weekend to attend a well-known designer's fashion show. The idea was that all three of us would be at the embassy on the same Sunday, and that we could easily corner Arngrímur since it was very unlikely that any of the rest of the staff would be there that day. We would introduce him to Fabían, the witness, and get him to write a confession. We assumed that it might be necessary to threaten him, and for that purpose hid a knife inside my candlestick, one of the two that were going to the embassy. It's mostly hollow and there was ample space in there for a knife like that. I sealed it in with plaster of paris, but it was easy to break—you only needed to bang the candlestick on a hard object of some kind."

"But then Arngrímur didn't show up," Birkir said.

"No, he didn't show up. Everything had gone according to plan until the reading started. I asked the ambassador about the counselor I was supposed to meet with, but Konrad said he'd been unexpectedly called to Stuttgart because of an accident there. As a result Konrad would hold the meeting with me himself. What a letdown. All that preparation and effort for nothing. We weren't going to get our hands on Arngrímur that day."

"What did you do then?"

"Well, Jón recited his poetry, and we played our parts as if nothing had happened. Afterward the ambassador took us across to the Icelandic building and we had a party. Then this strange man, Anton Eiríksson, suddenly showed up. Jón and Starkadur were feeling a certain sense of anticlimax, and they decided to get drunk on the booze the embassy provided. Jón threw himself into reciting poems, and the ambassador had a ball—he ordered food for us and we stayed there well into the night, as you know."

"But who killed Anton? Who knew about the knife?"

"I have no idea who killed Anton. We all knew about the knife."

"David as well?"

"Yes."

"And Lúdvík?"

"Yes. Lúdvík was supposed to be on hand to intimidate Arngrímur if necessary. He knows about that kind of thing. He used to be a heavy for the loan sharks for many years. He knows how to spook a guy."

"Why was he included in the gang?"

"He was a kind of mercenary. He does most anything for money, and Jón was going to pay him well."

"Doesn't that make him the most likely person to have murdered Anton?"

"I don't know."

"The rest of you had no idea what he was doing during the hour he was supposed to have been sick in the restroom. He could have gone up to the fourth floor at any time during that period. Isn't that so?"

"We were in the conference room. We didn't observe anybody's movements outside the room."

"So Lúdvík has no alibi?"

"No, I guess not."

"Where can I find him?"

"I think he's still abroad."

"No, he's not. Where does he live?"

"He lives with a woman up in the Mosfell suburbs. The address must be in the National Register."

Back outside, Birkir called Dóra, who agreed to come pick him up right away. She was in the apartment building at Austurbrún, talking with any tenants she could find at home—but that could wait.

Birkir called Magnús. "I must have a meeting with you now," he said when his superior finally answered. "The Sandgil fire is still in the picture. I've come across information that conflicts with your testimony. We need to get to the bottom of this."

"I'm just driving Gunnar home," Magnús said. "I'll meet you at my place afterward, same as yesterday."

"Bring Gunnar with you, he needs to be in on this. I can take him home later."

Birkir heard Magnús exchange words with Gunnar before replying, "OK. Gunnar's coming with me. I'll see you at home."

It was a full fifteen minutes before Dóra arrived in her car. Birkir got in.

"Sorry to keep you waiting," she said. "As I was leaving, I met the guy who lives in the apartment directly beneath Anton's. He said he heard drilling off and on over a period of two days. Not continuously, though, and not in the evenings."

"Did he see anybody?"

"No, but Anna seemed to have found something interesting. She went two hours without a smoke while she was investigating it, or so I was told."

"Any idea what?"

"Footprints, or something."

"Oh, just footprints," Birkir said, disappointed. *That might or might not be relevant,* he thought.

"It's something to work with," Dóra said.

Birkir asked her to drive to Magnús's home.

"This case is turning into something very strange," he said.

"What do you mean?"

For a long time, Birkir did not reply. Finally he said, "Let's hear what Magnús has to say."

In the driveway next to the house, Magnús's Land Cruiser was parked in the shade.

"Come in with me," Birkir said to Dóra. "You need to be a party to this meeting."

They walked up to the house and Birkir rang the doorbell. Nobody came to the door; there was no sign of life inside the house, no lights visible.

"They must be in there," Birkir said. He called Magnús's cell but got the automatic response saying it was either switched off or out of range. He tried Gunnar's, which rang until voice mail offered him the option of leaving a message.

"What's Gunnar's ringtone?" Dóra asked.

"He keeps on changing it," Birkir said. "Last I heard, it was a referee's whistle."

"I'm sure I just heard a sound like that," Dóra said. "Call the number again."

Birkir did, and Dóra pointed to the driveway. They followed the faint sound past the house and around the corner toward Magnús's car. The trilling of the phone grew louder as they approached.

"There's someone in the passenger seat," Dóra said.

Birkir opened the front passenger door to find Gunnar sitting there gasping for breath, both hands scrabbling at his neck, which someone had bound with heavy-duty packing tape to the headrest behind him. Gunnar was trying to pull at the tape with his pudgy fingers to relieve the pressure on his throat. The still-ringing cell phone lay on the floor behind the seat.

"I have scissors in my bag," Dóra said calmly, pushing Birkir aside. She fished out a pair of delicate nail scissors and carefully cut through the tape, which Gunnar immediately tore away from his neck. He then leaned forward, puffing like a whale.

"Where's Magnús?" Birkir asked.

"They . . . they . . . got him," Gunnar gasped.

Birkir was on the phone already, calling for help.

"They *who*?" he asked, as soon as he'd confirmed that an ambulance was on the way.

"I . . . I . . . don't know."

"Is your neck hurt?"

"I don't know. It's difficult to breathe."

After a while his breathing settled. "It's getting a bit better," he said. "But it still feels like I have a lump in my throat."

"We'll get you checked out."

Gunnar's head drooped. "I was so goddamned scared," he whispered. "I thought they were going to strangle me."

"What happened?"

"They jumped into the seats behind us the moment Magnús pulled in. They grabbed the seat belts and pulled them tight around our necks."

"How many?"

"I only saw three."

"Did you try to fight back?"

Gunnar found it difficult to talk. "My back and ribs were already killing me," he whispered. "There was nothing I could do. I gave up immediately, and they tied me up like this with the tape.

But Magnús fought as best he could. I think he eventually passed out because they kept pulling so hard on the belt around his neck. Then they taped his hands and feet. He looked totally limp when they dragged him out of the car."

"Did you see their faces?"

"They wore wool hats and some kind of cloth covering their faces. I couldn't see them properly."

"Could it have been Jón the Sun Poet and Lúdvík?"

"I don't know. At least one of them was big, like Jón. Why would they do this?"

"They think Magnús lied in his evidence about the Sandgil fire. Same with Arngrímur Ingason. They're probably going to try to force them to confess it was Arngrímur who caused the fire."

Gunnar looked at Birkir. "This has turned into a disaster," he said. "You need to contact the chief of police."

At headquarters, pandemonium broke out over the news that the superintendent had been kidnapped, and that the same gang had probably also taken another man. The word *terrorism* was bandied about. Birkir had to detail his business with Magnús from that evening and explain the connection with the events at Sandgil. After much discussion, the consensus was that Jón the Sun Poet was top of the list of suspects. They needed to search his home, and Birkir asked that he and Dóra perform that task. Everyone agreed, provided that a SWAT team accompanied them; the police administration was worried there might be violence. Another group was sent to visit Lúdvík Bjarnason in Mosfell.

Birkir and Dóra headed over to Jónshús with a seven-man SWAT unit. Two special officers went to cover the back of the house, and two took up positions watching the front. The others approached the front door. "Shall we break it down?" the unit leader asked.

"Let's give them two minutes to answer the door," Birkir said.

Half a minute after Dóra rang the bell, Rakel opened the door. Dóra handed her a piece of paper and said they had a warrant to search the house.

Rakel stepped aside without glancing at the paper. "Everybody is always welcome here," she said, not showing any expression. "We've got nothing to hide in this house."

Birkir was the last to enter. "Who's at home?" he asked.

"Only me and Fabían," Rakel said. "The other residents are having a get-together. They all went out to a restaurant."

"Is Jón Sváfnisson with them?"

"No. Jón went out of town."

"Do you know where he is?"

"No."

"Do you know what he's doing?"

"No."

"Do you know if Lúdvík Bjarnason is with him?"

"I have no idea."

"Is Jón somewhere with Arngrímur Ingason?"

"I don't know," Rakel said. "Look. Fabían is very sick. He hasn't been able to keep down any food. I had to give him intravenous fluids. If Jón and Lúdvík are somewhere together on some business, they've chosen not to get me mixed up in it. I can't leave Fabían. I took time off from the hospital to take care of him. There's nothing I can tell you."

"Why isn't Fabían in the hospital?"

"They can't do any more for him than I can. He feels marginally better in his own room, where he can smoke his grass. A doctor stops by twice a week. I follow his instructions."

"Is it OK for me to disturb him?" Birkir asked.

"Yes, I was sitting with him when the bell rang. He's awake."

"Does he know anything about where Jón might have gone?"

"No. Please spare him any questions about Jón," Rakel said earnestly. "He knows less than I do, and questions would only upset him."

Birkir went upstairs to Fabían's room and found the door ajar. He entered, and found Fabían sitting up in his bed, smoking and reading a book by the light of a small reading lamp. A bottle with some fluid in it hung from a bracket above the bed, and a tube connected it to a needle in his arm. Beautiful music wafted around the room. A Mozart piano concerto, Birkir guessed.

"Good evening," he said.

Fabían nodded and smiled listlessly.

"You're reading," Birkir said.

Fabían showed him the book, a collection of translated short stories. "I never start a long book now," he said. "I don't like the idea of leaving a story half read. These days I only read short stories—very short ones, preferably. I only manage a few lines at a time."

"I spoke with Helgi Kárason earlier today," Birkir said.

"He was well, I trust?" Fabían said. Though soft, his voice was remarkably clear.

Birkir nodded. "He told me you knew more about the fire in Sandgil than you've let on."

"I find that difficult to talk about," Fabían said.

"I understand. I won't push you. Helgi told me everything I need to know, I think."

"That's good. I've smoked too much this evening. I'm a bit high. It dulls my memory."

"The house is very peaceful tonight," Birkir said.

"It's always peaceful here. We try to be quiet after eight o'clock. Most of us go to bed early."

"Almost no one is at home tonight."

"They've all gone out."

"But Jón the Sun Poet isn't with them. Do you know where he is?"

Fabían shook his head and looked away. "Have I told you about Sun?" he asked.

"Yes, but I wouldn't mind hearing more."

Fabían looked at Birkir and said, "Sun was the loveliest person it's been my pleasure to know during my fragile life. There was not a hint of malice in her. She was pure goodness and wished everybody well." The words came slowly, as if he had to weigh them, one by one, before committing them to speech.

"What did she look like?" Birkir asked when he judged that Fabían had finished.

"What did she look like?" The question seemed to surprise Fabían. Finally he said, "It would be idle to say that she was beautiful. She had red hair and freckles, a small upturned nose, and a crooked front tooth. But her green eyes and her smile that always went straight to your heart would outshine any beauty queen's."

"I hear she was a good singer."

"Yes, she was. It was a rather deep voice, and so musical and true that it hardly needed accompaniment. But she played her guitar, too, with a kind of innate talent. She didn't know many chords, but they were enough for her to be able to create songs that would have done the most well-trained composers proud."

"People have told me that her death was more than you could cope with."

Fabían responded slowly, "For some unfathomable reason that child of the sun had to die, and we, her friends, have never been the same since. Why did this have to happen? What could we have done to avoid this tragedy? Those questions wake us every morning and send us to sleep every night. No one who has met such a creature and lost her so uselessly will ever recover their former self."

Birkir didn't know how to respond to this speech, and for a while neither of them spoke. Finally he asked, "Have you noticed any unusual comings and goings here?"

Fabían looked at Birkir in surprise. "Nothing here is either usual or unusual. Sometimes people turn up and sometimes people leave. Like the moon, waxing and waning."

"Have you seen Jón Sun Poet this evening?"

Fabían smiled weakly. "All my life people have been asking me questions. 'Who are you?' 'Where are you?' 'What is there behind the darkness?' I think I've only given confident answers to one or two of those questions," he said.

Dóra popped her head around the door. "We can't find anybody here," she said. "We're just finishing in the basement."

Birkir stood up to leave. "Thanks for the chat," he said to Fabían.

Outside on the landing, Rakel was waiting for him. "This scares me," she said. "I know you're a good man and that I can talk to you in confidence."

"What are you scared of?"

"I'm scared for Jón. I think he's having one of his manic episodes, and it bothers me that he's not at home. He can lose his sense of judgment under these circumstances."

"You really don't have any idea where he might be?"

"No. Somebody called him Saturday evening—some guy. Jón doesn't have a cell phone, so if anyone wants to get ahold of him, they call the landline. He left the house yesterday morning carrying an old cassette recorder, and I haven't seen him since."

"Did you hear any of the phone conversation?"

"No. Jón didn't really say anything. He just listened. Then he scribbled something on a piece of paper and took it with him."

"What sort of paper?"

"You know, a white piece of paper. Lined."

"I mean, where did he get the paper?"

"There's a pad by the phone for messages and stuff. When folks answer and need to pass on a message, they write it down and pin it to a corkboard next to the phone."

"Can you show me?"

Rakel nodded and led him down the stairs. By the front door was a little telephone table with a chair next to it. Rakel pointed to the small notepad and ballpoint pen on the table.

"Do you use this a lot?" Birkir asked, carefully picking up the pad.

"No," Rakel replied. "Most of us have cell phones so folks can call us directly, or text us. Or e-mail us. It's mainly Jón who gets messages here."

"Has anybody used this pad since Jón wrote on it Saturday?"

Rakel glanced at the corkboard. "No, these are all old messages. There's nothing new here. I don't think anybody's used the pad since then."

"Can I take this with me?"

"Sure."

"Thanks."

"Listen."

"Yes?"

"Please be gentle with Jón if you find him. He's a good man. He's just not too well at the moment."

The chief of police had instructed them to set up an incident room to coordinate the search for Magnús and Arngrímur. Birkir looked in and saw several people either talking on the phone or examining a large map of Reykjavík. They'd decided on a systematic search of empty houses in the city—there were plenty of them, thanks to the financial crisis—and some on the team were at work making lists of these places. Then there were others who evidently felt it would help to talk loudly or march back and forth waving documents.

In Mosfell, the SWAT team had found a small frightened woman in an apartment that, according to the National Register, was supposed to be Lúdvík Bjarnason's address. She swore he was abroad and not expected back anytime soon. She was not actually certain that this was his home at all, because their relationship was somewhat vague. Lúdvík came and went, and didn't tell her much about his movements. The woman was able to show the policemen a few boxes containing Lúdvík's personal things, as well as some clothes in a wardrobe. That was all.

Birkir found Anna in the forensic lab. She was standing by a sink, and quickly extinguished a cigarette under the tap when she heard someone coming.

"Oh, it's you," she said, relieved.

"You're still working," he said.

"Yes. I'm completing a preliminary report on the Austurbrún case, the dead safe-breaker. We'll continue tomorrow." She nodded at some photographs lying on the table. "We have footprints."

Birkir looked at one of the photos, which showed an indistinct print in something that could be a very fine layer of dust, with a red-and-white ruler laid next to it. The image had been computer-enhanced and the outlines exaggerated with a black line. It was a print from a shoe with a plain sole.

"Pretty ordinary," he said.

Anna picked up another photo and handed it to him. "This seems to be the other foot."

Birkir stared at the picture. It showed a smaller print, a shade wider but significantly shorter.

"It looks like a specially made shoe for a crippled foot," Anna said. "This could be a big help to us."

"Where do you get shoes like this?"

"We'll find out tomorrow," Anna said. "This will do for tonight."

"Just one more thing," Birkir said, carefully fishing Jón the Sun Poet's notepad out of an envelope. "I need to know what was written on the last bit of paper before it was torn out," he said, laying the pad down on the workbench.

Anna took out a magnifying glass and peered at the pad. "I'll have a look at it. You go home. It'll be on your desk tomorrow morning."

"Thanks," Birkir said. "But please call me right away if you detect an address or some sort of location."

Anna nodded.

22:10

Birkir found Gunnar at home in his kitchen. He had a stiff medical collar around his neck, and his mother was helping him eat.

"Want the rest of the meat stew?" Gunnar asked hoarsely.

"Yes, please, just a small amount."

María fetched a bowl and set it in front of Birkir.

"What did the doctors say?" Birkir asked when he'd taken a spoonful of soup.

Gunnar was having trouble swallowing. "They took an X-ray of my neck," he struggled to say. "Said it's just a sprain. A bad sprain, actually, and very inflamed, so I've got to wear this thing until it gets better."

"Oh, well, you got off easy," Birkir said. "I hope you stay home the rest of the week and try to recover."

"I'll come in tomorrow. I'm too restless to stay home while we're still working this case. I can at least take phone calls."

"You sure?"

"More or less. See how it is in the morning. I'll be in if I'm not feeling any worse. What's happening at the station?"

"The police chief set up a special team—with him heading it—to supervise the search. We're supposed to work with them."

22:30

This was a long day for Anna. She often made life more difficult for herself through her reluctance to delegate when in the thick of things. She trusted no one. In a crime-scene investigation, she preferred to deal with all the menial tasks herself. That could mean working well into the night, and now Birkir had added this notepad to her workload.

She began by removing the top leaf from the pad and examining it in different types of light. When that brought no useful results, she went out to the parking lot for a break to consider the best approach to what was an unusual challenge for her.

After some fresh air and two cigarettes, she felt clear on how to proceed. She went to the equipment room and got a bag that contained a small metal box—an Electrostatic Detection Device, or EDD. She set the device on her workbench and switched it on. A fan started up, creating suction through the perforated top platen, which gripped the sheet of paper when she put it in place. She then covered the paper with a very thin Mylar film, over which she waved the attached electrostatic wand for several seconds to create a positive charge in the paper.

Another part of the kit was black toner powder, and she now carefully scattered some of this over the film's surface. She knew the theory: The pressure of the pen used to write on a notepad causes the filaments of the paper below to break—and waving an electromagnetic field over the paper imparts a positive charge to the ends of those broken filaments, which attracts the negatively charged toner. But still it was like magic when the powder Anna dusted over the plastic film created a vivid copy of the last thing that had been written on the pad. Underneath, she could see a fainter image of an older message, probably a household shopping list for Jónshús.

What Anna read was not an address—just a few rows of numerals. No reason, therefore, to call Birkir now. This would be tricky to decipher.

23:00

It had begun to snow when Birkir parked his Yaris in the reserved spot behind his house. He remained seated in the car for a little while, reflecting. Finally he made a decision—instead of going inside, he'd walk over to Jónshús and check the situation there.

The falling snow was heavy and wet, and soon the ground was completely white. Birkir felt the snow pile up on his shoulders and in his hair, and now and then he stopped to brush the worst of it off. Between stops, he walked briskly and soon reached his destination. In a parking space just across the street from the house were two men in a car, its engine running and windshield wipers sweeping to and fro against the snow. These must be the plainclothes policemen the chief had put on watch there in case the Sun Poet showed up. He tapped on the side window, and the one sitting at the wheel rolled it down.

"Good evening," Birkir said.

"Hi."

"Any signs of life?"

"No."

"I wasn't really expecting there would be," Birkir said. "I'm just going to check on the folks in there."

"You do that," said the cop, who then yawned.

In Jónshús, all the lights seemed to be off—except for the glimmer of light coming from one of the living rooms. Birkir caught a glimpse of Rakel at the window.

He trod his way through the yard and went up the steps to the front door. He pressed the bell once, briefly. After a while, the light above him came on, and someone peeked through the drapes covering a small window next to the door. Birkir knocked and shouted, "Detective division, Birkir Li Hinriksson."

The door opened and Rakel peered out.

"Sorry to disturb you," Birkir said.

"What do you want?" Rakel asked. "I haven't heard anything from Jón, and Fabían is asleep. I gave him a large dose of painkillers."

"I want to ask you a few questions."

"You do, do you? I don't suppose there's any point in my refusing."

"I'd be very grateful if you'd cooperate."

Rakel opened the door and stood to one side. "You're welcome to come in. We'll see about the questions."

It was dark inside. Rakel was wearing a thick bathrobe, and she led the way into the house. She said over her shoulder, "Everyone went to their rooms long ago. They weren't very happy this evening."

"Why not?"

"There's something scary in the air."

"Is there something you know about?"

"No, it's just a feeling."

She ushered Birkir into the living room. A fire was dying in the fireplace, and Rakel added a couple of logs to its embers. Quiet music came drifting from the stereo. A scratchy vinyl record revolved on the turntable. Birkir knew the song but couldn't work out who the performer was.

"Who's the singer?" he asked.

"Joni Mitchell. The album's *Blue*, from 1971. This is my kind of music. The old hippie records. We have a bit of a collection."

"Were you listening? I'm sorry if I disturbed you."

"I was just sitting here alone, thinking," Rakel said, offering Birkir a seat. "There's so much going on. Times change."

She sang quietly along with the music—"Blue songs are like tattoos"—but stopped after one line.

"Were you into the hippie culture?" Birkir asked her.

"The hippies had the most beautiful vision of the twentieth century, but many things in the movement also went wrong. The Woodstock festival was in many ways the pinnacle of that era, but the Manson murders, in the same week of August 1969, were its nadir. Sadly, few could properly handle the freedom the hippies created for themselves and the rest of that generation. I just try to focus on the beautiful things."

"You're worried about Jón, aren't you?"

"Yes."

"Has he been unbalanced lately?"

"He's been agitated and restless."

"Were there symptoms of mania?"

"I don't know. Maybe. He's not stable, that much is certain. His bipolar disorder is usually only a problem when he does a lot of heavy drinking. But he's been sober lately. And he hasn't been talking to us—when he's manic he's usually very gregarious and loud."

Birkir said, "I know that those of you who lived with Sunna in Sandgil have wanted to talk with ex-Sheriff Arngrímur Ingason Esjar. Helgi told me the whole story. Are you aware of some kind of action that Jón has planned?"

"No."

"Do you think it's plausible?"

"Maybe."

"What were they going to do to Arngrímur?"

"I don't know. They haven't included me in their plans lately. I've always been so cautious. They called it fear."

"But would you have wanted to get Arngrímur to confess?"

"Yes, that would have been good. None of us emerged from those events unscathed. We survived them, each in our own way, but there was always this question: Why did it have to happen?"

"I know you were all very fond of Sun. What made her so special?"

"She was my best friend."

"Tell me more."

Rakel pointed at a framed drawing hanging on the wall, its paper yellowed and creased where it had been folded. "That's a picture of Sun that Fabían drew a long, long time ago," she said. "It's the only one of her that we have."

Birkir stood up to take a closer look. It was a fine drawing of a beautiful girl playing a guitar.

"But it's better than any photograph could have been," Rakel added. "Sun was singing when she woke up and singing when she went to sleep. She loved life as only the young can. She never argued with anyone, and soothed all who were bitter. The rest of us attempted to embrace the hippie way of life, but she was simply a child of nature. She came from the sparsely populated country of Northwest Iceland and didn't feel the need to copy anybody. She was a genuine flower child. The two of us went for long walks in the area around Sandgil, sometimes a long way into the hills, and even all the way up Mount Thórólfsfell—there was a view into the Thórsmörk National Park when visibility was good. Sun loved everything that was beautiful—landscape, music, poetry, pictures."

"Was she completely perfect?" Birkir asked.

Rakel smiled. "She was scared of mice."

Her smile disappeared as she added, "And fire."

TUESDAY, OCTOBER 20

06:20

Birkir got back home just after midnight. He slept soundly for most of the night, but toward early morning he woke with a start from a dream in which Jón the Sun Poet had caught him and was forcing him into a foul-smelling hessian sack. He lay a long while thinking about the dream. In it, he hadn't been scared of Jón—it was the smell. Sometimes he dreamed about an unfamiliar smell—it could be a good smell or a bad smell, but it was always something he didn't recognize from daily life. Something from his childhood, likely from Vietnam. He closed his eyes and inhaled through his nose, trying to find some image that went with this smell, but nothing came to him. It was as though he hit a wall whenever he thought about the day he arrived at that Malaysian refugee camp. He couldn't recall anything in context before that time, just obscure fragments that popped up in response to some everyday event.

He remembered, suddenly, that he had lots of work to do at the police station, and he got out of bed and rushed to get himself ready for an early start. He switched on the kettle to boil some water while he took a quick shower and shaved, after which he made himself a cup of tea and a piece of cheese on toast. Having eaten his breakfast, he headed out.

On his desk was an envelope from Anna. It contained a print-out of the image she'd retrieved from the notepad in Jónshús. She had erased all traces of earlier stuff, leaving just the most recent message—the one Jón had written:

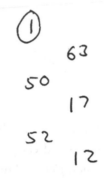

What did these numbers mean? Did they have any bearing on the case?

He was scratching his head over this when Gunnar hobbled in on his crutches, wearing a cervical collar. It took him a good while to sit down.

"You should have stayed home," Birkir said.

"Yeah, yeah, yeah, that's what Mom said, too." Gunnar sneezed and wiped his face with the sleeve of his jacket. "Goddamned cold," he said nasally.

Birkir passed him the roll of paper towels he'd fetched for him the previous day.

"Thanks," Gunnar said, blowing his nose. "Anything new?"

Birkir showed him the paper with the numbers on it. "What do you think these are?"

"Bingo numbers?" Gunnar said.

"I figure they're directions to someplace," Birkir said, and explained where the paper came from.

"I pass," Gunnar said. "I can't make any sense of this."

Birkir's cell phone rang. It was the front-desk duty officer. "There's a woman here wants to speak with you."

It was Rakel. She handed Birkir an envelope. "I went for a walk this morning like I do every morning. I came across Jón, waiting for me by Hallgríms Church—he knows my regular route. He said the cops were watching our house, so he couldn't come home. He said they were probably bugging his phone, too."

"That's possible," Birkir said. He didn't know what measures the chief of police had set up.

Rakel continued, "He gave me this envelope and asked me to give it you. I brought it straight here."

Birkir opened the envelope. It contained an old audiocassette, nothing else.

"I don't know anything else about this," Rakel said. "I swear. You take it and do with it whatever you have to. I hope I can go back home to look after Fabían. You know you can find me there."

Birkir nodded and watched her go. Then he went to see the chief of police, who'd just arrived at his office.

"I guess we're meant to listen to this," Birkir said, showing his boss the cassette. He explained how it had come to them.

"Do we have such a thing as a cassette player?" the chief asked.

Birkir said, "The old radio in the kitchenette has one."

"Let's check it out," the chief said, and stood up. They headed to the kitchenette, which was soon pretty crammed as others joined them. Birkir inserted the tape and pressed "Play."

The voice sounded tired, but spoke clearly. "My name is Arngrímur Esjar Ingason. I was appointed sheriff of the Rangárvellir district on April fourth, 1972, and remained in that office until February sixteenth, 1975. Since May fifth, 1975, I have worked abroad for the Icelandic Foreign Ministry."

There was a brief pause and then the voice continued, "This declaration is made at the request of persons who have me in their power. Although it's made under duress, it is, nevertheless, a relief to be able to make a statement about a matter that has weighed heavily on my conscience for thirty-four years. Why have I not done this before? Well, maybe because I was weak and unworthy. Perhaps I convinced myself that I would be in a better position to atone for my mistakes if what I had done remained under the radar. But that's not good enough anymore, and now it is my sincere wish that the truth be told.

"In all my duties on behalf of the Icelandic state overseas, I have tried to do my very best to serve my country and my fellow countrymen. I have responded to every request, be it night or day, when anyone has needed my assistance; I have tried to show discretion and compassion; I have tried to be a good man, all in the hope that on my last day on this earth I can say to myself: I have done more good than harm during my life. But one event, a combination of blind obsession and dreadful accident, weighs heavier than all the good deeds a man can possibly perform during however long a life. All my years I have been trying to make up for the mistake I made on the evening of February thirteenth, 1975, out there in Fljótshlíd.

"In the summer of 1973, when I had been sheriff in Hvolsvöllur for just over a year, five young people—Jón, Sunna, Helgi, Rakel, and Fabían—moved to Fljótshlíd and established a hippie commune in an old farmhouse on a plot of land called Sandgil. Their efforts at making a living from peddling artwork out there in the sticks amused me, so I let it pass. Although, they should probably have applied for some kind of license. On Friday afternoons if the weather was good, Sunna would sometimes come into the village to play the guitar and sing outside the co-op store. I began pretending I had some business there so I could listen to the music and watch this beautiful young woman. It pained me to see the self-satisfied way the locals tossed trivial amounts of small change into her guitar case after they'd stood there listening to her entrancing songs. Her music was unique, and her singing came from the heart. I fell in love with this wonderful being. As time passed, however, I realized that there was a chasm between the two of us—it wasn't so much the age difference, but rather the fact that I represented the authority, the system, that Sunna and her friends wanted nothing to do with. To her, the uniform I wore was at least a ridiculous clown's outfit. At most it was a threat and a symbol of power.

"I took to greeting Sun when she played outside the store, and I would sneak bank notes into her case, sometimes fairly large sums. I thought that the smile she rewarded me with meant something more than simply the joy of life she was so full of and bestowed on everybody in her generosity. I got this absurd idea that I could make this goddess fall in love with me.

"Then the authorities began to suspect that the hippies were cultivating cannabis at Sandgil. We received an inquiry from the detective division in Reykjavík, where somebody had fingered Jón and Helgi as dealers in various bars and clubs. Then we got an informal tip from an employee of the power company about the unusual amount of electricity that was being used in the house. We started watching them, and it turned out that most Fridays two or three of them would drive off to Reykjavík, staying there through Sunday and going methodically from one club to another selling their product. So one Friday, the police moved in and picked up Jón, Helgi, and Rakel with a considerable quantity of marijuana, all neatly packaged and ready for use. I was supposed to go back to the farm and arrest the two who had stayed behind—Sunna and Fabían—and confiscate the plants and all the equipment.

"That evening, I drove with Constable Magnús Magnússon into Fljótshlíd. When we arrived at the farmyard, I asked Magnús to wait in the car, as I wanted to go inside and talk to Sun on my own. What I had in mind was to explain to her what bad company she had gotten involved with, and offer to get her out of this situation if she agreed to move into the sheriff's house with me. It was an incredibly stupid plan, but I was obsessed with this girl. In my stupidity I imagined that my position, my personality, and my looks would make her fall in love with me on the spot. I thought she would realize I was there to save her and would appreciate that. It was the kind of delusion that could only occur to someone who has always had everything in life handed to him on a silver platter—wealth, education opportunities, a career, and the respect of his fellow citizens. Someone who has never been denied anything.

"I knocked loudly on the front door. It was unlocked, so I walked in. I found Sun in a large living room that was set up as a kind of workshop. She was sitting at a worktable, making candles. She was, of course, scared stiff when she saw me, but I took her hand and made her sit next to me on the sofa. I told her that her housemates had been taken into custody, and that she would be joining them behind bars unless she let me save her. All she had to do was to move in with me and she would be safe. I would take care of everything. I told her that I loved her and wanted her to be my wife. I tried to embrace her—and was even about to kiss her—but she tore herself from my arms and ran up the ladder into the attic, slamming the trapdoor behind her. Naturally, she thought that I'd gone mad, that I was capable of anything—and I suppose I must have been, because I followed her and began trying to smash through the trapdoor. Then I realized that the boy, Fabían, was standing in the kitchen doorway, watching me. I decided to grab him and get him into the police car before continuing my struggle with the trapdoor, so I jumped down. But he fled through the kitchen and out the back door, and disappeared into the darkness. I chased him out there, and spent some time searching fruitlessly before returning to the house.

"What I didn't know was that the boy had been melting candlewax in a pan on the stove. You have to watch it really carefully, because the wax easily ignites if it gets too hot. When I got back into the kitchen I saw black smoke coming from the pan, and instead of just covering it with a lid and turning off the heat, I grabbed the pan, intending to throw it out. But just at that moment the wax reached flash point, and a column of flame shot up in the air. I dropped the pan, and burning wax spilled all over the floor, which was covered in newspaper because somebody had been painting the kitchen. Wax also splashed all over my hands and arms. I had to beat out the flames with my bare hands, and I was badly burned—though I didn't feel the pain until much later. I tried to stamp out the fire on the floor, but to no avail, so I grabbed a bowl of water from a nearby table and chucked it at the flames, but that caused an explosion, and I only just made it out into the living room. There I leapt up the ladder, yelling like a maniac to get Sun to come downstairs. At that point Magnús entered the house. He'd seen the fire and felt his way through the smoke to find me. By then I was semiconscious, and he dragged me out. My screaming must have so terrified Sunna that she didn't dare come out until it was too late and the place was ablaze. Either that or the smoke drove her back when the fire first started. I can't bear to think about it.

"I was completely overcome from smoke inhalation and the pain from my burns. The constable used the radio transmitter in his car to call the fire department, but the house had almost burned to the ground by the time the men arrived. The boy had disappeared. Magnús put me in his car and drove me straight to Reykjavík, to my parents' house. Once there, I broke down in tears and told my father what had happened—how my actions had resulted in a lovely girl's death. I'm afraid my father had little patience for such displays of weakness. He called a doctor friend of his and got him to treat my burns and sedate me. Meanwhile, he instructed Magnús to draw up a report to the effect that the house was already on fire when we got there, and that I broke in to save Sunna but was unable to reach her. This was the cause of my burns and the smoke inhalation. He told Magnús he would arrange a good position in Reykjavík for him, and that his future would be secure. My father was a man of such influence that nobody dared oppose his wishes, and at close quarters he was quite overpowering, so Magnús decided it would be for the best to bow to his will. In any case, he had not actually witnessed what occurred inside the house, and had assumed that it was an accident that had nothing to do with me. It was simply a question of which came first, the fire or I, and this was a perfectly plausible interpretation of events. The occupants of Sandgil were an irresponsible bunch, and anything could happen in that sort of setting, in his opinion. I don't want him to pay for my actions.

"My parents kept me in their home to recover, and during that time my father made plans for my future. He had me resign the sheriff's office, and arranged a job for me at the Foreign Ministry, with a posting to Moscow, where my uncle was the ambassador.

When I left, he laid down some rules about my life. I was to drop the Esjar family name and instead adopt the patronymic Ingason, based on his second name, Ingi. He'd made a deal with the minister that I was to work abroad in Icelandic embassies for the rest of my life, in whatever capacity the ministry determined, provided only that they would never make me ambassador. This was documented in a protocol that successive chief secretaries at the ministry have regularly renewed. And so I left Iceland, and the gloss they gave of what I did in Fljótshlíd was that it was an 'accident involving the reckless manufacture of candles in unsuitable conditions.'

"My father was able to maintain his reputation and status in society for the rest of his days. He died many years ago. I've worked abroad ever since that time and not been back to Iceland until now. My career is unusual in that I have never had to return to work in the ministry in Reykjavík—I've been able to remain for longer periods in each posting than others, and I have never applied for the office of ambassador. Many people in the ministry know of this arrangement, but very few people know who instituted it, and nobody knows the reason behind it. Rumor has it that I am unable to tolerate the Icelandic climate because of a lung condition, and I've done nothing to correct that. 'Seek foreign fields when distant duty calls,' the saying goes. Or in my case, when you are not welcome at home.

"The crime I committed has long since lapsed in law, and my only punishment will be whatever my captors here determine. I hope they will have more mercy on me than I showed the wonderful Sunna, whom they loved so much."

Arngrímur finished speaking, and there followed the sound of the microphone being moved. Then they heard Magnús's voice, feeble and tremulous, "My name is Magnús Magnússon. I was a police constable in Hvolsvöllur when the farm at Sandgil was destroyed by fire in 1975. I can confirm that Arngrímur's account corresponds with what I witnessed of the event. My testimony that is on file about this event may not be accurate."

The recording stopped, but then resumed, and Magnús's voice sounded unnaturally high-pitched as he added, "I confess that I lied when I testified about the fire at Sandgil."

After this short declaration, there was nothing else on the tape.

"Where are they?" the chief of police asked, at a loss for what to do.

Birkir showed him the image Anna had recovered from the notepad. "I suspect that these might be directions to the place," he said. "We need to crack this."

He made an enlarged copy of the image and fixed it up on the board for everyone to see. Theories abounded as to what the numbers might mean: GPS coordinates; the television station Screen One, as the symbol at the top clearly resembled the logo of the station; pages in a book; a bank account number.

Anna tapped Birkir's shoulder. "Good morning."

"Thanks for the picture," he said.

"No problem," she said. "I've got something else for you."

"Tell me."

"I sent a sample from the embassy for chemical analysis. We have the results."

"Chemical analysis?"

"Yup. The coins that were on the table with the bits of plaster. The ones that were probably used to break open the base of the candlestick to get the knife out."

"Yes?"

"They were sticky."

"Sticky?"

Anna nodded and said, "Among other things, two sunflower seeds were stuck to one of the coins with some sort of lotion. I sent it for analysis. They found substances that typically occur in warm underground seawater—silicon, minerals, and algae."

"What does that tell us?"

"It's a skin cream produced by the Blue Lagoon company. Mineral Intensive Cream. Does any suspect have skin problems?"

10:10

Gunnar snuck out after he had listened to Arngrímur's account. Or tried to, as well as his crutches allowed. Anyway, he didn't tell anybody that he was leaving.

A taxi was waiting for him outside.

"Bank Street," Gunnar said, when he had managed to cram himself into the rear seat. Then he named a café. He was going to have breakfast and see his buddy Emil Edilon.

The writer was very organized, and had reserved a table for ten o'clock—a table for two, but the café owner had removed one of the chairs so that the author could drink his coffee and think in peace.

Ten minutes later, Gunnar hobbled in on his crutches. Just inside the door he spotted an empty chair at a table for four, and he hooked it with a crutch. Two young women loudly protested that they were expecting more people, but they broke off as they looked up and saw Gunnar's face. He just grinned and said, "Disabled people have priority." Then he pushed the chair ahead of him across the floor and plopped himself down opposite Emil.

"Hello, Maestro," he said loudly enough to attract Emil's attention.

The writer glanced reluctantly up from his papers and took a good look at Gunnar's head, which was even more of a mess than usual, his beat-up appearance exaggerated by the surgical collar and ugly black eye.

"Have you been hit by a garbage truck?" Emil said.

"I've got a riddle for you," Gunnar said, ignoring the question.

"Did I ask for one?"

Gunnar signaled to the waiter. "I'm hungry," he said. "I'd like bacon and eggs, two rolls with cheese, and a Danish. And a pot of coffee, please."

He put his hand in his pocket and fished out a folded piece of paper, which he opened and pushed across the table to Emil. It was Jón the Sun Poet's numbers—a photocopy he'd made when no one was looking.

"These are directions to a place," Gunnar said. "How should one read this?"

Emil looked at the paper and examined it a little while. "I'll admit that you can be entertaining from time to time," the writer said, "but this time you're just boring."

"Look," Gunnar said. "A guy gets a phone call and information about some place. He writes these numbers down on a piece of paper. What does it all add up to?"

"I don't know."

"Come on, just take a look. You're so clever at math."

Emil looked at the paper and soon said, "One hundred ninety-five."

"Eh?"

"Didn't you want me to add up the numbers?"

Gunnar shook his head and looked up at the waiter, who was bringing a large tray to the table. He put two plates in front of Gunnar, together with a big cup and a pot of coffee. He filled the cup and asked if there was anything else.

"No, that's it for now," Gunnar said and turned back to Emil. "I'll tell you a good story if you help me."

"A story?"

"Yeah, one I just heard down at the station."

"Is it worth it?"

"Sure, but you have to keep quiet about it."

"Let's hear it."

Gunnar repeated, word for word, what he'd heard on the cassette recording earlier that morning.

"Ah, so that's what happened out there," Emil mused.

"Yeah, and you can't tell anyone. Not yet, anyway. It'll start to leak out this evening. At least ten people heard this, and some of them are notorious canaries. They won't be able to keep quiet for long."

"I won't say a word," Emil said.

"And now for the numbers."

"Yes, what was it about these numbers?"

"Directions, remember?"

Emil looked at the paper again. "What sort of directions?"

"That's precisely what I don't know," Gunnar said.

"Local?"

"I don't know. Hardly. More likely out of town."

Emil thought about it. "How would you go about giving me directions? For instance—what if I wanted to go see Geysir?"

"I'd tell you to head east to Selfoss, or nearly. Turn left before you get there."

"Isn't the road numbered? A numeral?"

"Yes, Route 1, going south."

Emil looked at the paper. "Isn't that the ring road?"

"Yes."

"One in a circle."

Gunnar glanced at the paper. "Right. What next?"

"I don't know. Maybe kilometers."

10:30

In the yard of Jónshús, a man stood at an easel. He was painting a picture of a snow-covered red currant bush surrounded by a scattering of little multicolored birds.

The artist noticed that Birkir was looking at him. "Sorry, I can't stop for a chat, buddy," he said. "The light will be changing soon, and I've got to get this."

"Sorry to disturb you," said Birkir, and turned to approach the house.

As before, it was Rakel who responded to his knock. "Jón hasn't been in touch at all," she said.

"This time it's not Jón I'm after, I'm afraid I have to speak to Fabían. It's important."

"Fabían is tired. He's asleep. But do come in. I might be able to help you."

Rakel showed Birkir into the kitchen and offered him a seat. "I've just made some tea. Why don't you have a cup with me?"

"Thanks."

Neither spoke as Rakel poured tea into two cups and placed them on the table, and then stretched up to a shelf and retrieved something from among a stack of papers. Sitting down across the table from Birkir, she handed him a plain, unaddressed envelope. Birkir opened it and extracted a cassette tape and a small piece of paper. He read:

I, the undersigned, Fabían Sigrídarson, confess to the murder of Anton Eiríksson at the Icelandic embassy in Berlin in the early hours of today, the twelfth of October.
Signed: Fabían Sigrídarson
Witnesses: Helgi Kárason, Rakel Árnadóttir

It was dated the evening of October twelfth, this year.

"This is why you came, right?" Rakel asked.

Birkir nodded.

"Fabían said it wouldn't take you long to reach this conclusion."

"Did he?"

"But he asked me to give you this envelope. How did you know it was him?"

"We found traces of a skin lotion at the scene. I saw packaging from it in his room. Am I supposed to listen to this tape recording?"

"Yes. He wants you to hear this."

Birkir looked at the cassette. It was old, reused. Someone had written "Bob Dylan" on one side and then crossed it out. Birkir asked, "Why didn't you bring it this morning? With the other envelope?"

"I was hoping we'd get more time. A few days, at least."

"Can I listen to it here?"

"We have a cassette player in the living room. There's nobody in there, so you can listen in peace. Take your cup with you."

Rakel led the way into the living room and switched on an ancient stereo. Birkir inserted the cassette and pressed the "Start" button. The recording was clear, but the voice on it sounded weak. Sometimes there was a pause in the account and you could hear Fabían sipping a drink, and at other times there were fits of coughing, from which he took a while to recover. But the tape kept running, and little by little the whole story emerged.

"My name is Fabían. My mother died when I was eight years old and in foster care on a remote farm in the Northwest. I'd been sent there when she became too ill to take care of me. There were five of us foster children. When I had been there for a few months, a new farmhand joined the household—Anton Eiríksson. Eighteen years old, he was the cowman, and drove the tractor during haymaking season. In him I found a friend, something I hadn't had since I was taken from my mother. Anton always found time to talk to me, and sometimes he brought me candy when he came back from the village. He whispered in my ear not to tell anybody—he didn't want to give the other boys candy because they were bad boys. But I was a good boy, and I was his friend. Of course I felt proud of this, being the cowman's chosen friend—he was a guy all the other boys looked up to. I dreamed of being like him, driving a tractor and combing back my hair with brilliantine.

"Then, late that fall, the farmer and his wife were going to take us boys to Reykjavík. We'd visit the National Museum and go to the theatre and the movies. A two-week trip including the journey on the coastal steamer, and Anton was assigned to look after the farm in the meantime. I wanted to go, too, of course—to go on the steamer and see the National Museum—but Anton said that I should ask permission to stay behind and help him with the animals. He said he didn't want to be left all alone. I was supposed to say that I didn't want to go to Reykjavík. He asked me so nicely and said I wasn't his friend if I refused. I tried to promise that I'd stay behind next time, but then he became very sad and said he'd expected more from me. So I went to the farmer and said I didn't feel well and that I would prefer to remain with Anton rather than go on the steamer, and they agreed to it. Anton and I watched as the others headed off in the jeep to catch the boat.

"Anton raped me every single day for two weeks. When the family returned, I was seriously ill—but that didn't arouse suspicion, as I'd complained of not feeling well before they left. I couldn't keep anything down, and I became severely dehydrated. Anton had told me in graphic terms what would happen to me if I revealed to anybody what he'd done. It was so upsetting that I lost the power of speech. I was admitted to the local hospital in Ísafjördur, where they tried to get some food and liquid into me. They succeeded, gradually, but then we found that I'd become incontinent. They said it was intestinal cramps and would get better, and they sent me home. But the truth was that Anton's repeated assaults had severely damaged my anal sphincters. The outer muscle, the *musculus sphincter ani externus*, operates voluntarily, while the action of the inner muscle, the *internus*, is entirely involuntary. Together they normally perform the important task of controlling bowel movements and keeping the anal canal clear, but mine were so ruptured and bruised that they retained only very limited function. I'd soil my pants at the slightest exertion. I was so ashamed and did everything I could to conceal my condition. I learned to make a diaper from toilet paper, and that caught most of the fecal leakage—but my bowel functions were an ongoing problem, and the resulting contamination caused sores around my anus. I soothed them with constant applications of udder ointment, of which there was, fortunately, a plentiful supply in the cowshed. Anton had resigned his job and disappeared while I was in the hospital, so I didn't have to be scared of him anymore, but the other boys started bullying me, saying I stank of shit. I stopped eating, hoping that would keep my pants clean, but I ended up back in the hospital suffering from malnutrition.

"My foster parents could no longer cope with my problems, and—because I hadn't shown any mental or physical progress over a period of two years—the authorities put me into a home for retarded people. As it happened, I fit in pretty well there, since some of the inmates' toilet habits were, you could say, unconventional. At least I wasn't the only one who smelled of excrement. I stayed there for three years and did my best to fit in with the others. I just sat by the window all day, looking out and waiting for my next bathroom visit.

"One fall I had to go into the hospital again when the sores I was getting around my anus became infected, causing a high temperature. Antibiotics took care of that, but the doctor realized that my plumbing was not as it should be, and with some simple tests diagnosed that my sphincter muscles were defective. They couldn't treat that in Ísafjördur, but until I could see a specialist in Reykjavík the doctor suggested that I plug the leak with tampons. He gave me some to try, and told me to insert one up my rear end between trips to the bathroom. That worked reasonably well, and my sores healed. But nothing came of my seeing a specialist at that time. The doctor was a busy man, and I guess he forgot about me. I just didn't have the initiative to follow things up, and it wasn't clear who was responsible for my physical health.

"For a while, I lived with some good people down in Fljótshlíd, but, following a tragic event there, I ended up in a mental hospital. I had been there twelve years when I became seriously ill, and they diagnosed malignant colon cancer, a long-term consequence of my rectal damage. Because the muscles weren't functioning properly, there were always fecal remains in the anal canal, a condition that eventually causes cell changes leading to cancer. I had surgery to remove part of the bowel, followed by radiotherapy, chemo, the whole package.

"I had a colostomy, and for the first time since I was nine years old, I didn't have to worry about whether I'd soiled my pants. This was a huge improvement to my life, but—unfortunately—the cancer has now recurred and will soon finish me off.

"So now we come back around to Anton Eiríksson. I recognized him immediately when he joined the ambassador's party after the reading in Berlin. He had been plump as a young man but had gotten considerably fatter since then. He didn't appear to recognize me. I kept to myself, and we hardly said a word to each other until I told him that his face looked like a pig's ass. That was when he first took notice of me, and seemed to be trying to place me. I was in turmoil and wanted to banish all thoughts of him from my mind—it made me nauseous to look at him. I had absolutely no intention of revealing to the other guests what he'd done to me. It would have been interesting to to see how he would have reacted, had I spoken up and told them about our encounter back then, had I described how he'd mauled the little wisp of a child that I was, night after night, ripping my insides apart. But I said nothing. I'm not used to people taking me seriously or believing what I say. I am, after all, a chronic mental patient.

"But later, while looking for a bathroom on the fourth floor, I ran into Anton alone. He remembered me then, though our conversation was brief. I never managed to tell him about my condition, since he was too busy babbling on about how kind he always was to the children he abused. That was the final straw for me. Everybody sees me as an invalid, someone incapable of any great exertion. Anton, certainly, exhibited no signs that he feared me, so I seized the opportunity when he was preoccupied with making a telephone call. I extracted the knife that I knew was concealed in my friend Helgi's candlestick—and I plunged it into Anton's stomach. The blade was razor-sharp, and it took very little effort for me to slice a big gash in his belly before losing my grip on the handle. At first Anton screamed and tried to stand up, but I easily pushed him back into the chair. He was quiet after that.

"I noticed that my arm was covered in blood and innards, so I took off my jacket and turned the sleeve inside out. I went to the bathroom, rinsed my shirt, and turned up the sleeve. The shirt was black, so the staining wasn't as conspicuous as it would have been otherwise. Then I went back downstairs. There was some commotion having to do with the ambassador's wife, and nobody paid any attention to me. We all left the embassy shortly afterward.

"I know that a confession like this may seem far-fetched. People may even suspect me of taking the blame for someone else. But that's not the case. The jacket and the shirt I was wearing that evening will prove this—I lied when I claimed I'd left the jacket in Berlin.

"Why didn't I confess at once? Maybe I thought I could get away with not saying anything. That might have been an easier option. But I don't want anybody else to be accused of what I did, which is why I made a written confession as soon as I got back to Iceland. There are witnesses to my signature. If the police charge somebody else with the murder, or if the case still continues after I'm gone, my friends will present my confession, and this recording is to accompany that document.

"I am fully aware that when the police receive this, they will charge me with the murder. But I received my sentence a long time ago—I'm hardly going to worry about the judgment of any court. My health is not up to incarceration, and it's in no one's interest to hospitalize me. I think that a fair sentence would be house arrest here in my home until the mortician comes to collect me. It won't be long now.

"And that is the end of this account."

The recording was over, and Birkir rewound the cassette. He looked at Rakel. "You know Fabían well, don't you?" he said.

"Yeah, I guess. Better than most, I think."

"As witness to his confession, do you think he is physically capable of doing what he describes in this statement?"

Rakel replied, "Fabían has never been capable of any kind of physical exertion. He's very skinny, the dear boy. But in my profession, working with addicts and mentally ill folks, I have seen the most improbable of wretches take violent action when pushed to the limit. I think that Fabían could have wielded a knife if the occasion really demanded it."

"Would you feel able to testify to this?"

"Well, of course I didn't actually witness the deed, but I have confirmed with my signature that Fabían himself wrote this confession of his own free will and of clear mind. He did it the moment he returned from Berlin because he is always so afraid that he might not last the day. He taped this statement after your first visit, and I wrapped up his bloody jacket and shirt and put them in the freezer to preserve the evidence that will prove his story. He couldn't bear the thought of someone else taking the blame for this."

"I'm afraid I'll have to disturb him for a bit," Birkir said.

"Go ahead, then. Actions have consequences, of course. Fabían will have to deal with that."

Birkir hesitated, and said, "We're investigating another murder that's linked to this one. Do you know anything about that?"

"Another murder? No, God forbid. Fabían hasn't left the house since he came back. He can't possibly be guilty of that."

MONDAY, OCTOBER 12, REVISITED

01:45

*D*o you remember me?"

The voice came from the restroom doorway. Inside, the fat guy rinsed his hands at a shiny steel sink.

"Yeah, we talked earlier this evening," *he replied without looking up.*

"Yes, but I mean . . . do you recognize me from the past?"

"Should I?"

"Maybe you can't, Anton. It was a long time ago—I was only nine years old."

Anton picked up a clean towel and carefully dried his hands. Then, lifting the towel to his puffy face, he wiped the sweat from his brow.

"Nine, huh," *he said, pausing to check his reflection in the mirror.* "That's a good age."

After a prolonged silence, the other man said, "That was the last good year of my life."

Anton studied the man in the doorway. Then his small, deep-set eyes came to life as a hint of a smile twitched at the corners of his mouth.

"Yeah, I remember," he said. "I kept an eye on you for a few years after our encounter. You were the first one."

"The first one?" the other man said, almost whispering.

"I remember being kind of clumsy. I might have hurt you a little."

"You did."

Anton threw away the towel and walked toward the door. The other man moved aside as Anton stepped into the hallway. At first he headed for the stairs leading to the lower floors, but then he turned back and entered a room directly across from the restroom. The other man followed.

It was an impressive office with a large desk at one end. Anton flicked on the light switch by the door and said, without looking around, "It was impatience and inexperience. I was only eighteen—and much too impetuous the first few times."

"Yes," the other said. "I guess you were."

Anton drew a cigar from his jacket pocket and lit it with an elegant lighter. His jowly cheeks rippled as he puffed a few times to get the glow going.

With his lighter still in hand, he lit two tall candles on a low table nearby and continued: "But it didn't take me long to figure out how to do it right. Once I did, I never hurt anybody again. Now I know how to make the boys feel good. I even teach them about themselves."

The men scrutinized each other. Finally the other one broke the silence. "So you are still abusing children?"

Anton shook his head in disdain. "I have never abused anybody. That's the truth. To say otherwise is just spreading the ignorance and lies of those who have no concept of sincere friendship and tenderness. I merely guide my boys toward maturity. I open them up to new and wonderful dimensions. I allow them to experience their bodies completely for the first time. If I get my hands on them before they're spoiled by adolescence, I always succeed. They cry with pleasure when we're done."

The other man gasped. "Who are these boys? How do you get away with this?" His voice trembled.

"You just need to be careful. People are so prejudiced. I mostly go to Indonesia. The boys there are beautiful."

"Doesn't anyone ever press charges?"

"Charges? No, of course not. I pay well, and everything is taken care of. I only do business with the safest houses."

"Jesus! People are selling these children to you?"

Anton moved across the room and sat down in a large, comfortable chair behind the desk. "The hosts know me. They know how gentle I am. They save the new boys for me because nobody else is as tender with them. Many of the other customers are monsters. Unfeeling trash. They can ruin a boy in ten minutes, frighten them so badly that they shut down forever."

"You need to be stopped," the other man said.

Anton went on as if he hadn't heard. "I have a gentle touch— the kind the boys find soothing. You have to be patient with them."

After a short silence, the other man firmly said, "Someone has to put a stop to this."

Digging some change from his jacket pocket, he stacked the coins in a small pile and slid them across the table next to the candlesticks. "Someone has to put a stop to this," he repeated.

Unconcerned with his visitor, Anton picked up the telephone receiver and dialed a long number, reading it from a piece of paper on the desk. After a brief wait, he introduced himself in English. He was speaking to a hotel employee in some city or other, booking a room for a few nights. He read out his credit card number and had to repeat it twice.

Meanwhile, the other man licked his right thumb and index finger and pinched out one of the candle flames.

TUESDAY, OCTOBER 20

11:00

While consuming his second roll at the Bank Street café, Gunnar tried Birkir's cell number a few times, but all he got was voice mail, so eventually he called Dóra.

"Get a car and pick me up," he said.

Dóra protested. She was busy examining evidence related to the murder in the apartment on Austurbrún. "Call a cab and go home and rest," she said. "You need to give yourself a chance to get better."

"Please," Gunnar said. "I have to test a theory. If it works, it'll lead us to Magnús."

"Listen, the chief is in charge of that. He'll send the SWAT team with you if you know something."

"I don't know if I know something. It's just a hunch. I need to check it out. Then I'll brief the chief. I promise."

"You're crazy."

"I know I'm crazy," Gunnar said, but Dóra had already said good-bye and hung up.

"Fuck," Gunnar said, and looked at Emil. "Hey, buddy. You got a driver's license?"

The writer laughed. "Driving a car is the lowliest activity the human species has ever indulged in. Besides which, I never go outside zip code 101 in this godforsaken city. So, no, I do not have a driver's license."

11:20

When Birkir entered his room, Fabían was sitting up in bed, smoking. "Good morning," he half whispered.

"Good morning," Birkir replied, and sat himself down in a chair next to the bed. He was silent for a moment, and then said, "Rakel gave me the envelope with your confession and the cassette tape."

"That's good. It was beginning to weigh heavily on me. Were you able to listen to the recording?"

"Yes, but I need more detail. Do you feel able to talk?"

"I'll try."

Birkir dug out his voice recorder, switched it on, and put it on the nightstand. Having dictated the usual formalities, he said, "Tell me how you found Anton in the ambassador's office."

Fabían put his joint in the ashtray. "I'll attempt to tell you everything that happened. I've tried to put that evening out of my mind, but I still remember it pretty clearly."

He took a tissue from a box on the nightstand and held it against his mouth as he coughed several times, and then wiped blood from his lips and threw the tissue into a wastebasket. When he started speaking, his voice was weaker than before.

"Late that evening in the embassy, I needed to take a leak and empty my colostomy bag. The bathroom on the second floor was occupied, so I went upstairs. I was feeling too weak to walk up the stairs to the third floor, so I took the elevator. Once I was in the elevator, I thought I might as well go on up to the fourth floor, that maybe the bathroom up there would more likely be free. But

I found Anton there. The door was half open and he was washing his hands, just as if everything was fine and dandy, and I was standing there with a full colostomy bag and a cancer eating up my insides, all because of that man. I asked if he recognized me."

Fabían's voice trailed off.

"And did he recognize you?" Birkir asked after a while.

"Yes."

"Did he apologize for what he'd done?"

"No. Admittedly, I didn't have the stomach to detail the injuries he'd inflicted on me. And he just went on talking, wanting to convince me that what he did to children was a pleasure and satisfaction for them. I couldn't take it. I visualized scared little boys looking at this fat, disgusting man who didn't even speak their language or understand when they begged him to leave them alone. For the first time in my life I had the urge to hurt someone. I knew about the knife in Helgi's candlestick—I'd been there when they'd hidden it, seen how it was done. And I knew which candlestick had the knife in it. Although they look alike, they're not identical. Anton lit the candles when we moved into the ambassador's office . . . I've no idea why. But once he started rambling on about his kindness and sensitivity, I'd had enough. I took some coins from my pocket and made a little stack of them on the table. Then I snuffed out the candle and wrapped my handkerchief around the candlestick before picking it up."

Fabían reached for a bottle of water and started to take a sip from it, but then grimaced and put it down, saying, "I can't keep anything down."

He resumed his narrative. "Helgi had told us that it would take a certain amount of force to break the base, so I took great care as I banged the candlestick down on to my stack of coins. Anton was talking on the phone and hardly seemed to notice the noise.

When I lifted up the candlestick, the knife lay there on the table, and I picked it up and concealed it with my arm. I moved toward the door, but then turned and approached Anton, who was still on the phone, looking out the window. When I was almost on top of him, he looked up with a weird look of surprise. I grasped the knife with both hands and plunged it into the center of his belly and pulled downward, letting go when I felt something warm splashing my hands. Anton let out a kind of howl and tried to stand up, but I gave him a push and he slumped back down again, staring at his lap as if unable to understand what all this mess was. I saw that this man would not hurt any more children, and all I could feel was relief. I turned away and went to the bathroom. It took me a while to clean up and change my colostomy bag. Also, I tried to clean the sink so as not to leave any evidence. I rinsed my shirt sleeve the best I could, and I scrunched up my jacket. Then I began to feel cold. I went downstairs and told Helgi what I had done. He took charge and got me back to the hotel, where I gave him the whole story. We flew home to Iceland later that day."

Birkir asked, "Did you take a credit card from Anton?"

Fabían hesitated. "Yes," he finally said. "I took the credit card he'd put on the table. He was on the phone booking a hotel room, and he'd read out the number on the card."

"Why did you take it?"

"I don't know. Maybe as a kind of symbol. It all seemed so unreal that I had to take some form of proof that it hadn't been a dream. Or a nightmare, rather. The blood on my clothes should have been enough, but I put the card in my pocket nevertheless."

"Who took the credit card from you?"

"I can't remember. I showed it to Helgi while telling him what had happened. Then to Jón and Starkadur when we met later.

Maybe it's around here somewhere. Maybe Jón took it. I don't know. Do you need it?"

Birkir shook his head. "Don't worry about it," he said. "The credit card isn't important anymore."

12:30

Back at headquarters, Birkir reported to his superiors that someone had come forward with a credible confession to the embassy
murder, and he requested that the forensic department analyze
the frozen bundle of clothing Rakel had handed over to him. Then
he dispatched a couple of cops to pick up Helgi Kárason—Birkir
needed him to confirm the role he'd played in the case, but was
fed up with visiting his studio and having to bang on the door.

Birkir asked Dóra to be present during Helgi's interview in
case they wanted to charge him with concealment—after all, he'd
known all along who'd killed Anton Eiríksson but had kept quiet.
So when Helgi arrived at the station, Birkir informed him that he
had the legal status of defendant and, accordingly, had the right
to call his lawyer or to refuse to answer questions.

"No, I don't want an attorney," Helgi said. "I have nothing to
hide. I want to tell everything I know."

Birkir said, "On the evening of Monday, October twelfth,
you countersigned—as witness—a confession made by Fabían
Sigrídarson. Is that correct?"

"Yes."

"Fabían Sigrídarson wrote this confession and signed it of his
own free will."

"Yes."

"So you've confirmed the authenticity of that document. Do
you have any further information regarding the case Fabían confessed to being involved in?"

"Yes."

"Will you please give the details of what you know?"

Helgi said, "As far as the party at the embassy is concerned, I made a statement about that on a previous occasion, to which I have nothing to add. But at the end of the evening, when we were about to return to our hotel, Fabían suddenly sat himself down next to me and said he'd just killed Anton in the ambassador's office, using the knife I'd hidden in the candlestick. I was totally astonished, as Fabían hadn't previously exhibited such forcefulness. But I didn't want anything to come out that night. We would have to find a way to move forward, and preferably get back to Iceland, because no way was Fabían well enough to survive custody in a German prison. The ambassador's wife created a commotion when she couldn't find her shoe, which worked very well for us—and in fact I did my best to make the shoe even harder to find.

"Fabían was shivering with distress—and with cold, because he'd taken off his jacket and bundled it up, and his sleeve was soaking wet where he'd rinsed off the blood. I made him put on Jón's jacket, and told Starkadur to take David out to one of the taxis waiting outside. Then I woke Lúdvík, who'd fallen asleep in one of the restrooms, and I told the ambassador and his wife that the four of us were leaving. Konrad asked about the other guests, and I said they'd gone off together in a taxi. He and his wife came outside with us, and Konrad had to help Jón in his argument with the night guard over his lost guest pass—we were supposed to hand them back in exchange for our passports.

"Back at the hotel, I made Fabían tell me the whole story. We already knew that something dreadful had happened to him when he was a young boy, but it really shocked me to hear him describe exactly what Anton had done. All things considered, you could hardly blame him for bumping off the guy who'd destroyed his body and his whole life, especially after he'd bragged about continuing to abuse children.

"Fabían and I agreed we would go back to Iceland together later that day. We didn't tell Jón or Starkadur anything about what had happened until we all met in Iceland last Thursday. That's when Jón and Starkadur decided to make one final attempt to finish things with the ex-sheriff, Arngrímur. But I said I'd take no part in that. The whole thing had become too much for me. Before, I'd been prepared to deal with Arngrímur and accept the consequences—be convicted and maybe have to serve a sentence. But now I'd had enough. My nerves can't take stuff like this."

Birkir said, "We suspect that Jón Sváfnisson and Lúdvík Bjarnason have taken two men prisoner and are holding them somewhere. Do you know anything about that?"

"No."

Birkir continued, "You told me on a previous occasion that you and Jón and Starkadur had made plans to kidnap Arngrímur. Is that correct?"

"Yes," Helgi nodded. "I guess that's correct."

"Where were you planning to keep him captive?"

"We didn't know. We planned to find a suitable place if and when we needed it. It never got that far."

"What sort of place did you have in mind?"

"An abandoned house somewhere. Somewhere remote."

"Out in the countryside?"

"I don't know. Maybe, but not too far from Reykjavík, though."

"Do you know what will happen to Arngrímur after he has admitted his part in Sunna's death?"

Helgi was silent, and Birkir repeated his question.

"I don't know," Helgi finally said, "but I think you should try to find him as soon as possible."

"Why?"

"At some point someone suggested we should chain Arngrímur by one leg, near a burning candle. When the candle burned down, it would set the house on fire."

"He was to be burned alive?"

"He was to be given a chance to escape, which was more than Sun got."

"How?"

"Within his reach would be a saw so he could cut off his leg and free himself from the chain."

Birkir's cell phone rang. He saw on its screen that it was Gunnar.

"Hi," he said. "Where are you?"

"I'm stuck in a snowdrift up in Borgarfjördur."

"What in the hell are you doing there?"

"I think I've found the place."

"What place?"

"The one that the directions refer to. The numbers Jón wrote on the notepad."

"How?"

"I got a car and then headed up to the Vesturlandsvegur ring road."

"Are you actually driving?"

"Yeah, I'm not doing too badly. I just can't look to either side."

"How do you manage to go through an intersection?"

"I unfastened the rearview mirror and use it to see right and left."

"My God. Where did you get the idea for all this?"

"Just came into my mind—you know how it is."

"OK, but what's this place you're talking about?"

"So . . . I went up to Vesturlandsvegur and set the odometer to zero where the ring road begins. Then I drove sixty-three kilometers north to Borgarfjördur, where I came to Route 50, the third number on the list."

"I get it. So, then you drove seventeen kilometers along that road?"

"Well, not immediately. First I crossed the bridge to Borgarnes and had a bite to eat. You know how hungry I always get when I see Borgarnes."

"OK. And then what?"

"Then I went back and turned up Route 50, and drove for seventeen kilometers till I arrived at the exit for Route 52, just like it said on the list. I made a left and continued for twelve kilometers and came to a driveway. The house is called Setberg—there's a sign down where the driveway meets the road. Everything's covered in snow up here, and my car got stuck. You'll have to send backup."

"I'll do that," Birkir said. "Can you see the house?"

"Yeah, up on the hill. About five hundred meters."

"You've got to get up there right away. There may be an incendiary device on a timer. We don't know when it'll start the fire. It could happen at any moment."

"I'm supposed to switch it off?"

"Yes, but be careful. I'll have the Borgarnes police hit the road immediately."

"I'll try to investigate the house."

"Call me before you go in."

14:10

The tightly packed snowdrift in which Gunnar was stuck reached nearly halfway up the side of the car, and it took him some time, and all his strength, to heave the door open far enough to squeeze out, all the while trying not to strain his already painful back and neck. At last he was on his feet, and able to fish his crutches out from the backseat.

The house on the hill looked lifeless and abandoned—he saw no light in the windows, despite the overcast skies and waning day. This old farm had clearly not been worked for a long time. Though the house had been restored, probably for use as a summer house, the outbuildings were small and in bad shape—definitely not an establishment that would satisfy a present-day farmer's needs. The fences around the miserable fields had all collapsed, and there were no signs of livestock anywhere. The only vehicle in sight was an ancient rusty tractor standing in the farmyard.

He moved off up the driveway, step by step. Something big had driven there recently, and he was able to walk in the tire tracks, but his crutches sank into the snow under his weight; the frost gnawed at his face, his swollen eye was sore, and, apart from the surgical collar protecting his neck, he wore only an old suit and a thin shirt.

From time to time he looked up, scanning the house for signs of life. Or signs of fire. Smoke or flames. He saw nothing, and the house—a single-story with an attic, and standing on a concrete basement—seemed totally deserted.

When he finally reached the farmyard, he called Birkir as promised. "I'm by the house."

"Great," Birkir said. "The Borgarnes police are on their way, and a fire engine is about to mobilize. Can you get into the house?"

"Hang on," Gunnar said. "Let me check." He struggled up the few steps and tried the front door. It was unlocked.

"I'm inside," he said, still on the phone.

Birkir said, "Use your best judgment, but stay in close contact with me."

Gunnar was now in a narrow foyer and saw a hallway beyond. At first he thought of sneaking from room to room to check the place, but then reflected that a well-shod horse had more chance of moving quietly around the house than he did in his present condition, and so decided to tackle the situation head-on. "Hello!" he shouted as loudly as his husky voice could manage. "Anybody here?"

He listened, and immediately heard the faint response, "Help, help! We're in the basement."

"Coming!" he called in reply. From where he was standing, he could see stairs leading up to the attic, but no entrance to the basement. He proceeded along the hall.

"How do I get down?" he shouted.

"Help, help!" was the only reply he could make out.

He entered the living room but couldn't see any way down. He turned back and moved to the kitchen at the other end of the house.

"*Help, help!*" He heard it clearly now.

"How do I get down?" he repeated.

"There's a hatch in the kitchen," someone shouted.

Gunnar spotted a trapdoor in the corner. Throwing aside his crutches, he got awkwardly to his knees, hooked his finger through the loop set into the trapdoor, and lifted it.

"Hello!" he called.

He heard Magnús's voice saying, "Hurry! The fire'll start any minute."

Gunnar looked dubiously at the ladder leading precipitously down into the basement. "I'm coming!" he hollered. He sat down and swung his legs into the hatch, feeling forward with his foot for a rung to step on, and began his descent.

On the fourth rung his lumbago caught him with a stabbing, immobilizing pain. "Aargh! My back," he yelped.

"Quick, quick!" Magnús cried.

Gunnar gritted his teeth and closed his eyes as he let go of the ladder. He slid down the ladder on his belly, bouncing on the rungs and crying out, "Ouch! Ouch! Ouch!" as he went. Landing on his feet, he felt sweat cascading from every pore on his body.

"Put the candle out!" Magnús shrieked.

With difficulty, Gunnar turned to see the flickering stub of a candle in a bowl in the center of the floor.

Magnús shouted, "It's in a pool of kerosene! There's a fuse connected to that gasoline drum!"

At that moment, the candle sputtered, and a sheet of flame shot up from the kerosene in the bowl.

"The fuse is lit!" Magnús screamed.

Still in agony, Gunnar fell to his knees and crawled like a giant cockroach across the floor. He grasped the burning fuse and yanked it toward him, away from the barrel. Confident now that there was no danger of the place going up in flames, he slumped onto his belly, breathless and exhausted.

"Thank God," Magnús gasped.

Gunnar lifted his head very slowly and saw Magnús sitting, legs outstretched, in one corner of the basement, his back resting against some piled-up sacks of fertilizer. His hands and feet were bound with strong packing tape, and a rope fastened to the wall behind him encircled his neck. Magnús would have strangled himself if he'd tried to get away.

Arngrímur sat at the other end of the basement. In contrast to Magnús, he was shackled to the floor with a tight steel cuff around his left ankle, attached by a heavy chain to a substantial anchor bolt in the floor. A small handsaw lay next to him. He was in a state of shock, staring in silence at the shallow, bleeding wound on his leg.

"He was going to saw his leg off when he couldn't get through the chain," Magnús said. "But it was no use, he only managed that scratch. You arrived just in time, thank God."

Raising himself up on all fours again, Gunnar crawled toward the barrel. He tried to get to his feet using it for support, but it fell over with a loud clang. He peered into the opening where the fuse had gone.

"This barrel is totally empty," he said. "There was no gas in it. There wouldn't have been a fire."

Magnús began to laugh—an odd, strangled laugh that changed into a kind of whimpering. "They lied, the fucking bastards," he stammered between sobs. "They let us squirm here thinking we were going to be burned alive. Goddamned thugs."

15:20

Ten minutes after Gunnar had reached the basement, police officers from Borgarnes arrived at the farmhouse, followed a few minutes later by a fire engine and an ambulance. The police released Arngrímur and Magnús from their restraints and, after the paramedics had dressed the wound on Arngrímur's leg, helped them up out of their prison. Then they drove the two of them to Reykjavík for medical treatment and to take their statements.

Getting Gunnar out was more of a problem. The only way was back up the ladder, and there was no chance he could attempt that in his current state. He had to wait for a doctor to come from Borgarnes and give him a couple of painkilling shots in the butt—one of them morphine, the other, Gunnar didn't know what. When the injections started to take effect, he managed to stand up and, watched and supported by the pair of apprehensive paramedics, he slowly eased himself up the ladder, step by step.

Back up in the kitchen, Gunnar found his crutches and was able to use them to hobble out to the ambulance, where he laid himself down on the gurney and asked that they take him to Reykjavík. Not to the hospital, but directly to police headquarters.

"They don't give you anything to eat in that hospital," he said by way of explanation.

One of the paramedics drove the ambulance, and the other took the car Gunnar had used to get to Setberg.

As they approached the Hvalfjördur Tunnel, Gunnar fished out his cell and ordered a pizza. "Send it to police headquarters and deliver it to Birkir Hinriksson. He'll pay. Don't give it to anybody else—if you do, it'll be gone by the time I get back to town," he said firmly. "And include a large Coke as well."

A piping-hot extra large pizza with pepperoni, onions, and mushrooms was waiting for Gunnar as he hobbled into the detective division, along with a two-liter bottle of Coke.

"I sure as hell deserve this," Gunnar said to Birkir, taking the first bite. "You want some, too?" he asked with his mouth full.

Birkir shook his head. "No, thank you."

"Oh, well, I'll have to eat it all myself, then," Gunnar said, and continued eating while Birkir told him about Fabían's confession.

"Does it check out?" Gunnar asked, when he had heard the whole story.

"Yes. Anna is examining Fabían's clothing—the shirt and jacket. We also have Helgi's testimony that Fabían told him at the embassy what he had done, immediately after the event. I think they've stopped lying."

"What will happen to Fabían?"

"He'll stay where he is. Everybody is of one mind about that."

"What about the others?"

"Jón and Lúdvík will presumably be charged with kidnapping, aggravated maybe. It depends on what Magnús and Arngrímur tell us."

"Have Jón and Lúdvík been found?"

"No, but they won't be able to hide for long. Keflavík Airport is under surveillance, so they can't leave the country. We're not worried about that."

"What does Magnús have to say?"

"He offered his resignation immediately when the chief of police called him in. Which probably means that his taped confession is the truth."

"So we'll get a new boss."

"Presumably," said Birkir, and stood up to go. "Want me to take you home?"

"No," Gunnar said. "I'm going to finish eating." He was only halfway through the pizza.

"And after that I'm going to go have a beer," he added quietly, after Birkir had said good-bye and left.

Few people remained in the office. In an incident room, Dóra was clearing the display board of the photographs and evidential notes about the Berlin killing—that case was solved, and they had to move on to the next one.

"Sorry I didn't help you earlier today," Dóra said, as Gunnar hobbled in and plopped into a chair.

"No problem," Gunnar said. "I know I can be a bit demanding at times. It all went very well, I think."

Dóra pinned up some new pictures on the board. They were from the scene in the apartment on Austurbrún where Búi Rútsson had been found murdered.

Gunnar watched her with keen interest.

Dóra explained where the metal rod had come from and how it had been used. "The killer made off with a large sum of euros," she said. "None of the people living in the other apartments seem to have seen him."

"What's that?" Gunnar asked, pointing at the picture Anna had taken of a footprint.

"We think the murderer may have hidden in a closet. He left footprints in the dust on its floor. He had a crippled leg, and we're collecting data on individuals who have custom-made footwear."

Gunnar stared at the picture, his mind working. Finally he said, "Give me a photocopy of that picture."

Dóra hesitated. "What did you just pick up on?" she asked.

"Just a hunch."

"Anything I can help you with?" Dóra asked as she handed him the copy.

"Nope," Gunnar said, folding the paper and putting it into his jacket pocket.

"Sure?"

"Yeah, but you can take me to the bar on Smidjustígur. There's a guy I have to see."

18:30

There was a new bartender. This really irritated Gunnar, because now he had to explain carefully what he wanted—a bottle of Holsten beer and a Jägermeister—and tell the guy where to find these things. And what to charge for them.

"Bring it to that table over there," Gunnar said. He'd already spotted Konrad sitting at one of the tables. The waiter followed Gunnar as he hobbled across the room on his crutches and sat down opposite the ambassador without asking permission.

"Were you in an accident?" Konrad asked, contemplating Gunnar's scruffy appearance, his bruised eye (now turned dark-blue), and the surgical collar.

"Several accidents," Gunnar said. "I have one whenever I leave the house." He picked up the Jägermeister bottle and drained it in one go. "This helps a little," he said, as he chased it down with a sip of beer.

Konrad said, "I just heard from the ministry that Arngrímur's had some kind of a crisis. Apparently some criminals kidnapped him, but he was rescued today somewhere in Borgarfjördur."

"Yeah, I rescued him."

"You did? So you were in a fight, then?"

"Nope. No fight. Just pure genius. My amazing powers of deduction coupled with superefficient procedures. That's how I do business."

"Cheers," Konrad said, raising his glass. "I also heard that somebody confessed to the embassy murder. That invalid, apparently, who came with Jón the Sun Poet."

"Yes."

"So you've solved all your cases, then?"

"No," Gunnar said, and bent down, grabbed Konrad's leg with one hand and swung it up onto his knee. Konrad was taken completely by surprise, and had to grab the table to stop himself from falling backward.

"What the hell are you doing?"

Holding the leg tightly, Gunnar used his free hand to extract the footprint image that Dóra had given him.

"What are you doing?" Konrad repeated, as Gunnar compared the short, broad sole of his shoe with the print.

"Exactly," Gunnar said, and let Konrad's leg flop back down to the floor. "As I suspected. You paid a visit to an apartment in Austurbrún a few days ago."

Konrad snatched the picture from Gunnar and studied it closely.

"Where was this picture taken?" he asked.

"You left this footprint behind in a closet in the apartment."

"That can't be." Konrad said.

Gunnar took out his cell phone. "I'll have to take you in."

Konrad lifted his glass and emptied it. "Wait, wait," he said. "We can come up with an arrangement."

"Afraid not," Gunnar said. "Even if you were to give me half of all the euros you took from Anton's safe, someone else would soon pick you up. There won't be any problem figuring out who made this shoe for you, and your name will be in their records."

Konrad hesitated and then said, "Let's have another round before we go to the station to correct this misunderstanding."

Gunnar thought about this. "OK. You're paying." He waved to the waiter and ordered more of the same for both of them. Then he said to Konrad, "Look, we have this footprint. You can bet we'll find a hair or something else that will point to you when we do DNA analysis. We'll be examining your clothes—when you banged that guy on the head, microscopic drops of blood would have sprayed all around him, and a lot landed on you, even if you didn't see them. We will find those. No doubt we'll also find some money in your possession."

"This is not looking good," Konrad said after a long silence.

"No."

"What should I do?"

"Be cooperative. That simplifies things."

"Does it?"

The waiter brought the drinks and set them on the table.

"Keep the rest," Konrad said as he handed the waiter a fifty-euro note. "And bring me another glass in ten minutes."

Gunnar produced his voice recorder and switched it on "You can begin by telling me what happened. We'll take a formal statement later. So, what were you doing in the apartment?"

Konrad was silent for a time. Then he said, "Some years ago Anton entrusted me with the task, should something happen to him, of going to his apartment and removing and destroying certain boxes of papers. Not many people knew about this place of his, but I sometimes visited him there when he was in the country. He gave me keys so I could get in if the need arose."

"What were these papers?"

"Various financial records and some pornographic material—the models seemed to be rather on the young side."

"When did you go to the apartment last week?"

"I arrived in Iceland late Thursday, and went there that night to deal with things. There was no one in the apartment, but I saw that somebody had tried to break into the safe. There were tools there, and one of the locks had been drilled out of the safe door.

I guessed that whoever it was had stopped to avoid attracting attention during the night."

"Why didn't you contact the police?"

"The safe caught my attention. I'm in big trouble financially. I sold our house here a few years back and put the money into bank shares. Everything disappeared in the crash. My wife thinks I invested in safe funds, and I haven't had the courage to tell her the truth. Now that we're moving back from Berlin, she wants me to buy her a nice house in Reykjavík."

"So what did you do?"

"I took the boxes of papers out to the car I'd rented. Three boxes, rather bulky and very heavy. Then I went back into the apartment and waited till morning. When the guy arrived at about ten o'clock, I hid in the closet."

"Did you recognize him?"

"I could only hear him, and it wasn't until, you know—afterward—that I realized that this was Anton's bodyguard."

"How did you manage to overpower him?"

"I sneaked up on him while he was drilling the second lock out of the door. He was wearing ear protectors and couldn't hear me. I was only going to knock him out, but the one blow wasn't enough, and I had to hit him again. Too hard, I guess."

"Did he die instantly?"

"I think so."

"What happened then?"

"I finished drilling the lock out and emptied the safe."

"What was in it?"

"A lot of euros. I haven't counted them yet. There was some gold, too."

The waiter brought Konrad a glass of whisky. He paid with a twenty-euro note. "Keep the change," he said, just as before.

WEDNESDAY, OCTOBER 21

10:30

Rakel called Birkir's cell.

"Fabían died this morning," she said. "Jón was with him. Starkadur is here, too. They're ready to turn themselves in. We'd appreciate it if you would come on your own to pick them up."

Birkir found the men in Fabían's room, where the dead man lay on the bed. A beautiful candle was burning on the nightstand. Everything connected with pain and disease had been removed from the room, and an extraordinary peace suffused the scene. Starkadur stood gazing out the window; Jón was seated, and didn't look up when Birkir came in.

Birkir sat down opposite him. "You're going to have to come with me," he said.

"In a moment."

"There's no hurry."

Neither spoke for several minutes. Finally Jón broke the silence. "Did you find the men you were looking for?"

"Yes."

"Were they unhurt?"

"Yes."

Jón showed no sign whether he considered this good or bad news.

Birkir asked, "Can you tell me about your involvement in this case?"

"You heard the sheriff's confession."

"Yes, I know all there is to know about the historical background, but I need to get a picture of what has happened during these last few days."

Starkadur turned away from the window and said, "I'll tell you about that."

"Wait," Birkir said. He fished out his voice recorder and switched it on. "Please identify yourself," he said.

Starkadur did so, and continued, "I planned the arrest, if that's the right word. I also got Lúdvík on board, for a fee. Jón knew nothing about it until Lúdvík called him after you arrested me last Saturday."

Birkir looked at Jón. "But you knew about the plan for Berlin, right?"

Jón nodded.

Starkadur said, "Yes, we all knew what was planned for Berlin. The idea was to corner Arngrímur at the embassy and have him confess then and there. When that didn't work, Jón and Helgi gave up. They'd reached the end of the road. But I wanted to make one final attempt, and I had the idea of tricking Arngrímur into coming to Iceland. I called the embassy and introduced myself as assistant secretary to the foreign minister. I said we needed Arngrímur in Iceland for a meeting that same day to discuss the embassy's future, and that he would shortly receive a confirming e-mail. I tried to make the call brief, and hung up abruptly, saying that the minister was calling for me. I knew a way of sending an e-mail that at first glance appeared to come from the ministry. Then I bought the airline ticket with the credit card Fabían took from Anton in Berlin. Lúdvík and I went to the airport not really knowing what to expect. I'd written in the e-mail that a ministry driver would pick up Arngrímur from the terminal."

Birkir asked, "Lúdvík pretended to be an official driver?"

"Yes. He drives a black Range Rover that could be taken for a ministry vehicle."

"How did you overpower Arngrímur?"

"That was the simplest part. I waited at the place where Lúdvík had to stop the car to pay the parking fee. Arngrímur was sitting in the front passenger seat, and I opened the rear door and grabbed his seat belt—it was easy to pull it tight around his neck as I climbed into the rear seat. Arngrímur couldn't do a thing to defend himself. We had practiced this many times. Lúdvík drove on, beyond the airport area, to a place where we could stop. I tied Arngrímur's hands and feet with tape, and we put him in the back and covered him with blankets."

"How did you get access to that house in Borgarfjördur?"

"The owner's someone Lúdvík knows. He lives in Spain and only uses the place during the summer. Lúdvík looks after it in the winter, so he has a key. After capturing Arngrímur, we took him straight there. Lúdvík attached an anchor bolt to the basement floor, and we shackled our prisoner to it with a chain and a steel cuff round his leg. That way we could leave him there while we prepared the next move."

"You left Arngrímur alone in the house?"

"Yes," Starkadur replied. "We left him some food and a bucket for him to do his business in. And a mattress and a blanket for sleeping. It was warm enough down there. We told him he would stay there until he'd told us everything about the fire at Sandgil.

Lúdvík went back the following day, and I was going to join him that evening with video- and audio-recording equipment. But then you guys arrested me, and Lúdvík had to contact Jón for help with the rest."

"Was that the first Jón heard of the kidnapping?"

"Yes, Lúdvík asked him to bring something so they could record Arngrímur telling his story. Jón's not familiar with that part of the country, so Lúdvík described the route carefully to him over the phone. Next day, Jón got somebody to drive him to Borgarfjördur. He brought an old cassette recorder that was good enough for our purposes."

Birkir asked, "Did Arngrímur make his confession willingly?"

"Yes, he was very cooperative. He just seemed pleased to be able to talk about this. I think it was a relief for him, in a way."

"Why did you grab Magnús, too?"

"When Jón and Lúdvík heard what Arngrímur had to say, they realized that the cop had also been involved—that he'd deliberately written a false report. I heard about it when Lúdvík and I spoke on the phone after you released me on Monday. We didn't think it was fair for him to get away unpunished."

"How did you manage to kidnap him?"

"Lúdvík and Jón came back to town to pick me up. We then waited outside Magnús's house, and when he came home and parked, Lúdvík was able to get into the rear seat and trap him with his seat belt. When we saw he wasn't alone, we needed Jón to help us. There was much more resistance than when we took Arngrímur, but finally, after Lúdvík had all but strangled Magnús with the seat belt, I managed to tie him up. It was easier to deal with the passenger, in spite of his size, since he gave up right away. We left him in the car but took Magnús off to Borgarfjördur, where we made him listen to the recording of Arngrímur's story, which he confirmed was an accurate account."

"I heard as much," Birkir said, "but why did you let them think you were going to burn them alive?"

"Through all these years, we've discussed different ways of dealing with Arngrímur. There've been a lot of different suggestions, one of which was to burn him alive in the same way that Sun died. Then someone had the idea of leaving a handsaw beside him so he could escape the fire by sawing his leg off. That was a chance that Sun didn't get. The shackle would be made of a heavy-duty steel that the saw had no chance of cutting through. Finally, the day before yesterday, we decided to use a variation on this idea. We set up the fire trap, but unbeknownst to them, there was no gasoline in the barrel. We've clearly gone soft with age. And it's a nice house—we didn't want to burn it down."

Birkir looked from Jón to Starkadur and back again. "Did you ever think you would get away with this?" he asked.

Starkadur replied, "Maybe, if we'd stuck to the original plan to kill Arngrímur and dump the body where it wouldn't be found. Or we could have burned him alive. The idea was to fix it so no one could prove we were responsible, but things quickly got way out of our control. But we're ready to face the consequences for our actions. We did it for Sun and for ourselves."

Birkir shook his head. "Having listened to all your statements these last few days, I've managed to put together a picture of this girl, and I'm not convinced she would have wished for such retribution."

Starkadur looked at Jón. "Probably not," he said. "But we don't have her ability to forgive and forget."

"Do you know where Lúdvík hangs out?" Birkir asked.

"He is asleep here, in the house," Starkadur replied. "He knows we plan to turn ourselves in. He's coming with us."

Birkir stood up. "I guess it's time to go. Are you ready?"

"Yes," Jón said, and rested his hand momentarily on Fabían's forehead. "Will we be allowed to go to the funeral?"

"I don't know, frankly," Birkir replied. "That's not my decision. I think you should say good-bye to him now."

"I already have," Jón said.

AUTHOR'S NOTE

I visited the Icelandic embassy in Berlin in the fall of 2006, and I was given an exhaustive and most enjoyable guided tour around the embassy and the Felleshus by members of the embassy staff, who readily provided comprehensive answers to my many questions. I took great care not to ask about the security arrangements in the Nordic Embassies complex; everything I have written about such matters in this story is my fabrication, and is undoubtedly very different from reality.

The poem translated on pages 41–42 is by Adalsteinn Ásberg Sigurdsson and was written especially for this story. Adalsteinn and I have made it our custom that he writes poems for all my books. Three such poems have been set to music by Eyjólfur Kristjánsson and released on CD.

Early in 2009, the ceramic artist Margrét Jónsdóttir held an exhibition of her works at the Akureyri Art Museum in northern Iceland. The exhibition was named *Hvítir skuggar*, or *White Shadows*. A year previously she had reached out to a number of writers, requesting assistance with a particular aspect of the exhibition. She asked that they each write a description of an item of pottery—the only condition being that there should be no mention of color—and she would then make a piece that fit what they had written. The writers reacted positively, and there were many interesting pieces in Margrét's exhibition created in this manner. I was lucky enough to be one of the writers that she approached; at this time I was working on the first half of this story, and I sent her the text on pages nine and ten of this book. Margrét subsequently made two candlesticks from the description, and those were displayed in her exhibition.

ABOUT THE AUTHOR

Viktor Arnar Ingolfsson is the author of several books, including *Daybreak*, which was the basis for the 2008 Icelandic television series *Hunting Men*. In 2001, his third novel, *House of Evidence*, was nominated for the Glass Key Award, given by the Crime Writers Association of Scandinavia; his novel *The Flatey Enigma* was nominated for the same prize in 2004. His numerous short stories have appeared in magazines and collections.

ABOUT THE TRANSLATORS

Icelandic native Björg Árnadóttir has lived most of her life in England; her British husband, Andrew Cauthery, is fluent in Icelandic. They have worked together for many years, translating both English texts into Icelandic and Icelandic texts into English. They have worked on a wide variety of manuscripts, including books on Icelandic nature and technical topics, as well as literature. This is their third translation of Viktor Arnar Ingolfsson's work, following *House of Evidence* and *Daybreak*.